The Cheyenne Horse Copyright © 2018 by Robert J. Brown

Cover photo by Gary Cook

This book is a work of fiction. Names, characters, places, and incidents either are products of the author's imagination or are used fictitiously. Any resemblance to actual persons, living or dead, events, or locales is entirely coincidental.

Robert J. Brown

First Printing: 2018

ISBN-978-1-9805-8515-2

*Robert J Brown studied zoology at Liverpool University and for the past twenty-five years he has worked as a countryside ranger. He lives in North Yorkshire with his wife, three dogs, two horses and two ponies. The Cheyenne Horse is his first novel.*

*For Melanie.*

# THE CHEYENNE HORSE

Robert J. Brown

Robert J. Brown

# CHAPTER ONE

## Colorado
## April 1863

As dawn broke the grizzly set himself for an ambush near the waterfall. He'd caught a yearling elk from the same spot last year, although there had been no intent that time. It had been an unplanned twist of fortune, but like any other bear, he could learn from experience and he didn't forget a fulfilling meal. That day he'd emerged from the den he had dug under a massive boulder, high up on the steep valley wall, but still a bit drowsy, he'd lain against a slab of granite warming in the afternoon sun. Pretty much surrounding him, was a thick, virtually impenetrable screen of brush, but to his front the scrub opened out and directly below him lay the riverbank. A female elk had sauntered past with her youngster in tow. They were part of a sixty-strong cow and calf herd that was walking upstream in the search for willow and alder shoots. The wind was blowing up the valley wall, so the elk couldn't smell him and even if he'd moved, they couldn't hear him for the sound of the waterfall. They moved closer, completely unaware of the impending danger.

For a creature weighing over 1300lbs, the grizzly's eruption from the rock wall had been stupendously quick. With massive, gravity-aided strides, he'd almost reached the calf before it had registered the danger; almost. The calf had turned away and leapt for its life, but on landing, its right front leg had landed between two deadfalls and it had stuck. Momentum carried its body onwards and the cannon bone shattered. The calf flipped over, dislocating its shoulder and as it landed it shrieked in pain, just as the bear hit it like a freight train. Mercifully for the calf, the end was near instant. The hunt still fresh in his mind and with little else going on in his calendar for April, the bear lay down to see what would happen.

Somewhere beyond the mountains the sun broke the horizon and blushed their snowy crests pink. Down in the meadow where the grass was still armoured in silver frost, a mist rose from the ground and hung around the horse's belly as he dozed. The silence was deep and profound and even the horse's sensitive ears could only detect the rumblings of his own belly. Suddenly, a wolf howl ripped through the air like a sabre through silk and the horse's head jerked wildly. He skittered a few steps in the meadow, frightened and unsure of where to go, muscles twitching in his flanks, nostrils flaring and ears swivelling. He whinnied explosively and stamped a fore hoof into the turf. The echo of the howl bounced and reverberated in the pure mountain air and then faded to nothing. Silence settled back in around the horse's huffing, only to be disturbed a few seconds later by the whisper of a raven's wings. It glided down from on high, a black angel, flared its wings and tail and rattled into the top of a lodgepole pine at the edge of the meadow, giving itself a 'kronk' of satisfaction for a well-executed landing. Gradually, the horse relaxed a little as he realized that the howl had been way off in the mountains and that the wolf, for now, was only a distant spectre.

The horse regained his stock-still pose and without his movement the weak spring sunshine warmed his flanks. He stood, eyes half closed in a bliss of warmth. He watched his breath move in the air for a while and when he'd warmed enough he bent his head down to graze.

The wolf howl had also startled John Keller into wakefulness inside his cabin and he peered out of the sole grimy widow and through the grass, which grew in the turf just under the sill, to check that his horse, Doc, was still there and still okay. Doc looked fine, chowing down on the grass as always, and resplendent in the golden light of dawn. To Keller's relief, it felt like there was finally some strength in the sun. The moss at the bottom of the pane steamed gently, slowly emerging from a delicate carapace of ice. The winter cold had been punishing and even though he'd expected it, experienced it the year before and prepared for it, its depth and tenacity had still disturbed him.

When Keller had built the cabin he'd sunk it five feet into the ground, mainly to allow him to stack the log walls without help, but it had had the additional benefit of preventing the wind being able to search for gaps amongst the timbers. He'd covered the roof with sod for insulation and now the whole structure merged with the pasture it was hewn from.

Although the cabin wasn't tall, it was long, as Keller had made it both his home and Doc's winter quarters. Keller had room for a bed and a table and chair at his end of the cabin and this was separated from Doc's space by the stove on the back wall and a rail that ran front to back. He'd sloped the floor gently down towards Doc so that he wouldn't have to wade around in the horse's copious piss, but he was happy to share Doc's, not inconsiderable, body heat. The horse hadn't just been a source of warmth in the depths of winter - the routine of looking after him had kept Keller sane. He'd fed Doc twice a day, boiling up various mixes of bran, wheat, barley and molasses. He'd given him hay from an outside store, which he'd bought last summer and had brought up by wagon at fairly considerable expense. When the weather had been tolerable Keller had let him out covered in blankets and sacking tied on with rope.

This high up in the Rockies wasn't the best place to winter a horse, but this was where the gold was. Of course, he could have gone down the mountain and wintered somewhere more suitable, especially as he couldn't look for gold with the river frozen, but he liked it up here and he had no real interest now in other humans. Turning away from the window Keller put on a shirt and pulled his pants on over his long johns and then he heaved his feet into his boots. His legs were now starting to feel a bit stiff in the mornings and he had to admit to himself that at forty, he was no longer in the first flush of youth. It didn't help his joints and sinews that he'd spent the best part of two years digging up the creek bed in the search for gold. Some mornings he now woke with his hands in spasm, hooked like an eagle's talons, a result probably, of slamming a pick and shovel into gravel and rock countless thousands of times and sluicing pebbles and sand in cold water. Still, despite the aches and pains, Keller was content with his lot, especially now that the winter was fading.

As Keller prodded the fire in the stove back to life through a wispy veil of his own breath, he realised that he had gone almost five minutes from waking before he had thought of Sally. It was undoubtedly a record. With a pot of water on for coffee he stumbled out into the new day not sure if he should be glad that perhaps his constant dwelling on the past was waning, or guilty that maybe Sally was fading away from him.

The grass outside was wet with melting frost and glittering spider webs, which looked beautiful, but soaked his boots and pant legs almost instantly, making them stick uncomfortably to his skin, but he didn't feel he could complain as the sun continued to banish the mist. It was a beautiful day and Keller was mercifully unaware that it would be his last full day and so could enjoy it to the full.

Doc's head came up at the sound of the cabin door slamming shut and he looked at Keller and then cantered over in the hope of getting a handful of oats or something similar. Keller thrilled at the sight of his horse; he was chestnut with a thin, kinked, white stripe down his nose and a black mane. He felt Doc's canter through the ground as the horse neared and he marvelled at the horse's grace and power. To Keller's mind, how a creature as big and powerful as a horse could be grown from grass was a truly mysterious miracle.

He'd bought Doc in preparation for his journey west, but it had taken him several days to find the right horse. After his seventh day of fruitless searching he'd gone into a saloon for a beer and had met a physician who just happened to be selling a horse. The doctor had never named the foal born to his carriage horse and he seemed to have little interest in it at all, but he told Keller that as it had grown, a friend of his had been breaking it in and teaching it the rudiments of living with men. Seeing it the next day, Keller thought it a splendid looking animal and that as it had come from the family of a physician he'd call it Doc. He'd bought it there and then, thinking only that his transport problem was solved. However, it was only as he led the horse away from the stable, its withers level with the top of his head, had he realised the enormity of what he was about to do. He was a tradesman and had never really ridden horses and now he was intending to ride west, up into the distant Rockies on a huge beast with a mind of its own. Committed to his mission, he had trusted his life to an unknown horse. He'd later thought it very auspicious indeed that Doc hadn't tried to kill him on the first day.

Keller saddled up Doc and they set out to go prospecting for the day. They followed the trail by the creek that they had worn together into the turf, heading upstream through patchy snow. Doc's hooves plodded forward, his head nodding gently. The raven took off from its perch in the pine, curious as to what these two unlikely companions might turn up in the way of food. As the soporific motion of the horse lulled him, Keller's mind drifted.

For most of his adult life Keller had been a carpenter. He'd built houses and barns and churches along the towns of the east coast. He'd met Sally at the age of twenty-eight and they had married a year later. A blissful nine years had passed until she had begun to show signs of consumption. It had been a terrible, painful and drawn-out way to see someone die. Their marriage had been childless and with no ties to hold him and unable to bear the pain of life in an empty marital home, he had decided to start a new life out west. The Pikes Peak gold rush had hit in 1859 and although he had missed that particular boat, he liked the idea of searching for something in the untamed wilderness. He wasn't quite sure what to search for, possibly gold, or furs, or silver, or peace, but he thought he could make up his mind as he travelled.

Like many of the west-bound migrants he'd followed the Smoky River across the plains of Kansas and into Colorado Territory, nominally following a course to Pikes Peak for want of a better target. On the way, to his surprise, he hadn't liked the plains at all, although he couldn't exactly put his finger on why. He'd felt terribly exposed under the huge sky with nothing around him to break the distance of the horizon and the lack of trees somehow unnerved him. Although the buffalo he'd seen were spectacular and the pronghorn antelope delicately beautiful and stunningly athletic, the unfamiliarity of the plains wildlife had contributed to his feelings of alienation. The Rockies though, thrusting vertiginously out of the earth, had embraced him like a lover as he had climbed and he had relished the return of the trees.

On their journey west Keller found himself becoming emotionally tied to his horse. Doc was a very gentle and responsive horse and Keller found himself believing that Doc was making allowance for his inexperience as a rider. He would go whenever a touch of heels asked him to go and, more importantly, he would slow whenever asked. As early as the second day Keller had felt that he could trust the horse not to throw him and he couldn't help but admire the beauty of the creature and the way he looked at him with those trusting brown eyes. Keller talked to him as they rode and as they made and broke camp and the horse always listened and never once argued. They became a tight partnership.

They'd reached the beaver meadow where the cabin now stood on a warm May afternoon and Keller had stopped initially for a rest, but the open aspect catching the sun and the friendly welcome of an inquisitive gray jay had tempted him to set up camp in order to explore. He was tired from the night before where he'd camped by a lake. Intermittent splashes from the shore had jolted him awake several times, adrenaline jetting into his bloodstream with the fear that what he was hearing was a bear hunting fish. An east coast city-boy unused to the wilderness, he'd lain on the floor of the tent gripping his new Spencer rifle, but even that hadn't reassured him much. Part of the problem was that he couldn't see anything through the tent walls, but was worried that if he stuck his head out to look and a grizzly was there, it might swat his head off before he had time to blink. Unnerved, he lay back fiercely gripping his gun and tried to listen for clues above the roar of blood in his ears and his racing heart. It seemed an interminable age after each splash that he calmed enough to sleep and so the night had been a long one. It was as he was getting ready to break camp the following morning that he had seen a beaver dive with a slap of its tail on the water and he'd laughed with relief and admitted to himself that it might take some time for this city boy to become a mountain man.

The following morning under a hot sun, he'd explored upstream of the beaver meadow and had found a 300 yard rocky section of creek in a defile of rock. At its head was a waterfall with a clear, cold plunge pool around five feet deep, into which he'd dived for a swim. During his ablutions he thought he saw something glitter in the depths and sure enough, after groping around on the bottom, he'd come up with a tiny gold nugget. It was a find that made the purpose of his journey clear; he was to become a gold prospector.

Despite beginning the task of panning through the creek bed, initially his primary motive wasn't the gold, but just using the task to take his mind from Sally. Slowly though, he grew into the job at hand. The rhythm of digging and panning was soothing. As his muscles hardened to the work, he drove at it with a steely determination, the repetition of it was occasionally punctuated with the thrill of a find. The plunge pool and the 200 yards downstream of it proved a rich hunting ground and he'd quickly amassed several thousand dollars-worth of gold. He felt the solitude of the mountains was important to him now and so despite hitting a rich vein of gold he'd decided to gamble and not stake a claim. He figured that if he did, it would surely spark a stampede and he didn't want a clamour of other men for company. Instead, he'd travelled far and wide in cahoots with Doc, in order to exchange gold for cash. The rest of it he'd buried for a rainy day. He didn't know how much he was worth, but he knew for sure he didn't have to work again, especially as his outgoings were so low.

Late that summer he'd made the decision to overwinter and so had built the cabin. Much of the timber he'd used, especially for the tops of the walls, was deadfall from the meadow edge and so had lost most of its weight in the desiccating summers. Doc had helped him move logs and the two of them became bound by the sweat of a shared endeavour. Keller loved working with the horse, who always did as he was asked without complaint, unlike many craftsmen he'd worked with.

The mist lifted early and the day passed for Keller in a pleasant blur of digging and panning. Doc grazed contentedly, tail switching, occasionally giving Keller the once over whilst he worked. A raccoon provided the entertainment at lunch, running head first down a tree, which Keller found amazing. He noticed that the raccoon had turned its back feet through 180 degrees in order to slow its descent. It had stopped about four feet from the ground and studied something intently in the grass, eyes shining and nose twitching. It had then pounced and sat upright with a grasshopper in its front paws, which it quickly dismembered. Keller thought the raccoon delightful.

The whole day, Keller found nothing of monetary value, but without realising it, he had regained one more tiny fragment of the spirit he had lost to grief. As the sun headed back down towards the mountain tops man and horse made the journey home, satisfied with their respective days. A quarter of a mile from the cabin, with the sky turning red, Keller spurred Doc into trot and then canter. He stood up in the stirrups and revelled in the rocking motion of the horse. Doc decided to go for home and broke into a gallop. As Doc's hooves thundered in the turf Keller grinned maniacally, half balancing and half clinging on, riding the very edge of disaster. His eyes streamed tears in the cold air, making the ground below him blur even more. The world flew by, Keller's sense of it reduced to the ground below him, Doc's forelock dancing up between his ears and a red sky above. The speed was breath-taking and Keller was suddenly overcome with an upwelling of pure, unadulterated, joy.

"Whooo Doc. Ain't it great to be alive?" he cried.

Doc didn't reply, but he sensed the excitement in the man above him and it made him gallop even faster. He enjoyed the sensation of his own body stretching out and working hard and his nostrils flared to suck in the cool air. Doc was tiring as they neared home, but pleased with himself, he gave a little buck of his rear end, which Keller rode with a wry smile. They slowed up as they emerged onto the meadow, easing down through the gears, canter then trot and into a steady breathy walk. Keller dismounted, yards from the cabin as the shadows of evening were growing long. He removed Doc's saddle and leaned his forehead against Doc's neck and for a moment watched wisps of steam rise around his face.

"Thanks for the ride." He whispered.

Above them, in a gap between the trees, where the trail crested the pass, two Cheyenne, Red Bird and Half Bear, watched Keller's ride in from the backs of their own horses. They had been riding themselves for six days. They had taken part in the first buffalo hunt of the spring with the rest of the village and then they had decided to take a few days together for a jaunt into the mountains to hunt elk and to see their friend Keller, who had been a great source of amusement last summer. Then, as they had followed the trail over the pass in the search for elk, they had first seen the cabin. They'd stayed in the timber, wary of strangers, the word for which in the Cheyenne language, was synonymous with 'enemy' and watched Keller's comings and goings for two days. They'd seen him tend his horse and dig and wash the creek bed. His antics in the river seemed crazy, but they had heard of prospectors in other places looking for the yellow metal that the whites seemed to crave. Despite digging up the creek and making it too silty to drink, which seemed lunacy, he obviously cared greatly for the horse and so they had named him, Loves His Horse.

Red Bird and Half Bear had been friends ever since they could remember, although they were both only twenty-three summers old. They made a great partnership, as they were both intelligent and physically able men. Red Bird was the greater thinker and Half Bear was more the man of action and between them they seemed able to cope with whatever life was able to throw at them. Half Bear was five feet ten inches tall and powerfully muscled. He'd plucked the hair from the sides of his head with shells used as tweezers, leaving a long mane down the centre of his head. In contrast, Red Bird was only five feet six and thin and wiry, the muscles in his forearms standing out like ropes. He'd kept his jet-black hair, which he wore tied back in a loose pony tail.

Now, from atop their own horses, Red Bird and Half Bear grinned at each other as they watched Keller with his head against his horse, amused that Loves His Horse had already been caught living up to his name. Red Bird let out a 'whoop' and waved his bow above his head. A second later, down in the pasture, Keller's head jerked up and he waved back and the Indians went down the trail to join him.

Red Bird had a half-sister, named Susan Sumner. Their mother, Sun Woman, had married a fur trapper, John Sumner, after Red Bird's father had been killed falling off his horse and breaking his neck on a buffalo hunt. As a result of Sun Woman's relationship with Sumner and the birth of his half breed, half-sister, Red Bird had learned the white man's language.

At first the white men had come into Cheyenne territory slowly, like the growth of a tree. But now, that trickle of men was becoming a flood. Spurred by the growing influx of whites, who were clearly not going to go away anytime soon and keen to avoid major conflict, the Cheyenne, along with the Arapahos, Sioux and Crows had met at Fort Laramie in 1851 and signed a treaty allowing the whites to put some roads across their land, but without giving up claim to it, or the right to hunt, fish and travel anywhere over it. In that treaty the Cheyenne territory was recognised as being a vast area between the North Platte River in modern Wyoming and south west Nebraska to the north and the Arkansas River to the south in western Kansas. It went west into the Rockies of Western Kansas Territory (later to become Colorado). Both the Indians and the whites swore to maintain good faith and friendship. Since then however, the whites had rampaged through the Cheyenne homelands, spurred on by the discovery of the yellow metal. Wagon trains forged up the Platte River and a chain of forts had appeared. Then stagecoaches started running and the forts got closer together, Pony express routes appeared and eventually the 'talking wires' were strung out. A huge wooden village, known as Denver, sprang up in 1859 and so many more miners came, along with ranchers, that the buffalo became scarce. Despite all of that, on the whole, the Cheyenne bore the invasion with great patience.

Only ten years after the Fort Laramie Treaty, the US government established the Territory of Colorado and dispatched a governor there. Soon politicians were clamouring for land to be taken from the Indians and in 1861 invites were sent to the Cheyenne and Arapahos to come to the new fort at Big Timbers, later renamed Fort Wise, near modern Lamar in Colorado to discuss a new treaty. Only six of the forty-four Cheyenne chiefs deigned to attend, but they were made a fuss of by luminaries such as A.B. Greenwood, the Commissioner of Indian Affairs, who gave out gifts, including impressive medals. The six Cheyenne chiefs did sign the treaty, although they were misled as to what they were signing. The whites were consigning them to a reservation only one thirteenth the size of their old territory, in an area along the Arkansas River to the Northern boundary of New Mexico, where game was scarce and it was too dry to grow crops. On their part the Cheyenne thought that they were still keeping their freedom to move and hunt buffalo anywhere on the plains. None of the other chiefs ever did sign the treaty and some bands of Cheyenne including the Dog Soldiers continued to hunt buffalo in Colorado and Kansas and harassed the gold seekers on the Smokey Hill River. However, Black Kettle, chief to Red Bird and Half Bear, had signed the treaty and he was determined to keep the peace in order to keep his people safe.

Keller went inside to light the fire while Red Bird and Half Bear rode down the trail. Half an hour later as the sun slid down below the mountain peaks, the three men were drinking coffee, sat cross legged on the floor beside Keller's stove.

"It's good to see you Red Bird. How are you?" Keller asked.

"I am well Loves His Horse. Please wait a moment and we will smoke," Red Bird then switched to speaking Cheyenne. *"Half Bear, Loves His Horse asks how we are, but I have said we will smoke before we talk."*

Half Bear nodded and pulled his pipe from a bag at his side. Slowly and deliberately he filled the bowl with a mix of tobacco and dried sumac leaves and lit it with a spill from the stove. He stood and pointed the pipe stem to the sky, the earth and the four points of the compass chanting, "*Spirit above smoke, Earth smoke, North smoke, East smoke, South smoke, West smoke,*" Half Bear then passed the two-foot-long pipe, bowl down, to Keller, who as owner of the 'lodge' had the right to smoke first. Keller drew in smoke and passed the pipe left, as was custom, placing the bowl on the floor with the stem vertical, allowing Half Bear to pick it up without the risk of it being dropped.

"How did you find the winter in the mountains?" Red Bird asked, exhaling a stream of smoke.

"Very long and very hard. But we survived it. I was pleased to see and feel the sun today."

Red Bird nodded and quickly translated for Half Bear. It was Keller's turn to smoke again, but Red Bird couldn't pass the pipe straight to him, as that would entail it passing in front of the door, so he placed the bowl down and handed the stem to Half Bear who did the same for Keller and in this way the pipe was smoked for half a circle and then passed back for half a circle, until the tobacco was gone. The men talked of winter provisions, horse care, hunting and prospecting.

After two hours of talk the men were silent for a moment, the fire popping in the stove, its flickering the only light now that night had fallen. Red Bird shifted his weight gently side to side and Keller could see he was wrestling with an important question.

"Loves His Horse, are there more whites coming to our land? How many white people are there?" Keller was momentarily embarrassed knowing the answer, but pressed ahead and told the truth.

"Yes Red Bird, more whites will come and I am afraid there are millions in the east and millions more waiting to cross the sea from Europe."

"Millions? This isn't a number I know. My grandfather once told me that there used to be so many buffalo that they were like raindrops in a storm. Is that millions?"

Keller nodded, "And I'm afraid the coming whites will be like a storm. I think more would have come already, but they are fighting amongst themselves in a civil war."

Red Bird nodded. He already knew of the battles between the bluecoats and the greycoats. Soldiers of each hue had been roving around looking for each other in a war that had already been raging for almost exactly two years. Red Bird had also heard that the war was being fought over the rights of the black man, which seemed odd to Red Bird, as neither side seemed to care for the rights of the Cheyenne, or any other tribe. He translated Keller's words for Half Bear who shook his head dejectedly and began refilling the pipe.

Keller excused himself and stepped outside, picking up a blanket as he went. The sky was black velvet covered in thousands of diamonds and the air so crystalline and cold that it felt like it might break if a sudden movement were made. An owl screeched and Keller called to Doc. At the sound of Keller's voice the horse stamped his right rear hoof into the turf. It was his signal that he was pleased to see the man and Keller smiled, recognising the stamp for what it was. Doc had begun doing it on winter mornings when Keller was setting about making up buckets of food. The stamps were a 'hello', but were followed by snorting if the service wasn't quick enough. After two quick stamps Doc trotted over. Keller threw the blanket over him and tied it on, deciding that as the night was so still he would leave Doc outside with the Cheyenne horses. The two Cheyenne watched, amused, as Keller fussed his horse and settled him with a bag of hay.

*"If the horse is going to bed perhaps we should also sleep"*, suggested Half Bear. *"We could start early tomorrow to hunt elk."* Red Bird and Keller agreed, but first the three of them smoked the restocked pipe. They sat in silence, mesmerised by the flames of the stove and immersed in their own thoughts. They turned in for the night, Keller on his bed and the Cheyenne wrapped in blankets on the floor.

Keller had woken up to find his guests missing. They hadn't gone far though, as he found them in front of the cabin, sat on a buffalo hide rug out of the dew, with their backs against a large rock.

"Good morning fellas." Keller greeted them.

"Good morning Loves His Horse. We were just admiring the sunrise," Red Bird poked his chin at the pink in the heavens.

"Uh, huh. What you got planned for today?"

"We would like to try to find an elk." Keller absorbed that information for a moment.

"You guys got a gun?" he asked.

"No, we have bows."

"Ok. We'll hunt an elk with my gun. I know a good spot where they gather in a valley bottom. It's a deep, narrow valley and you can shoot across it. My gun has a range of about five hundred yards."

Red Bird translated the conversation to Half Bear, who asked, *"What is five hundred yards?"*

"I'll show you," Keller said when Red Bird asked him Half Bear's question. He held up a finger, asking them to wait a moment and then he walked away from them, pacing as he went and trying not to stumble in the tussocks and look like a clumsy oaf white man. Eventually he turned back to face them and shouted, "It's five hundred yards from me to you."

*"That is a long way,"* Half Bear muttered with an edge of disbelief.

*"It is. We need to see this gun.* Loves His Horse, go get your gun. We want to see it," Red Bird shouted, his voice bouncing back off the pines and sending a gray jay into an outraged ferment.

"We'll have breakfast and I'll show you the gun," Keller shouted as he ran back, pleased with the interest he had generated. He checked Doc was quiet with the Cheyenne's horses and then began making porridge. Red Bird and Half Bear didn't like the look of the porridge and made a show of needing to eat their travel cakes instead. They had two types with them, choke cherries pounded with buffalo meat and tallow to make a pemmican and bull-berries and currants pounded up and dried into cakes. They ate these with a tea of red leaf wood, suspicious of and relieved that they had avoided the porridge. Keller, on his part, thought that what the Indians were eating looked vaguely like it had already passed through somebody else's digestive system. 'Still, it'd be boring if we were all the same', he thought.

Keller brought his gun from the cabin.

"There are seven bullets in here," Keller said, pointing to the stock. "You jack a round into the chamber like this." With his fingers in the trigger guard he pushed down and back up again in a swift motion. "You cock it to fire by pulling back the hammer," which he did with his thumb. "I'll aim at that aspen," he said pointing at the only grey trunk in a sea of lodgepole pines over three hundred yards away, "but I can't guarantee I'll hit it." He took aim and fired. All three horse heads leapt up from the grass at the report as flakes of bark exploded from the trunk of the aspen and a blue cloud of smoke billowed in front of the impressed spectators, who nodded sagely, trying hard not to look amazed.

*"Let's find an elk for Loves His Horse to shoot."*

"Saddle up, eh?" Keller asked, guessing the sentiment of Half Bear's words.

Red bird nodded agreement. "Yes....please, lead the way to your elk valley."

As they rode side by side on the way to the valley Red Bird looked over Doc.

"He is a fine looking horse," he said to Keller in admiration. "Is he fast?"

"Wanna Race?" Keller said in reply.

"Okay. *Half Bear we're going to race Loves His Horse's horse. You ready?"* Half Bear nodded his assent.

"You shout 'go'", Keller said.

"Go!"

*"Hokahe!"* Cried Half Bear as he whipped his horse's rump gleefully.

Keller jabbed his heels to Doc and with the reins in one hand slapped them from side to side across Doc's neck. All three horses erupted into gallop, throwing clods of turf up behind them. They pounded through the grass, manes up and tails streaming behind them. Doc pulled ahead and gradually stretched the lead. After a mile Keller pulled him to a stop and waited a few seconds for the others to catch up from over twenty lengths behind.

"That is a fast horse," Red Bird exclaimed in wonder. "He runs like the wind. If he was mine I'd rename him, *'Minninnewah'*

"What does that mean?"

"It means Wild Wind."

"I like it, but I'm going to stick with 'Doc'." Keller slapped Doc's shoulder, proud of his friend's physical prowess.

Ten minutes later the trees to their right opened out and they could see across the valley they had gradually been descending. Sure enough, on the valley floor were some elk. The bear was watching them too. It was his second day of waiting. The first had been mainly sleeping, but he wasn't in a rush. He was unaware of the arrival of the horses due to the continual roar of the waterfall. Doc stood only fifteen feet from the bear as Keller raised his gun. The three humans held their breath as he aimed. The instant Keller fired, his world went into slow motion. Doc danced up onto his hind legs and skittered sideways some ten feet towards the waterfall. Through the smoke of the gun discharge Keller saw the elk begin to buckle, but his eye was drawn to a huge boar grizzly that exploded from some brush at the water's edge. It ran under Doc's upraised front hooves, its shaggy coat shaking with movement and held on by skin seemingly too loose for its body. The two creatures collided a glancing blow and Keller was whiplashed from the saddle. He fell downhill, facing the sky, which he noticed, was brilliant blue with only one white cloud.

The deadfall pine had lain for twelve years, unmoved and untouched by all except invertebrates and the scratching feet of squirrels, who had used an opening within it to store pine seeds. Despite the years of weathering, the splintered remains of the branch had not softened one iota. It was the perfect spearhead and it reached up for the sun in homage. Keller landed on it and it lanced through his right kidney, blasting through his abdominal wall and back into the sunlight. The force of the impact took all the wind from Keller and his head smacked onto the trunk giving him a mild concussion. At first he felt nothing but blunt impact, but three seconds later the rush of pain from the tear in his body struck like a thunderbolt and he screamed.

In theory a person can live with only one kidney, but nobody could survive the massive internal bleeding that Keller was suffering for long. The bear had gone in a second, unaware of the carnage left in the wake of its unintended hit and run. Half Bear and Red Bird were off their horses like acrobats and scrambling down the ravine to get Keller before the smoke from the gun had had time to start drifting. They lifted him from impalement and had him back on the flat ground under a buffalo hide rug within five minutes, but already his body was shutting down with shock.

Keller grabbed Red Bird's forearm with a strength he had barely had before. Pale and cold, with eyes half closed he pleaded, "Red Bird, take my gun. There are more bullets in boxes under my bed." He gasped for air in a ragged hiss. "Look after Doc for me. I want him to have a good life. Run with him. Promise me." Red Bird nodded.

"I will take him. Don't worry," he reassured him and Keller seemed to relax a little. Doc moved towards Keller, curious as to his companion's unusual prone position. He bent his head down and Keller held his muzzle in both hands. It was soft like velvet and despite his agonising pain, he felt the wonder of it. His eyes fluttered and his hands dropped. The last thing he saw was his own reflection in Doc's eye.

Doc knew in an instant that the spark of life had left the man. He nuzzled him hard on the chest, trying to bring back breath like a dam would with a new born foal, but it was hopeless. He felt confusion at the loss of his friend and anxiety flooded in knowing that his leader was lost in an uncertain world.

"Is he dead?" Half Bear asked. Red Bird nodded.

"Help me get him on his horse and we'll take him back to his lodge."

Getting back to Keller's cabin was much slower than the journey out. Red Bird and Half Bear kept having to stop to readjust Keller's body on the horse. Doc was nervous and not keen to be led, spooked by the scent of blood. A raven followed them all the way, fluttering short distances between trees and keeping its eye on the bloody carcass draped over the back of the horse.

It was late afternoon by the time they made it back. They wrapped Keller in a blanket from his bed and tied him into it with rope. The raven's head bobbed in frustration at this added complication. Following Cheyenne custom they bound some of his valuables in the blanket with him, his pipe, a knife with a finely carved handle and a pouch of flakes of the yellow metal that the whites seemed prepared to die for. Red Bird kept the rifle, as Keller had specifically asked him to keep it. The same was true of Doc, who would have gone into the afterlife with Keller if he hadn't asked Red Bird to care for him. Red Bird was pleased about this, as it would have been a shame to kill such a fine horse. They were sure that by now Keller would be following the footprints of those who had gone before him to the milky way and to the camp of the dead beyond, where he would surely be met by the wife he had told them of. All that was left to do was to dispose of his body. Then they would leave him in case his ghost was near and did them some mischief.

Sometimes the Cheyenne would lay a body under a pile of rocks, but often bodies were put on scaffolds in trees, or even just laid on the roof of a lodge. Men thought it well that their bodies would be of use to, and scattered by, the likes of wolves, eagles and ravens. Red Bird and Half Bear left Keller's bound body on the roof of his cabin where it could still appreciate the touch of the sun. They took what was useful to them from the cabin and then they rode off, Red Bird leading Doc on a short rope.

The raven came down onto the cabin roof to inspect its prize. The blanket was tough and it might take a while to get through. It threw its head back and cawed in consternation, the sound of which carried and brought in another raven, which soared high over the clearing, assessing the situation below. Soon their activity would be noticed by brother wolf, who would help them in the task.

# CHAPTER TWO

## Ash Creek, Kansas.
## April 1864

The sun hadn't been up long and the tipis cast long shadows on the prairie grass. There were nearly a hundred arranged in a circle with a diameter of almost half a mile. High above the village a kite circled and it could see only occasional people amongst the tipis, which nestled under a blue haze of smoke from the hearths, but there were many dogs sauntering around looking for opportunities to scavenge a morsel and a herd of several hundred horses grazed close by. The surface of the river glinted in the sun where the water rushed over a riffle and the kite wheeled away to keep its vision clear.

The striped gopher had burrowed into its hibernation chamber in October surrounded by a vast ocean of grass. It had slowed its respiration from over one hundred breaths per minute to one breath every five minutes and it had then slept the sleep of the dead. But now, the warming April soil had awoken it from slumber and it dug upwards and popped its head out into daylight, only to see a man looking at him amongst a metropolis of towering tipis. Red Bird smiled at him. The gopher rotated his head almost a full circle and his tiny shiny gopher eyes were clearly startled and asking, 'What the hell?'

Red Bird was sat in the grass as the bewildered gopher's head popped back down into the soil. He leaned back against the tipi pole and resumed his train of thought. Although he'd never told anyone, not even Half Bear, the death of Keller had disquieted him. He didn't know why he should particularly care about the white prospector he barely knew, but throughout the winter he had been worrying over him more and more. He was sure Keller was some kind of portent. Wild Wind of course, was a reminder of him and Red Bird told himself how lucky his contact with Keller had been. The magnificent horse and the gun with over five hundred bullets were surely gifts from The Great Spirit.

As one of Red Bird's best horses, it was Wild Wind's turn to be picketed outside his tipi. He was a good, quiet horse and was head down grazing with his ears periodically flicking off the early spring flies. Tomorrow, if not for the impending war party, Wild Wind would be rotated back out into the village herd and a replacement brought in, so that there was always a good horse available for an emergency.

Red Bird went back to his task of finishing his new war whistle. He'd taken the humerus of a whooping crane he'd found dead on the prairie and had cut off both ends. He'd then made a notch near one end and partially filled it with pine gum, so that when he blew down it, the air whistled out over the top of the gum. It was a loud noise and with many wailing together in a war party they made a frightening crescendo. Whooping crane whistles were highly valued, as the crane was a fierce bird of great courage. If it was wounded and couldn't fly it would even try to fight off a man. As the crane had no fear, the whistle would transfer that fearlessness to its bearer. Red Bird had decorated his whistle with tiny beads and all that was left to do was attach a deerskin string so that it could be hung around his neck.

When the whistle was finished Red Bird began painting Wild Wind ready for war. As he did so he sang a song to bring strength to the horse. He painted black circles on the horse's shoulders and white zig-zags on his hips. Over the winter there had been three attempted raids near the village by Utes and though they had been intercepted each time and there had been no loss of life, or loss of horses, Old Owl Man had had his arm broken by a Ute war club as he'd tended the herd. Now a party of twenty warriors, including Red Bird and Half Bear, were going to see if they could find some Utes and at least capture some of their horses and hopefully administer some retribution. It would be a small war party, as many of the other men were out on a buffalo hunt and the remainder would stay in the village to protect the women and children.

The leader of the war party and the bearer of the war pipe, Leaping Panther, had already set off with Wounded Buffalo. The rest of the group would leave in pairs throughout the day and they would all meet up several miles from the village to camp the first night and to smoke the war pipe. Each man would carry several days-worth of pemmican, although they intended to hunt along the way, and a blanket and ropes with which to lead captured horses. They each set out riding a common horse with their best war horse in tow so that it would be fresh for the fight.

Half Bear walked over to Red Bird leading his chosen two horses. "*You ready to go?*" he asked. Red Bird nodded as he finished tying a blanket to the back of his saddle.

"*If I can prove myself a good warrior and maybe capture some horses on this war party, then I think I will give them to She Wolf's father,*" Red Bird said without preamble.

*"You and She Wolf are getting married?"* Half Bear asked with a smile and eyebrows raised. He was really pleased that his friend was finally getting around to marrying the girl he had seemed destined to marry since childhood. Red Bird nodded confirmation. He felt that this war party was a crossroads in his life and things were changing, as surely and as profoundly as the seasons were shifting.

The air was perfectly still and as scouts Red Bird and Half Bear rode up the hill, the rest of the party left down in the valley, the only sound beyond their movements was the chirring of grasshoppers. They split up either side of a narrow gorge and ended up roughly twenty yards apart. Near the crest of the rise Half Bear dismounted and Red Bird followed suit and they crept the last few yards to the top. Red Bird carried his rifle and Half Bear clutched his bow.

Red Bird lay flat in the grass breathing the scent of humus accumulated over the last ten thousand years. He looked to his right and saw Half Bear, similarly prone in the turf, give him a grin of acknowledgement and shared conspiracy. They looked forward and began scouring the landscape for anything out of place and within two seconds they both saw movement at the same time. Two Ute scouts were jogging up the hill towards them to do exactly what they were already doing. About a mile below them was a cluster of about twenty-five or thirty riders.

Red Bird's heart beat crazily in his chest. The Utes were directly below him and coming straight at him. He could shoot at them, but that would give the game away. He looked to Half Bear and signalled him to use his bow. Half Bear had already thought the same and barely looked at Red Bird as he concentrated on the motion of the approaching Utes. Keeping his bow horizontal in the long grass he rolled to his side and drew back the bowstring. The arrow took to the air with a thwack and buried itself just below the clavicle of the Ute on the right. As the arrow was in mid-air Red Bird leapt up with his knife in hand and charged the other Ute. The man hit by the arrow flipped over on his back, momentarily no longer a threat. Startled by his friend's gymnastics, the other man was slow to see Red Bird coming. Straining every sinew in his body to get there, Red Bird leapt at the man and drove his knife up into his diaphragm and both of them crashed into the grass.

Half Bear was in motion a split second behind Red Bird. The man hit by the arrow staggered up to one knee and started to raise a revolver in Red Bird's direction. Half Bear's fist whickered audibly through the air and smashed his knife into the man's throat, knocking him backwards again and wrenching the pistol out of his hand without it firing. Both Cheyenne lay for a moment, eyes wide with adrenalin and their breath hissing like a white man's railroad train. After a few seconds pause they were up in a crouch and cutting the scalps from the dead men. Task complete, they jogged back over the crest of the hill and lay on their backs next to each other, Half Bear clutching a new pistol along with the scalp.

*"They might not have seen that,"* Half Bear panted, referring to the warriors a mile away.

*"That's what I'm thinking. I think we get everyone up here and then signal the Utes to come up. If they don't recognise us we'll get them in ambush, but even if they do, they'll probably still come up to chase us."*

*"Let's do it."*

Red Bird jogged back down the hill to where Wild Wind was waiting patiently. His knees popped slightly and his thighs trembled with the effort of keeping upright on the steep slope and from the adrenaline still coursing through him. He jumped up onto the horse and rode a zig-zag in trot, down the hill, indicating that the enemy had been spotted. He then rode in a circle asking the rest of the war party to join them. Down below, the Cheyenne horses bolted into action and a couple of minutes later the plan was laid out for the party to consider. All agreed without hesitation and Red Bird and Half Bear rode back over the hill to ride circles to draw up the Utes. They then came back over the crest and the Cheyenne waited, spread out in a line below the ridge.

Eight of the Utes crossed the crest of the hill shoulder to shoulder and attracted a simultaneous and withering hail of arrows. Red Bird fired the gun at the belly of the man nearest him and the bullet smacked into the bridge of his nose. It deflected upwards and cut a groove around the dome of his skull before exiting through his jaw. He was dead before he left contact with his horse. Four other Utes were dismounted by arrows and the rest turned to flee. The Cheyenne whooped and gave chase, some of them, including Red Bird, renting the air with their war whistles.

A crashing torrent of forty-five horses galloped downhill raising a storm of dust that could be seen for miles. The ground thundered with hooves and the ride was so fast and so rough, that nobody could fire a gun or a bow. Mad Beaver pulled alongside a Ute and swung his war hammer at him. The hammer, a heavy, sharp-edged stone lashed to an ash handle caught the Ute on the shoulder blade with a sickening crunch of bone, but the Ute held on and pulled his horse away from Mad Beaver. Several Cheyenne, including Mad Beaver, whooped again as he was seen counting coup. Touching an enemy warrior in battle was known as counting coup and brought great prestige to the man who accomplished it, much more so than killing, or scalping a man, which was relatively inconsequential. A man could also count coup by touching a dead warrior during the battle, but only if he was one of the first three to do so.

Sleeping Elk also drew alongside a Ute and reached over to grab him and both of them fell to the ground in an explosion of dirt and grass. By now the Utes were starting to split up and the ground was beginning to level out. Red Bird raised his gun just as Wild Wind put his front right hoof onto the soft soil of a gopher mound. His hoof sank and his head pitched forward and down almost to the turf. The sudden jerk sent Red Bird sailing over Wild Wind's head. He rotated slowly in mid-air, his feet arcing high above his own head as Wild Wind moved away from him and he landed with a tooth jarring whack on his right buttock, with a force that whiplashed his neck and drove the breath from his lungs.

Red Bird lay for a moment, the sound of battle receding and replaced by the grasshoppers' chirr, all of whom seemed oblivious to the action that had just passed over them. It took almost half a minute for his senses to return and his first thought was to find his horse. Then he thought of the gun. Wild Wind would be easy to find, but the gun was laid in long grass and if he moved far from where he was now he knew he would never find it.

He tried to stand and collapsed again as a shooting pain ran down his right leg and up into the small of his back. For a moment none of the muscles in his leg seemed under his control and he burst into a panicked sweat thinking that his leg was paralysed. From the corner of his eye he saw movement and looked up to see a Ute running at him with a knife in one hand and a scalp in the other. Instantly Red Bird recognised the white shells that Sleeping Elk had woven into his hair and a wave of anger swept through him. The Ute was forty yards away and closing fast. Red Bird scanned the grass for the gun and to his relief, he saw a glint of metal in the sun. He hobbled towards it, unable to put weight on his damaged right leg. He dived for the gun with the Ute less than ten yards away and as he jacked a round into the chamber he made a plea to the Great Spirit that the muzzle wouldn't be blocked with dirt. The blast was point blank and the Ute collapsed, his spine blown into two just above the hips as the bullet went clean through him.

Red Bird sat down at an angle, his weight on his left butt-cheek. He was dizzy with pain and filled with grief for Sleeping Elk, who had been his friend all of their lives. Still, it had been a good way for a warrior to die, his ancestors would greet him with pride.

Wild Wind had been startled by the first gunshot of the engagement, but he had steadied himself in an instant. He had heard the sticks that flashed light, smoke and ear-splitting sounds many times before. The man who had taught him to carry a rider had often made a stick explode with sound and he and his friends had yelled at him before reassuring him that they meant him no harm. The men were noisy at times, but they were kind to him.

After the gunshot, the chase had begun and Wild Wind was caught up in the excitement of it. His herd raced after another herd of strange horses downhill and he galloped faster than he ever had before, until his leg collapsed under him and the man riding him flew off over his shoulder. Without the man's encouragement Wild Wind lost his focus and he began to slow down. He needed to get his breath back and calm himself after the fearful din of the screams, whistles and gun shots. A red tailed hawk flew low overhead, carving a graceful circle in the air and bringing back a sense of normality. His breathing slowed towards normal and his feeling of excitement subsided. Way below him, he could see the dust cloud of the receding chase and he watched the patterns of it for a moment as the mounted herd split up. Suddenly, there was another gunshot and he jumped slightly. He looked in the direction of the sound and saw Red Bird sit down in the grass. Curious as to why the man was sitting in the grass he walked over to investigate.

Red Bird was delighted to see Wild Wind coming back to him. What a fantastic horse he was. As Wild Wind ambled over, Red Bird moved on all fours to the downed Ute and took his knife from him and cut off his scalp. He picked up the scalp of Sleeping Elk and sat down to watch the remains of the chase below.

The Utes had been routed and the Cheyenne were gathering together and riding back up towards Red Bird at a walk. Red Bird counted them. Everyone was there, except himself and Sleeping Elk. Suddenly, there were whoops from the party and the horses burst into a laborious uphill canter. Red Bird turned behind him to see one of the four Utes dismounted in the first seconds of the skirmish running away. He felt a small pang of pity for the man, knowing he was not going to escape. Swooping Eagle was the first to reach the man. He thrust at him with his lance, but missed as the Ute stepped sideways, but as he staggered away from Swooping Eagle's lance he collided with the shoulder of Young Bull's horse and fell. As he tried to get up Mad Beaver's horse ran over him and even as far away as he was, Red Bird heard the sound of crunching bone. Swooping Eagle's horse spun around, tail flailing like a snake and this time the lance went through the man's back and into the prairie below him.

The battle was over and the war party took stock. Sleeping Elk had been killed and Red Bird was the only one injured. Between them they had killed nine Utes and captured their horses. Before they could leave, Sleeping Elk's body had to be cared for. No warrior wanted to be buried in the cold earth and so he was wrapped in his blanket and placed in a sunny position on the hillside. He would return to the earth with the help of the prairie animals. The wind blew across the prairie and the grass rippled like waves on a lake and Red Bird thought this was a good place to lie.

After helping Red Bird back onto Wild Wind they took the captured horses in tow and rode hard for home. For Red Bird the return journey was two days of agony. On nearing home they camped early, two miles from the village, so that they could time their ride in to coincide with dawn. As the sun broke the horizon the following day Leaping Panther signalled the village with a mirror that they were coming in and that they were one man lost. Overnight they had prepared the captured scalps and mounted them on poles. If the fallen warrior hadn't had the honour of counting coup during his death, they would have had to have thrown the scalps away, but as it was, they could be shown as trophies and danced over in a scalp dance. Had none of them been killed, they would have painted their faces black with burned willow sticks for the ride in, but this was dispensed with out of respect for Sleeping Elk. The two leaders rode hard into the village and wove in amongst the tipis waving the scalps on poles. The celebrating lasted all day and all night, with even Sleeping Elk's widow joining in the scalp dancing, although her heart was breaking.

It was three days since the war party had returned and the celebrations had finally receded. Red Bird and Half Bear sat on a boulder on the riverbank and watched the sun glow red with effort as it hauled itself into the sky. Earlier, in the half-light of the pre-dawn Half Bear had taken ten of Red Bird's horses and tied them to picket pins outside the tipi of She Wolf's father, Eagle Wing. When Eagle Wing, roused by the commotion, had emerged from the tipi bedraggled with sleep and surprised at the herd around him, Half Bear had told him that Red Bird wished to take his daughter for a wife and that he offered these horses to him as a gift. With that Half Bear had walked away to join an anxious Red Bird waiting down by the river.

The melody of the water rolling over rocks filled the silence between the two men until Half Bear finally said, *"I notice you didn't give Wild Wind away, even though he's your best horse."*

*"I know. I don't know why really, other than I promised Loves His Horse I'd look after him."*

*"Yes, but Loves His Horse was a white man we hardly knew,"* Half Bear said, slightly taken aback by Red Bird's explanation.

*"I know, but there is something about that horse..."* Red Bird's words trailed off and he picked a flake of rock from the boulder and tossed it into the river. *"Anyway, I've offered ten horses for She Wolf, that's a lot and they are good ones."* Half Bear nodded his assent. Everyone would know the horses were good and two of them were captured from the Utes, making them the highest of compliments.

By now the village was waking up behind them and several boys came down to the river for their morning swim. A group of three boys of about twelve years of age led a horse down to be washed, although with the messing about that ensued, the boys got wetter than the horse. Half Bear and Red Bird watched them, amused by their antics and reminded of themselves only a few short years ago.

Red Bird, Half Bear and She Wolf had been born the same summer and their parents were friends, always putting their tipis close together as the village migrated over the plains. As a result, the three of them had played together since being able to walk and their friendships were unbreakable. Over the last two years though the bond between Red Bird and She Wolf had grown into something different and though Half Bear had been quick to see the first glimmer of romance and might possibly have felt excluded, or jealous, he didn't feel either. In fact, Half Bear had eagerly pushed the other two together, moving aside to let them talk together without being too obvious and encouraging them to dance together at every social event or celebration. By the time She Wolf and Red Bird were feeling differently about each other, Half Bear's eyes and heart were roving elsewhere.

Time crept on and Red Bird lay down on his left side to take the pressure off the buttock and leg he'd injured in the fall chasing the Utes. He was walking with a limp, which he was doing his best to disguise to prevent his peers making fun of him. Half Bear kept looking back towards Eagle Wing's tipi where there was still no sign of movement. By tradition Red Bird's proposal would be accepted, or refused within twenty-four hours and the horses either kept, or returned. *"He's making you sweat,"* Half Bear said with a wry smile.

*"I know, but surely he couldn't find a better son-in-law than me."*

*"I wouldn't get too sure of yourself,"* Half Bear goaded, *"he mightn't want his daughter marrying a cripple and who's to say you didn't damage other marriage-relevant areas?"*

Red Bird swung a half-hearted slap at Half Bear's shoulder.

At last the door to Eagle Wing's tipi was drawn aside and he emerged and led the horses away. Half Bear gently punched Red Bird's shoulder in fraternal celebration and, for Red Bird at least, the rest of the day passed in a blur. Eagle Wing distributed Red Bird's horses amongst She Wolf's cousins and news of the wedding spread like a fire in the wind. Each receiving cousin then sent back their best horse to Eagle Wing, who rounded up some of his own best horses and brought the whole herd together, with various gifts of blankets and arrows and the like.

She Wolf emerged from her father's tipi dressed in her finest clothes and she was put onto the best horse in the newly formed herd. She Wolf's mount was led by her friend, Mountain Sun, and behind them, She Wolf's mother led six horses on ropes laden with gifts. The rest of the horses were all led by She Wolf's female friends and relatives.

As the procession had reached Red Bird's father's tipi, Red Bird's relatives emerged and spread a blanket on the ground and She Wolf was lifted off the horse and sat on the blanket and the young men carried her into her new in-laws' tipi. Once inside, Red Bird's sister and female cousins redressed her and braided her hair and Red Bird then joined her.

Next morning, She Wolf had been put on a horse and sent with more horses and presents back to Eagle Wing, where the presents were redistributed. She Wolf's mother cooked a feast for the friends and family of both the newly-weds, whilst her father gave away more of his horses to show his approval of the marriage. She Wolf's mother had also made a new tipi in which the new couple would live.

It was now mid-May and Red Bird stood in front of his marital tipi. It was a gloriously sunny day and he lay down in the grass to enjoy the warmth of the sun for a few minutes. His backside and leg were still painful and he was glad to rest it. The leg was still not fully mobile, but at least the alarming yellow and black bruising and impressive swelling had receded.

From his prone position Red Bird could see chief Black Kettle's American flag flutter gently in the breeze on a pole high above his tipi. It had thirty-four stars on it, representing the thirty-four states. Keen to keep the peace, when Black Kettle and Starving Bear had been to Washington to sign the peace treaty they had met the Great Father of the whites, Abraham Lincoln. President Lincoln had put medals around their necks and Colonel Greenwood had presented them with the flag and told them that as long as the flag flew over them, no soldier would fire on them. Black Kettle was proud of that flag and Red Bird was sure he was doing the right thing by trying to keep his people in favour with the whites.

The village had spent the winter here on Ash creek, near Fort Larned in Kansas, so that they could trade with the whites and be under the protective umbrella offered by the fort. Black Kettle felt that if his people were out on the plains and a column of troops bumped into them, they might mistakenly be assumed to be hostile.

Half Bear was out with the buffalo hunt while Red Bird rested his leg, but just as he became drowsy in the sun there was the thunder of hooves and the hunting party raced back in. Half Bear rode up to Red Bird, his horse lathered in sweat and its nostrils flaring.

*"What's wrong?"* Red Bird asked over the sound of the horse's gasping breaths.

*"We saw at least eighty soldiers with big talking guns,"* Half Bear spat dust from his throat, *"heading towards the village."*

A few moments later, as Red Bird hobbled over to collect Wild Wind, the village crier was shouting out that Chief Starving Bear was going out to meet the soldiers to tell them that the village was friendly to the white man's army. Wild Wind in hand, Red Bird grabbed his gun and he and Half Bear joined the warriors who were accompanying Starving Bear in his peace mission.

When the hunting party had initially returned with their news, Black Kettle and Starving Bear had been outside Starving Bear's tipi drinking green leaf tea and reminiscing over old times; the two of them had been great friends since their earliest childhood and they were now in their fifties. Raven told them about the soldiers' arrival and Starving Bear got up and beamed a smile, *"Good, good. Excitement on a quiet day. I'll go and see what they want and make sure they know we're friendly Indians."* With that he ducked inside his tipi and re-emerged hanging the medal he had got from Washington around his neck and in his hand he carried a scroll from Abe Lincoln declaring that the Indian carrying it was a good friend of Americans.

Starving Bear mounted his horse and set off with a small party of warriors. Most of the village gathered to watch proceedings out on the plain. The reception party led by Starving Bear rode up the hill towards the soldiers. As they drew near they could see the soldiers had lined up and that there were nearly a hundred of them, with two cannons in their midst and some wagons strung out behind. Starving Bear reined in his horse and held up his hand to his men.

*"Wait here. We don't want to frighten them into doing something stupid. I'll go forward with Star and shake their chief's hand."*

Starving Bear and Star rode on, their horses relaxing now that the mustering and cantering was over. Red Bird waited at the head of the main party and moved his eye from the laconic twitch of Star's horse's tail to the troops ahead. He tried to make out the expressions of the soldiers, but couldn't gauge their mood. Then he caught a movement near the wagons and thought he saw a man tamping a ball into his Sharps rifle and his stomach flipped.

By now Starving Bear and Star were only about thirty feet from the soldiers. They were both smiling and Starving Bear picked the medal up off his chest to show it and raised his parchment in the other hand. Suddenly, Lieutenant Eayre shouted a command and the soldiers fired. Starving Bear and Star were thrown from their horses by impacting bullets and their horses skittered away, leaving the men writhing on the ground. As they lay there helpless some soldiers walked forwards and shot them again.

For a split second the watching Cheyenne were stunned, unable to comprehend what had just happened. Then Thunder Cloud screamed and as one they charged forward. Red Bird fired into the bluecoats before his view was obstructed by the charging warriors and then he urged Wild Wind forward. The howitzers fired, but no one was hit and the gap between the soldiers and the warriors closed. Small parties peeled off left and right and Wild Wind joined the stream to the right of the soldiers' line with Half Bear's horse at his shoulder.

Private Soams was in the Independent Battery of Colorado Volunteer Artillery in order to kill redskin heathens. He had joined in Denver only weeks ago when Lieutenant Eayre had brought the unit into town to buy supplies and the wagons to carry it. He'd been assured by corporal Hays that Eayre was out to kill any Indians he found, peaceful or not, with the full blessing of Colonel Chivington, the commander of the district of Colorado. That suited Soams just fine, because his brother had been killed by the Sioux last year and Soams wanted some revenge.

As Starving Bear and Star rode forward Soams loaded his gun.

"Hell are you doing?" private Anders asked him.

"What's it look like?" he replied tamping the round in place.

"Why ain't it loaded already?"

"Forgot."

"Dumbass."

Now that it had come to it, Soams was nervous and he was beginning to wonder if he had done the right thing joining up. He was a pasty, thin man, only five-feet-six tall and weighing less than one hundred and forty pounds. Although he could shoot, fighting wasn't his speciality and all four bar fights he'd been in had resulted in him taking some spectacular hidings. On seeing Anders, who was the biggest son-of-a-bitch he'd ever seen, at six-foot-five and as wide as a barn door, but less moveable, Soams had decided that if it came to close quarters fighting he wanted to be behind him.

Lieutenant Eayre's barked order and the fusillade of shots almost made Soams drop his gun, but as the Cheyenne charged up the hill, he recovered his wits and darted behind the wagon next to him to be joined quickly by Anders.

For a few moments the soldiers held their line, but the speed of the Indian advance was blistering and they were soon surrounded by a whirlwind of horses. The Indians screamed and whooped and blew on whistles, creating a deafening cacophony that unnerved the troops. More Indians were streaming up from the village and it was apparent within minutes that the militia had made a grave mistake for only eighty-four men to attack what were now, almost five hundred enraged Cheyenne. All order of fire was lost and with most of the soldiers only able to fire twice a minute, they were making little impact on the targets swirling around them. The horses were too fast and too erratic to hit and many of the warriors had slid around their horses' necks and were almost impossible to see.

In contrast to the soldiers' slow rate of fire, arrows were slicing through the air like snowflakes in a blizzard. The soldiers drew together around the wagons, badly frightened.

Sergeant Cunningham, manning one of the howitzers was hit in the neck with an arrow and dropped to the ground thrashing his arms and legs wildly, making a gurgling sound that terrified Private Coleridge next to him. Coleridge got up and ran back towards the wagons as Half Moon charged through their line and sliced down with a hatchet that bit into Coleridge's skull like a cleaver into a melon. Half Moon whooped his counting coup and charged on, slicing into another soldier who had broken into a run.

Anders kept his cool and knelt by the wagon, supporting the barrel of his rifle on the wheel. He kept a bead on Half Bear and fired. The bullet struck Half Bear's horse behind the shoulder and her front legs collapsed, throwing Half Bear clear as the horse summersaulted and slid to a stop. High on adrenaline, Half Bear rolled on landing and kept hold of his bow. He was up and running and getting his knife from his belt as his horse died. He charged Anders, who tossed his spent gun into the air and caught the barrel ready to swing at the running Indian. As the gun butt arced through the air towards him, Half Bear ducked and his knife-hand whipped up and plunged into Anders' groin. Anders' knees buckled and he collapsed with a wheezing groan. Soams stood to fire at Half Bear, who was now turning on him. Soams' world had gone into slow motion and it was taking minutes for the barrel of his gun to swing over to the running man. Finally, it was there and Soams' finger began to squeeze just as Wild Wind crashed into his back and sent him sprawling, the gun firing into empty space. Reining in the horse hard with one hand, so that he pranced on the spot, Red Bird pointed his gun straight down with his other hand and shot Soams in the back of the head. Several soldiers turned their fire on Half Bear, who jumped up behind Red Bird and Wild Wind leapt forward to re-join the race around the wagons, oblivious to the hail of lead around him.

By now Black Kettle had joined the melee. Despite being distraught at the death of his friend, he rode amongst the warriors yelling at them to stop fighting, fearful that yet more of his friends, family and villagers would be killed. It took several minutes of Black Kettle's imploring and shouting, but the warriors began to heed his word and pull back. As the storm of Indians receded, the soldiers mounted up and began a flight back to Fort Larned, feeling desperately lucky to be still alive and guessing, rightly so, that this would be far from the end of the incident.

As they trotted back into the village Wild Wind was relieved that the skirmish was over. He was lathered with sweat and wild eyed, even though he was getting used to the guns, the screaming and whistling. The initial shot of the engagement had been a surprise and had made his heart hammer wildly in his chest and only the firm hand and legs of the man above him had given him the confidence not to flee.

It had been terribly confusing to ride into the battle. The worst part had been when he had galloped towards the man with the long stick held out. Not wanting to hurt the man he had initially tried to change course to avoid him, but Red Bird had tugged on his bit to straighten him and had kicked his heels into his flanks to confirm that that was the course to follow. The collision had been firm and he knew that the man was frail and would be hurt, but, as he would do many times to come, he did as his leader bid.

# CHAPTER THREE

## Summer 1864

In the wake of the murders of Starving Bear and Star a war on the plains had broken out and much blood had been spilt, a great deal of it innocent, as peaceful Indians were killed by soldiers and non-combatant settlers were killed by Indians.

The day after the shootings of Starving Bear and Star, in a fit of rage, Cheyenne warriors attacked a farm on Walnut Creek where the owner's wife was Cheyenne. The woman was taken from the rancher and the man was told to leave, 'because every white man in the country was going to be killed'. It wasn't just the Cheyenne on the warpath, as the Arapahos, Kiowas, Apaches and Sioux were all retaliating against crimes committed against them. Ranches, stages, wagon trains and towns along the Platte and Smoky Hill rivers were burned and men, women and children killed, some almost in sight of Denver.

Despite the fighting, many Indians still wanted to remain peaceful, but many peaceful Indians were attacked by troops or civilians who assumed that any Indian was a bad Indian. In late June the Governor of Colorado, John Evans, issued a circular to the plains Indians telling them that if they were friendly they should report to Fort Lyon where they could be protected and fed whilst the war against the hostiles continued. Unfortunately, many bands of Indians were well scattered over the plains on summer hunts and didn't get the message and were attacked as hostiles. By late August Evans had issued another decree authorizing all citizens of Colorado to go in pursuit of hostile Indians, meaning any not camped a Fort Lyon.

Red Bird couldn't sleep. He lay on his back watching the yellow light of the fire flicker on the tipi wall. She Wolf lay on her side facing away from him, but her back and buttocks were pressed against him. He marvelled at the delicious heat of her warming him like no fire could. Despite the comfort of his bed and the warmth and soft touch She Wolf gave him, he was feeling a turmoil deep within him that had risen and fallen like an irregular tide throughout the whole summer and fall. Why was the inferno of war devouring the Cheyenne? He felt that surely there must be a reason behind the destruction and havoc being created by the whites and he couldn't help feeling that he was part of that reason. He flushed with sweat as a dread that he might unknowingly do something to make the situation worse swept through him.

Being careful not to wake She Wolf he got up and dressed quickly, picked up his rifle, bridle and saddle blanket and stepped out into the night. The cool air was a blessed relief and the pale moon a face offering no judgement. He walked quickly through the wet grass and found Wild Wind in amongst the herd by the river. He slipped the bridle on over his head and laid the blanket across his back and leapt up to ride him without the saddle.

Straight away some of his angst was removed by the motion of the horse and as the heat of his confusion subsided, he felt the chill in the air press around him. They hadn't gone far when they saw the bobcat. Under the pale light of the moon there was no colour, but Red Bird could make out the spots on the cat's legs and the bars on his stubby tail. Wild Wind had stopped, but Red Bird didn't know if this was due to the horse's own decision, or a response to his own unconscious command.

The faintest of breezes brushed against Red Bird's face and kept their scent away from the bobcat who had now slowed the pace of its walk. Its head had dropped below its shoulders as it stalked onwards, its shoulder blades rolling fluidly, but the broad cheek ruffs of its face remained steady as its eyes bore ahead to something unseen by Red Bird. It stopped. Its head tilted slightly, as if it was asking itself a question and it paused to think about the answer. Red Bird waited, fascinated to see what would happen.

The power in the pounce was stunning. The bobcat arced back to earth, its teeth lancing into a hapless ground squirrel and carrying it away in a blur of motion and a puff of dust. Wild Wind danced nervously, but Red Bird held him whilst staring at the grass where the bobcat had made its decision. It had asked itself a question and found the answer. Red Bird knew then that the bobcat was telling him to be still and seek a vision in which to find the answers he sought.

Running Otter was a medicine man, the son of a medicine man and the adopted son of another. He'd been born Sioux, but at the age of ten he'd been out riding with his parents when they had been attacked by a party of Pawnee. His parents had been killed and as the Pawnee left in a cacophony of whoops and yells taking with them the horses, he had been left for dead. Two days later The Great Spirit had sent his new father, Roaring Bull, to find him. He was now seventy-one summers old and though he was grey haired, reed-thin and only five-feet-five inches tall, he was remarkably strong and fit and could still run long distances. He sat cross legged under a tall aspen, his face partially shrouded in a mist of pipe smoke as he listened to Red Bird.

*"I'm hoping you will help me seek a vision to explain to me why we are being persecuted by the whites. I am afraid I may have inadvertently done something to anger the Great Spirit,"* Red Bird said, his words punctuated and underscored by the rattle of the aspen leaves above him. Running Otter nodded sagely.

*"I think you should swing to the pole. Now is a good time to do such a quest. I want you to cut a straight pole of cottonwood and together we will dig a hole and plant it on top of the hill,"* he pointed behind Red Bird where the land swelled upwards beyond the river. *"You will undergo your vision quest in three days from now, but until then I want you to eat nothing to purify your body."*

The morning of his quest Red Bird and Running Otter got up long before the sun. They walked up the hill to where the pole now stood, a rigid sentinel against the stars. Whilst Red Bird silently prayed to the Great Spirit to give him a vision, Running Otter lit a fire using a hot ember kept within a buffalo horn, as his ancestors had done for millennia. By the heat and light of the fire he then rubbed his hands four times over each of the two ropes to be used in the ordeal. He then lifted a coal from the fire and spread sweet grass over it, creating a smoke which the ropes were passed through four times. Running Otter, with proper care and deliberation, attached two deerskin strings to one end of each rope and then put them aside.

By now the sky was lightening and Red Bird stood facing the breeze as Running Otter painted his body with white clay. The fire crackled behind him and Red Bird was grateful for the warmth it gave at his back. Once painted he sat down and Running Otter lit a pipe and offered it to Red Bird four times. On each offering Red Bird smoked, the pipe held to his lips by Running Otter, as he was not allowed to touch it. As the sun broke the horizon Running Otter took a knife and thrust it through the skin and pectoral muscle on each side of Red Bird's chest. Through each slit he pushed a wooden skewer and tied the deerskin strings to each end. The other ends of the deerskin were attached to the rope, which in turn, was tied to the cottonwood pole.

Red Bird stood to face the rising sun, blood pouring down his chest and dripping into the grass. It was now his task to watch the sun travel its journey east to west whilst standing up and leaning away from the pole in an effort to pull himself free. Although Running Otter would leave him alone until sunset, he was watched by the buffalo skull placed on the ground to the south and by the buffalo chips piled to the east and west. They would be there watching to ensure that Red Bird completed his task. He could walk to and fro on a bed of white sage, but he must always watch the sun.

After an hour the initial agony of the assault on his body had dulled a little and he grew accustomed to the constant pain. He thought about launching himself backwards in a one off, massive effort to rip free, but as well as Running Otter having strongly advised against it, he knew he needed to be here all day to achieve his vision. It would only be by suffering all day that he would be able to reach the spirit world, so he leaned back far enough to pull and tear his flesh by tiny increments and he settled his mind to follow the sun and remain open to whatever may come.

A spell of dizziness and nausea welled up in him and Red Bird tried to focus on the feel of the sage piled beneath his feet and of the growing warmth of the sun until it passed. By mid-morning the sun was hot and it began to beat on his head making it throb and bringing the dizziness back. He stared, not directly at the sun, but just below it, marking its travel across the distant hills. It seemed years before the sun reached its zenith at midday and Red Bird sat down for the short rest he was allowed during the ordeal. In the few minutes he rested he watched a silver spotted skipper butterfly float gracefully over the grass and land on a flower. At rest its wings closed together vertically above its body, showing off a brilliant splash of white on the underwing. It unfurled its proboscis and probed the flower for nectar, dabbing quickly with dexterity and with an inherent knowledge of where to probe. Red Bird briefly marvelled that such a delicate and flimsy looking creature could survive the exposure that surrounded it on the prairie.

The afternoon dragged on for eternity and the sun blazed the earth until Red Bird became delirious with pain, dizziness, nausea and dehydration. His whole body was catching fire and in the conflagration within him, as he drifted out of consciousness, he saw a vision. Keller's gun fired and the magnificent elk sank to the ground. The light left its eyes and in a moment of embarrassment Red Bird remembered that in the wake of Keller's accident they had never recovered, or made use of its body and for that, Red Bird knew that the Great Spirit was angry and that this was the reason they were being punished. In his mind's eye he watched the flesh melt from the elk's skull in a time lapse process of decay. The skull shone white and then it began snowing and Red Bird knew he was seeing it in the time of the Deer Rutting Moon.

The image of the skull faded and was replaced by Wild Wind. He was swimming in a river and about to do something of huge import, but Red Bird couldn't grasp what it was. Wild Wind was immensely important, but the reason why was as untouchable as the smoke from the fire still smouldering behind him and this lack of understanding made Red Bird's stomach churn to the point of vomiting. His empty stomach could only retch bile as he wept with pain and frustration.

Running Otter came for Red Bird at sundown. He had collapsed to the ground and was in very bad shape. He was barely conscious and babbled nonsense, his face covered in vomit and his eyes, when they opened, were wild and bloodshot. He had managed to pull the right side of his chest free, but the other side was still attached and almost his whole body was caked in blood. Running Otter freed him and looping his arms under Red Bird's armpits, dragged him into the sweat lodge they had built on the site in preparation for this day.

Running Otter bathed him, cleaning off the blood and remains of the clay and dressed the wounds on his chest and got him to drink water. All the while the steam of the lodge purified him. It was a full twenty-four hours before Red Bird could talk coherently and was able to eat a little food.

By the evening of the second day in the lodge Red Bird was sat up and eating by the fire. *"Did you see a vision?"* Running Otter asked him.

*"I did, but I don't understand all of it."*

Running Otter nodded, this was not uncommon after a vision quest and he knew it could take years for its full meaning to unravel.

*"Tell me what you saw and I will try to help. Talking about it may make its meaning clearer to you."*

*"I think we have had bad times with the white men because the Great Spirit is angry with me. When Loves His Horse died he had just killed an elk with his gun and in the confusion of the accident we never recovered its body, or said the proper thanks for it giving itself to us. It was wasted. I saw it clearly. Its skull is where we left it and I must collect it in the Deer Rutting Moon. It may lift a curse, or it may have some importance for the future."*

*"That seems clear,"* Running Otter said, as he spooned more water over the rocks at the edge of the fire, causing a great hiss of steam. *"I take it there is more that isn't so clear?"*

*"Yes, the problem is Wild Wind. I saw him clearly in a river and felt deeply that he was doing something of great importance to us and possibly, something so huge it will affect all Indians and whites alike. But I cannot grasp what it is. What I feel though, is we must look after him as best we can until this point arrives."* Both men were quiet for a moment trying to think how a horse could affect the lives of men.

*"Don't fret over this,"* Running Otter said, *"I know from helping in many, many, vision quests that these things may take days, or months, or even years to work out, but don't try to force a meaning on it. It may come to you eventually, just as the vision did. Or, it may be that the meaning is only revealed when the event occurs, but until then you can help to make sure the conditions are right for the vision to become reality. "*

Red Bird, reassured by Running Otter's words, lay back and closed his eyes and tried to sleep. He now wanted to be outside so that he could talk to Half Bear and She Wolf, but he knew he must wait three full days in the sweat lodge for the ceremony and his pact with the Great Spirit to be complete.

Once Red Bird had promised the Great Spirit he would recover the elk skull the fortunes of the Indians seemed to begin to change. Despite the storm of warfare that had been raging, Black Kettle managed to bring the Kiowas, Arapahos, Comanches,

Sioux and Apaches together to try to reinstate the peace. He exchanged some of his own horses for white children held as prisoners by Indians so that he could arrange a prisoner exchange with the soldiers.

At the end of September Black Kettle and some of the other chiefs went to Denver with Major Wynkoop of Fort Lyon to make the exchange and to arrange safe passage for their people to Fort Lyon. But Colorado Governor, John Evans, wasn't keen to make peace with the Indians, saying that the Indians deserved to be punished and to that end, he had raised the Third Colorado Regiment for a period of one- hundred days to do that punishing.

Evans agreed in the end to meet the Indians and at the end of negotiations Black Kettle decided to move his camp to Sand Creek, about forty miles northeast of Fort Lyon in Colorado so that they could be seen as friendly. Red Bird was sure that the peace in camp at Sand Creek that Black Kettle's people began to enjoy was at least in part due to the promise he had made to the Great Spirit.

As soon as they left the forest soil Wild Wind found it difficult to keep his footing on the scree. At nearly every step the rocks shifted unpredictably and there was a sheen of ice over most of them. Now that they had left the shelter of the trees, the snow blew at them in tiny mean flakes like a gale-driven swarm of bees, making it hard to see. In minutes, Wild Wind's eyelashes were encrusted in white and he blinked myopically. Red Bird knew he would have to get off to help his horse, but he was reluctant as his backside and the insides of his legs against the horse were the only bits of him that were cold; the rest of him was freezing. With a heavy sigh and with numbing hands keeping tight hold of the blanket around him, Red Bird dismounted and ten yards behind, Half Bear mirrored him.

Both men were acutely aware that it would be touch and go as to whether they would get to Keller's cabin in the remains of the daylight, such as there was. Even the spare horses seemed tired and beaten by the weather. A clattering slide of rocks ahead made all six heads look up to see a herd of twenty or so bighorn sheep get up and run away from them. They had been laid down below the ridge ahead, sheltered from the worst of the wind and quietly chewing the cud and resting when they had spotted the humans. As they danced away from the intruders, even in the grey-white murk of the blizzard, their white rumps flashed conspicuously.

In the wake of the bighorn sheep departure Red Bird went back to his sullen thoughts and tried to remind himself as to why he was suffering here on an unforgiving mountain in the deer rutting moon instead of relaxing in a warm lodge by the hearth with his wife.

"*There's the cabin,*" Half Bear spoke from in front of him, startling Red Bird back to the present. He hadn't been aware of Half Bear overtaking him, or of the ground sloping down towards the meadow. He could barely look up as his neck and shoulders were so stiff with cold. At the cabin they led the horses inside and broke down the rails between the 'stable' and the rest of the cabin so that they could all squeeze in. Just stepping out of the wind made it feel at first as if they had walked into a heated room. Within twenty minutes the fire was roaring in the stove and they began preparing a hot meal for the horses from Keller's supplies, the bliss of which only Wild Wind had ever experienced before. With the horses tended, the men arranged gear to dry and wrapped themselves up to sleep.

The following morning dawned bright and clear and even under the snow, the trail to Keller's hunting ground was visible, a thread-like depression under the ermine shroud. When they got there, the carcass of the elk had been picked clean by predators and many of the bones were missing, taken by wolves, or badgers, or wolverines, but to Red Bird's great relief, the skull was laid near to where it had fallen and still unbroken, although the lower jaw was missing. The teeth of the upper jaw smiled maniacally despite their counterparts below being missing, and the eye sockets fixed Red Bird with an accusing glare. Red Bird carefully wrapped the skull in a blanket, attached it to Wild Wind's saddle and mounted his spare horse for the journey home.

Major Scott J. Anthony revealed his true colours almost as soon as he arrived at Fort Lyon the first week of November to assume command. Unlike the commander he relieved, Major Wynkoop, he was no sympathiser with Indians. He cut the rations of the Arapahos who were camped at the fort and even had his men fire at some of them as they came in to trade, laughing as they ran away in shock. News of the new unfriendly commander reached Black Kettle camped at Sand Creek and so he and a small party from the village went to see this new commander to impress upon him their friendly intentions.

Major Anthony made a show of friendliness and assured Black Kettle that his people were safe and under the protection of the fort and he told them also that they would be free to send young men east to the Smoky Hill to hunt buffalo to feed themselves until their allotted rations arrived at the fort. When Black Kettle's party had left, reassured by his words, Major Anthony told the Arapaho to pack up and leave. There were two bands, one led by Left Hand, who took his people to join Black Kettle at Sand Creek and the other led by Little Raven, who took his people across the Arkansas and headed south, not trusting Major Anthony at all.

Little Raven's suspicions were well founded, as Major Anthony was setting a trap. He wrote to his superiors to tell them he would keep Black Kettle's village quiet, some forty miles from the post until such time as reinforcements for an attack could be sent. To lull Black Kettle further he sent out a post trader to do business with the Indians. With their exact position known and many of their warriors away hunting buffalo, the trap was set.

On November twenty-seventh Colonel John M. Chivington arrived at the fort with six-hundred men, including the Third Colorado Regiment, who had Governor Evans' punishing to do. For Chivington, time was off the essence, the existence of the Third Regiment would be fleeting and he was determined strike whilst that particular iron was hot.

That evening fire danced warmly in the hearth and candles added to the glow, but the mood in Major Anthony's office at Fort Lyon was far from cheery. Chivington's officers sat around a table with a map spread out and held at the corners with plates. "Gentlemen, we will set out for Black Kettle's camp at eight pm. tomorrow night," Chivington addressed his commanders, pointing where Black Kettle was assumed to still be camped, "and we'll teach him not to attack our peaceful homesteaders."

"Sir, Black Kettle has been peaceful until now and has settled near here to be under our protection," Captain Soule interjected and unable to let this pass without protest. Chivington stared at the captain as if he'd just slapped him in the face. Undaunted by the colour rising above Chivington's black beard, Lieutenant Cramer felt the need to back up the captain.

"Captain Soule is right sir. We should find and pursue some hostiles. I'm sure..." Cramer's protestations were cut off by Chivington's explosion.

"Damn any man who sympathises with Indians!" he yelled, smashing his fist down on the table near Lt. Cramer's face. "I have come to kill Indians, and believe it is right and honourable to use any means under God's heaven to kill Indians."

"Yes, but..." Soule began again, but was shouted down once more by Chivington who was outraged and furious.

"Any man who refuses to join the expedition tomorrow will be court-marshalled. Get out of here and make sure your men are ready."

The officers stood and shuffled out leaving Chivington seething at the table. Outside in a bitter wind Captain Soule pulled aside his friends Lieutenants Cramer and Connor. "Listen, we'll have to go along with this madness, but I'm going to tell my men not to fire, or only in self-defence. When we get back to the real world I'll make a complaint about that old bastard." Cramer and Connor nodded in agreement and made a pact to do the same.

The following night, as Red Bird and Half Bear made their way back to the village with the skull of the elk, a column of over seven-hundred men set out towards Black Kettle's camp with murder in mind.

Private Jim Goddard was scared shitless at the prospect of a battle. Even without guns, the heathens had killed people he knew. Despite that he had still volunteered for the Colorado Third Regiment, but only so that he could avoid being drafted into the Union Army fighting the Confederates, all of whom did have guns, and cannons besides. He tried not to let his anxiety show, but his friend Sam Jenkins, poked fun at him tirelessly. The night was crystal clear as they marched and the stars glittered like no jewels on earth. The cold was intense, drawing their breath out on silky clouds and the moon silvered a thin layer of snow on the ground. Goddard had slung his rifle over his shoulder and was marching with his hands jammed in his armpits, desperately trying to keep them from getting so cold that they'd snap off.

"Hey shitbird, drink some of this, it'll keep you warm," Jenkins said, passing a flask of whiskey to him. Goddard took a slug and felt the whiskey burn down his throat. Many of the untrained militia in the column had had the same idea and it seemed that half the marching column was at least semi-drunk. Goddard was grateful for the burst of warmth that the whiskey gave him and as he looked around he was also grateful that he was on foot. He was freezing, but at least he was moving, whilst the men in the mounted regiments, sat still on horses, must be truly frozen.

Just as light was coming into the sky the column came to an abrupt halt. In the distance, to the north, they could see the Indian village. It was spread along the north bank of the big bend of Sand Creek. Smoke curled from the tops of some of the tipis, but that was all the movement Goddard could see. To the south of the creek and to the column's left was a huge herd of hundreds of horses. Goddard scanned the riverbank and counted almost a hundred tipis. He thought that maybe with four people per tipi there could be four hundred Indians below. However, there weren't that many, because most of the men were away on a buffalo hunt, as Major Anthony had encouraged them to do. About two thirds of the camp was made up of women and children and many of the men were old. Black Kettle was so confident of the protection of Fort Lyon, that there was not even a night-time guard out, except a few men to watch over the horses, some of whom could do themselves a mischief totally unaided.

Jenkins and Goddard finished the last of their whiskey as Colonel Chivington gathered his officers together for a few moments. Then it began. Wilson's First Regiment peeled off, under orders to cut off the horse herd. Electricity jolted through the horses as they galloped towards the Indian herd.

Dragonfly Woman was fetching water from a pool on the riverbed when she saw the shadows moving on the other side of the river and felt the earth rumble with hooves. "*Buffalo!*" she called to Magpie.

"*No, soldiers!*" Magpie screamed and they dropped their pots and ran up the bank towards Black Kettle's tipi. Black Kettle ran out, "*Don't be afraid,*" he called, "*we are under protection.*" As the women gathered around him he hoisted his American flag and a white flag of surrender above his tipi.

Old Running Badger saw the cavalry coming towards his horses and shouted out a warning to the other men watching the herd. As he ran towards the soldiers drawing an arrow into his bow, a volley of shots rang out and he fell. At the gunfire, a ripple of panic surged through the village and the women and children gathered, screaming, near Black Kettle. The few warriors still in camp snatched up their weapons and raced towards the horses as the gunfire intensified. Running Weasel leapt onto his war horse and stood forward as she charged up the bank. They were both cut down in a hail of fire only yards from the creek.

Within minutes Jenkins and Goddard, in amongst a mass of other infantry, were running down the banks of the creek and onto its wide, flat, sandy bed. The creek was almost totally dry, with only isolated pools of ice-cloaked water. The mounted troops had split and some of them thundered across the river in a spray of sand and snow and up the other bank, the horses' nostrils flaring as they turned to head into the main body of tipis. The rest of the cavalry stayed on the south bank and began firing across the river into the village.

As Goddard ran on, two squaws with three children stepped out from under the bank where they had been hiding. He fired in a drunken haze, catching a little girl in the belly and sending her sprawling in the sand. Jenkins fired, hitting a squaw and by then they were running past, but more shots followed behind them and the little group lay dying in the frost, under a pitiless moon. Gradually the troops slowed to a walk. By now most of the village had been driven into the riverbed and were fleeing away from the infantry, but the cavalry had them corralled on either side and were waiting for them further ahead.

Black Kettle called out reassurance to the women around him until some of them were cut down and at last he grasped his wife's arm and pulled her towards their horses. He called to his friend White Antelope to come, but White Antelope crossed his arms in front of him and began to sing the death song, *"Nothing lives long, Except the earth and the mountains..."* he was cut short by a bullet hitting his chest and he collapsed.

Red Bird and Half Bear were almost at the horse herd when the firing began. Red Bird was sick with guilt and bewildered, thinking that somehow this new horror was down to him. He must have misread his vision and not done properly what the Great Spirit had demanded. This was the end of the world. They spurred their horses on towards the village to help defend the women and children. Cut loose from his master, who was riding his spare horse, Wild Wind was left behind on the plain with the elk skull tied to his back, the small spring antlers poking out from the confines of the blanket. He came to a stop, afraid to move towards the gunfire and momentarily confused as to what was required of him. He pawed at the thin layer of snow and found old brown grass and began to graze.

The braves guarding the horses had been driven back to the riverbank, where they met with others fleeing along the river. Here they gathered themselves and dug into the sand and readied themselves to fight. Black Kettle joined them, exhausted, riven both by guilt for reassuring his people so foolishly and by grief for his wife, who had been shot in their flight along the river. He would find her later, wounded, but alive.

Private Goddard was now transformed into a man of bravado. With only unarmed women and children as opposition he had lost his fear and was firing at anything that moved. Up on the riverbank private Sanders' horse, Betty, was hit by a bullet and she screamed piteously as her entrails fell out onto the sand. Sanders fell off as she staggered, but she held her footing and stood back up with feet splayed, making a beseeching noise that brought Sanders close to tears. He took his pistol and shot her to end her suffering and leapt down the bank to join the infantry. As he half-ran down to the creek, trying to keep himself upright, below him Goddard saw movement and turned and shot him square in the chest. Everything was happening so fast that Goddard, running again, didn't even register his mistake. Sanders wasn't the only soldier killed that day by drunken friendly fire.

Red Bird and Half Bear galloped down the riverbed towards the infantry, their war whistles screaming. In the half-light Goddard and Jenkins saw two spectral banshees racing towards them on horseback and with nerves calmed by whiskey and by the ease of the killing so far, they both coolly knelt as one, raised their rifles and fired. By pure chance, Goddard's bullet smacked into Red Bird's cheek. His brain never had chance to register the impact before it was liquidised by the passage of the bullet and its shockwave through his skull. He fell backwards off his horse, which veered off up the riverbank and fled the field of battle. Half Bear charged onwards, determined to kill the two soldiers in front of him. His horse clattered into Jenkins who was knocked to the ground and as he landed on his arm, half propping himself up, one of the horse's rear hooves caught him full in face, killing him. As he rode over Jenkins, Half Bear swung his war club and caught Goddard in the forehead, splitting his skull open and killing him too.

There were seven women and six children in Running Otter's tipi and they cowered around the hearth in flickering firelight as gunfire sounded all around and they could hear horses galloping amongst the tipis like malevolent thunder. "*We need to let the soldiers know we are women and children in here,*" said Soft Wind, "*otherwise they may burst in and shoot us by mistake.*"

*"You and Pot Belly go out with a white cloth and tell them,"* Pawnee Woman suggested. Soft Wind nodded assent and picked up a white cloth and took hold of her three-year-old daughter's hand. With a calmness she didn't feel, she spoke to her daughter, *"Come on Pot Belly, let's go and tell the soldiers we aren't here to hurt them."* Pot Belly began to cry, but her mother took firm hold of her hand and they stepped outside.

Corporal Peter Tibbs was charging his horse back towards the river when the squaw and child stepped out of the tipi. He pulled hard on the reins and brought his horse to a standstill and dismounted. As his feet hit the dirt he pulled his pistol from its holster and jabbed it against the head of the squaw. Her head bounced away from the gun and she screamed, but the plea was cut short as he fired. Pot Belly was spattered with her mother's blood and erupted into a wail as her mother fell, but she too, was silenced by Tibbs' gun. Four infantry soldiers arrived and the five of them stepped into Running Otter's tipi and calmly shot everyone in it.

The flow of the battle had ebbed away and now most of the soldiers concentrated their fire against the warriors dug in on the riverbank. All around the edges of the village small groups of Cheyenne escaped onto the prairie. Half Bear rode up to Calling Calf Woman who was limping very badly and trying to carry her child. Her legs below her skirt were red with blood and her moccasins almost black with it. Half Bear dismounted and gave her the horse, helping her up and passing the child up to her. He then turned back towards the river to look for more survivors.

Wild Wind had been trying to graze amongst patchy snow for nearly an hour when a soldier approached him on foot. So far in his life the humans he had encountered had been good to him, or at worst ambivalent, but there was something not right about this one. The man was walking slowly, like a stalking predator and Wild Wind was suspicious of him. He felt a tingle of apprehension. He lifted his head and snorted. The man began swinging a rope and shifted to a strange sidling walk. Wild Wind pranced sideways away from the man, unsure of what to do.

Private Gant had been told to start rounding up loose horses while the battle petered out. Gant had deliberately joined the infantry and not the cavalry as he hadn't a clue about horses. This son-of-a-bitch seemed to have sussed him and he was starting to step away from him so Gant ran and flung his rope at the beast's neck.

When the man suddenly went from his odd stalk to an outright chase and threw something at him, Wild Wind's instinct to avoid the danger took over and he erupted into flight and galloped towards the river. As he went, the rope holding the elk skull to his saddle came loose and the skull swung down against his flank, sending him into a blind panic and a desperate charge away from the danger. In seconds he was by the river, where he could see a man he recognised, just as another stepped out from a bush just in front of him. He stepped sideways in an attempt to avoid a collision, but as he passed him, out of the corner of his eye he saw the man fall.

As Half Bear had reached the river a soldier in a thicket of alder stepped out, raised a pistol and took aim, but he swivelled at the sound of a galloping horse and as he spun around Wild Wind jinked away trying to avoid him, but the elk skull on its short lariat arced gracefully away from Wild Wind's flank and a tine of one of the antlers twirled through the air and gouged into the man's eyeball. He dropped his pistol and was lifted from his feet screaming and dragged several yards like a fish on a hook. As the tine worked free of the man's eye socket he fell flat on his back and Half Bear ran over, picked up the pistol, and shot him. He then raced on and caught Wild Wind, who felt reassured enough by the sight of Half Bear to come to a stop. Half Bear leapt up onto him and went to find more people to help.

Bob Williams looked at the body of the dead squaw. She'd been shot through the neck, but he could still see she had been a pretty woman. 'Shame', he thought, 'she had great tits and if we'd caught her alive we could have had some fun.' He lifted her buckskin skirt with the barrel of his gun. "Whooo-ee. Look at this squaw pussy," he called to Jeffers and Calhoun who were poking about through some stuff thrown clear of a tipi. They both looked over at Williams. "I'm gonna get me some of this."

Williams laid his gun down and drew his knife. In quick, savage movements he cut off the woman's genitals. "Look at this!" he crowed holding his prize aloft. Jeffers and Calhoun watched as Williams stretched the woman's privates over his hat as a hatband. Following Williams' example they too then set off in search of their own hat decorations. Williams then cut off the woman's scalp and the mutilation of corpses spread through the regiments like a fire on the prairie.

Up ahead Half Bear could see a grey haired man, 'Running Otter', he thought, supporting a limping woman he didn't recognise as she wasn't walking properly and her head was dropped down below her shoulders. He put his heels into Wild Wind's flanks and urged him on. The man and woman were above Half Bear, climbing a hill into an austere blue sky devoid of cloud, a wobbly trail laid out behind them in the mosaic of snow and bare ground. The sun was shining, but low in the sky and totally without warmth and as Wild Wind sliced through the still air it burned in Half Bear's throat. As the gap between them closed Half Bear could see that the man was indeed Running Otter and that the woman was She Wolf. The pair of them turned in fear at the sound of Half Bear's approach and then relaxed momentarily as they recognised the horse and rider. A split second after registering Half Bear as friend and not foe, She Wolf was afraid of why Red Bird wasn't with him, as the two were inseparable. With a tide of panic surging through her chest she wondered why Half Bear would be riding Red Bird's horse.

Half Bear climbed down from Wild Wind as She Wolf disengaged herself from Running Otter and asked, *"Where is Red Bird?"* Half Bear stepped forward and wrapped her in his arms. She sank into his chest and choked on a wail, knowing what was coming.

*"Red Bird was killed in the creek. He was shot and never felt anything. It was a warrior's death".*

The wail in She Wolf's throat escaped onto the vastness of the prairie to be absorbed by a billion blades of grass. She cried hard, shaking against Half Bear and pushing him backwards a step. A storm raged within her and Half Bear could do nothing but hold her until it subsided enough for him to ask Running Otter how badly injured they were.

*"I am fine,"* Running Otter said, *"Just old and tired. But She Wolf had a bullet pass through her hamstring and she can't walk properly."*

*"You get on Wild Wind and I'll push her up behind you,"* Half Bear said to the old man. She Wolf was insensate with grief and seemingly unable to understand anything said to her, so that it took the two of them pushing and pulling to get her mounted and in a position she could ride. She put her arms around Running Otter and slumped against his back. *"Go,"* Half Bear told them. *"Head for the hunters' camp on the Smoky Hill. I'll catch you up."*

It was fifty miles to the Smoky Hill, where the majority of the warriors were camped and spread out across the prairie, that was where the survivors of the Sand Creek massacre headed. Half Bear jogged as best he could across the frozen landscape, loosening his clothes to prevent himself from soaking them with sweat and in that way kept warm. In the late afternoon, whilst heading downhill towards a stand of cottonwood, he could see another group of survivors. The party ahead sat down, exhausted, and waited for him to catch up. Half Bear recognised them all. There were four young women, Trembles In The Wind, Picking Sticks Woman, Yellow Leaf and Antelope Woman and their six children, aged between one and eight years. The group was completed by two aged men, Old Yellow Sun and Old Eagle.

The women sat hugging their children in a fruitless attempt to keep them warm. No-one in the little bedraggled group was dressed to be outdoors in winter, as they'd been rousted from their beds and had fled at dawn. Half Bear was met with vacant stares and nobody spoke. He could see that the clothes of three-year-old Little Leaf were soaked in blood and her eyes were shut. All of the children had been barefoot, but Old Eagle had cut his robe into strips to bind their feet. Half Bear had never seen a more desperate looking group of wretches.

*"Let's get down into that stand of trees,"* Half Bear said trying to keep his voice bright and encouraging, *"They will give us some shelter for tonight."* As they walked the last hundred yards to the trees he wrestled with a dilemma, whether or not to light a fire. The sun was sliding below the horizon and a bank of dark cloud was gathering

ominously, threatening snow. A fire might draw the attention of the soldiers if, as seemed likely, they were in pursuit, but without a fire some of them might not survive the night.

Using a broken branch Half Bear swept the snow and leaves from a small hollow and lit a fire by striking his knife against a flint he always carried in a pouch on his belt. They gathered leaves and brush to make a bed to lie on and to cover themselves as a blanket and they rounded up wood for the fire, pathetic as it was under the black dome of the seething sky. Yellow Leaf sat and wailed with grief, rocking the now lifeless body of Little Leaf in her arms. The snow began to fall heavily in a premature attempt to bury them.

Half Bear began a cycle of feeding the fire and warming himself for a spell before getting up to find more wood and then returning to the flames. He kept the fire small as there wasn't enough fuel to make a big one and in any case a big fire would be more likely to draw the soldiers. Despite the heat from the fire it couldn't stave off the cold which was a living, biting parasite, burrowing into his skin and bones and creating a constant pain that made Half Bear want to howl at the night like a wolf. Yellow Leaf seemed impervious to the cold, sitting still as a statue, staring at the fire with Little Leaf locked in her arms.

After three hours Half Bear swept the fire and its hot coals six feet away from its original position. That done he roused everyone from under their leaf blankets and got them to make new beds on the fire-warmed earth. It was this that probably saved most of their lives, but despite his best efforts, when dawn broke Old Eagle and Yellow Leaf couldn't be roused.

The snow had stopped falling late in the night and the sky now promised sunshine. Before departing they placed the tiny body of Little Leaf in the cold arms of a cottonwood and laid Old Eagle and Yellow Leaf out in the sun. They felt bad about it, but they took the clothes from the dead to keep the children from freezing. All the adults knew that they would likely spend another night in the open before reaching the sanctuary of the hunters' camp, but they kept that terrible prospect from the children.

They travelled all day and saw no sign of soldiers. Their march ended by a dry river which was bordered by trees and so they built a fire. With plenty of wood and no sign of pursuit Half Bear built a big fire and the worst of the cold was pushed away. At daylight the drumming of hooves preceded the arrival of rescuers from the Smoky Hill with spare horses in tow.

# CHAPTER FOUR

## Smoky Hill River
## January 1865

She Wolf had cried almost continuously for three days and Running Otter had become concerned about her health as she became starved and dehydrated, but there were so many others in the village with terrible wounds in need of his help, that he couldn't give much attention to those with mental scars. Half Bear did what he could to get her to drink, but she was bloody-minded and not in the mood to be coddled. As a sign of grief, she cut off her hair and in a period of relative emotional calm, she cut off the top joint of her little finger, an act that would signify and testify to her grief.

Half Bear began to worry that She Wolf was going more than a little crazy as she wandered around the camp muttering incoherently, her un-bandaged hand dripping blood and her cropped hair spiky and wild. He began to doubt that she would ever really recover from her bereavement but he was wrong, a sea-change in her outlook was about to take place. It was late afternoon and snowing hard with big flakes that fell straight down with purpose. She Wolf was wandering around outside the tipi muttering about Red Bird's lost blanket when she almost bumped into Half Bear bringing Wild Wind to wait outside his tipi.

She Wolf stopped in her tracks and stared at the horse as if it had just slapped her. Wild Wind and Half Bear stood still, blinking snowflakes from their eyelashes, their breath wispy exclamations of life. She Wolf stared at them for a second and then she walked to Wild Wind and gently held his muzzle in her hands. Not only had this been Red Bird's favourite horse, but he had impressed upon her how important he thought the horse would be. His vision had been clear in that this most normal-looking of creatures would do something of immense import.

She Wolf stepped around Wild Wind and put her arms around his neck and rested her face against his deep winter coat, breathing in his smell and absorbing some of his heat. The two of them stood together for several minutes with Half Bear just standing and watching, snow collecting on his head and shoulders, not daring to break the spell.

Wild Wind's ears came forward and he stood patiently as the woman wrapped her arms around his neck. He could feel her warmth and although she felt incredibly frail to him, he could sense a strength within her. He also felt comfort in her embrace and he stamped his right rear hoof.

This huge but gentle animal, She Wolf told herself, was her connection to Red Bird and he was Red Bird's unfulfilled promise. She Wolf, like her husband before her, pledged to do her utmost to help him achieve his preordained role.

"*Can I ride him?*" She Wolf suddenly asked Half Bear, raising her head from the horse's neck.

"*Of course.*" Half Bear held up a finger in a 'wait' gesture and stepped inside to fetch Keller's bridle and saddle. Ten minutes later the woman and horse were a partnership walking through the skeletal winter cottonwoods on the bank of the river. Wild Wind shied slightly as an otter darted out from the trees and slid into the river through a hole in the ice, leaving only a rapidly diminishing ripple as evidence of its existence. Wild Wind resumed his walk and She Wolf was soothed by the motion of the animal and she let her mind register only the path of the horse and her conscious thoughts ceased.

Wild Wind came to a sudden halt and She Wolf was brought back to the here-and-now. Up ahead a wolverine was digging in the snow and earth. Soil sprayed up between its back legs as its front legs pistoned into the earth with thrusts of its powerful shoulders and its coat shook with the effort. The wolverine was so focused on the dig that it didn't see the horse and rider. Seconds later the buried prize it was digging for was rent from the iron-hard earth; the shoulder and leg of a deer it had buried sometime before. The wolverine, unaware it had an audience, turned towards She Wolf and then realised it had company, turned tail and rumbled off into the trees, the deer leg dangling from its mouth and clumsily catching on the vegetation as it went. Connected to Red Bird through his horse and seeing the wolverine recover a desperately needed, life-giving, winter meal, She Wolf realised that her life would also continue and that she needed to come to terms with the loss she had suffered. With a physical jolt she also realised that the otter had been trying to tell her something; just because she could no longer see Red Bird, it didn't mean he wasn't here. She could feel his ripples.

News of the massacre of Black Kettle's people spread across the plains and messengers rode between the Cheyenne, Arapaho and Sioux carrying war pipes, calling for revenge against the white men. Black Kettle was disregarded as a chief, his way of peace now seen as hopeless and the leading chief became Leg In The Water. The white men sent a peace emissary to him to appeal to him to make a new treaty. The emissary, who had lived with Indians for half a century, told Leg In The Water that there were not enough Indians to fight the whites, as they were as numerous as the leaves on the trees. Leg In The Water answered him, *"We know it, but what do we want to live for? The white man has taken our country, killed all of our game; was not satisfied with that, but killed our wives and children. Now no peace. We want to go and meet our families in the spirit land. We loved the whites until we found out they lied to us, and robbed us of what we had. We have raised the battle axe until death."*

It was now the Moon of Strong Cold and the Crier didn't want to be out long as he made his way through the tipi village at Cherry Creek in deepening snow. The falling snow gathered on the blanket over his shoulders and deadened his voice, but he was determined everyone would hear his news; the war party would set off in the morning to attack Julesburg. A raven perched above a tipi smoke hole kronked encouragement and agreement, its head and chest vigorously bouncing up and down with each call, the echoes of which, like the Crier's, were trapped in the snow.

She Wolf did her best to walk in the trampled, shallower snow, as she sought out Half Bear. Her injured leg caused her to hobble and her foot dragged, pulling snow into her moccasin and the pain was fierce. She should have been in bed resting, but she desperately wanted to be close to Half Bear and Wild Wind, both of whom, she knew, would be going out with the war party. She almost bumped into Half Bear as he came up from the creek, a pot of icy water in hand. *"I want to help you paint Wild Wind for the war party,"* she blurted out. *"I'm going to come as well with two spare horses."*

Half Bear nodded his assent, having expected nothing less. He took She Wolf's arm and helped her back to his tipi where he sat her by the fire to get warm. They sat together in the flickering light and spent time mixing buffalo fat, ochre, charcoal and various berries into paint. *"This might not end well,"* Half Bear said as he mixed.

*"What, painting Wild Wind?"*

*"No, I mean the war party."*

*"Oh. Well it's fine. Either I'll see white men killed, or I'll be killed and see Red Bird again. I don't care how it ends."* Half Bear looked at her crushing red berries and nodded to himself, realising that it was indeed fine either way and finding a peace settle within him. Wild Wind waited patiently outside, tethered to a picket pin and stoically enduring the snowfall.

The snow had stopped when Half Bear and She Wolf stepped back outside. Half Bear untied the rawhide strips that held three US Army blankets over Wild Wind's back and they began to paint him for war. Half Bear put spots and zig-zags on his shoulders and forearms, whilst She Wolf drew a red bird, a cardinal, on each hindquarter. They were beautifully drawn and coloured, even to the extent of the black area around the base of the beak. Half Bear was amazed at the result. So good and so unusual was the painting, that Wild Wind gathered clusters of admirers all afternoon.

Julesburg was a small town where the overland stage forded the South Platte and headed up Pole Creek towards the North Platte, Fort Laramie and the mountains beyond. There was a station made of cedar logs for the stage, a telegraph office, stables and corrals, stores and warehouses. A mile to the west was Fort Rankin where a company of the Seventh Iowa Cavalry was in residence.

A mixed party of a thousand Sioux, Cheyenne and Arapaho left Cherry Creek looking for revenge. A rainbow of colours snaked out over the white of the snow, with material of many hues and thousands of crow and eagle feathers fluttering in the wind from lances, headdresses and shields. They rode in silent determination to hit the enemy unannounced and marched close up to Fort Rankin, where they camped out of sight in a fold of the earth. The Sioux chiefs had led the way, as, after all, the war pipe had been offered to them first and they had smoked it, so they had place of honour, and in any event, they knew this region better than the other tribes. The women had followed the warriors with spare horses on which to load plunder, or the wounded, and amongst them was She Wolf, whose acute grief had now been replaced with a burning anger.

Before dawn broke Chief Big Crow came to speak to Half Bear. "*I want you to ride out to the fort with me and five others. We will ride down the ravine to where it meets the Platte in front of the fort,*" he pointed at the far end of the ravine, which was almost three miles from where they stood now. "*Hopefully we can get the soldiers to come out and chase us and everyone else will be hiding here behind this hill ready to surround them.*"

Half Bear felt honoured to have been chosen for the ride to the fort, but he suspected that much of the decision was based on the known prowess of Wild Wind and on the impressiveness of his war paint, which was surely a powerful protection against the white man's guns. He finished applying his own war paint. He had made one half of his face black and the other half yellow. Then he checked over the rifle he had recovered from Red Bird and the pistol he had taken from the soldier at Sand Creek. As well as the guns he had a war club attached to Wild Wind's saddle and a knife on his belt. Armed to the teeth as he was, he had lent his bow to Bright Moon, as he couldn't carry that as well.

Light was coming into the sky, but there was still no sign of the sun, as the seven men rode down the ravine towards the fort. The cold was stunning and Half Bear rode with the reins in one hand and the other hand in his armpit to keep warm. His rifle was attached to the saddle with a rawhide strip and a quick release knot and the pistol was in his waistband. To him and the others, it felt as if the sound of their movements were enough to wake the dead, but beyond a few yards from them the snow dragged sound to the ground and devoured it. The soldiers in Fort Rankin were totally unaware of their approach.

Finally the sun broke the horizon and the seven Indians, who by now had reached the end of the ravine, could see some men loitering outside the wall of the fort. Half Bear aimed carefully with the rifle and fired. The gunshot sounded cataclysmic in the frozen air and the horses exploded into life. They had gone several strides and were being brought into a controlled gallop by their riders by the time the man at the gates fell under the force of Half Bear's bullet. The Indians whooped and jeered at the soldiers in front fleeing into the fort, whose doors were slammed shut. They had galloped to within fifty yards of the doors to the fort when they swung open and Captain O'Brien and a body of cavalry came charging out. The Indians were delighted and grinning like maniacs, they spun their horses around and began a headlong retreat back to the hills, manes, tails, hair, feathers and cloaks flailing in the air to keep up. The cavalry fired at them, but at a gallop it was impossible to fire accurately. The shots gave notice to the Indians behind the hill that their part in the drama was just about to be played.

Unfortunately, some of the younger warriors couldn't contain themselves and as the shots grew close they got over-excited and broke early, ruining the chance to surround the soldiers. With the ambush blown the chiefs gave the orders to charge and a thousand warriors galloped out of cover and blazed towards the fort.

O'Brien and his cavalry saw the eruption of Indians from behind the hill and realising they were riding into an ambush, turned hard back towards the fort, spurring their horses into greater effort now that they had become the quarry in a deadly chase. At this point they were a mile from the safety of the fort. Private Grady's horse slipped on a patch of ice and its legs splayed out flat beneath him. Ironically, Grady kept himself in the saddle as the horse went down, but was thrown clear as it jerked back up. The horse staggered away and Grady raised his gun as Wild Wind bore down on him. Grady fired and the round blazed an inch to the left of Half Bear's ear. Wild Wind was beyond Grady before Half Bear could fire back, but Snake jabbed his lance into Grady's chest, catastrophically puncturing his pulmonary artery. He went down gasping, eyelids fluttering and was dead a minute later.

Half Bear could see that the soldiers' horses were tiring, but Wild Wind and the other six Indian horses were fading even faster, as they had run further in two directions already. The horses of the thousand Cheyenne behind though, were fresh and they overtook Big Crow's party and closed in on the soldiers. As O'Brien and his men made for the sanctuary of the fort another troop of cavalry came bursting out to help cover them, but seconds later the vanguard of the Indian party surrounded O'Brien's group and he saw several of his men hit by arrows and bullets. In a whirling cacophony of war whistles, whoops, screams and gunshots that seemed to last forever, but was in fact only seconds, O'Brien and his men broke through the melee to the greeting cavalry and together they made it into the fort.

Ira Laidlaw had been driving the stage for two years and he was getting jittery about the Indians. His friend Jed had been killed and scalped last year and his stomach had been churning all day, wondering if this would be his day of reckoning and so he was mightily relieved when they pulled into the station at Julesburg. When the horses had stopped, he stood up to get the kinks out of his ass.

Inside the station Ester Gainford had been busy since before sunup cooking breakfast for the stage and its passengers and as it pulled in, the table was laid with plates of steaming hot bacon, sausage and eggs. Outside, from his perch atop the stage Ira could see breakfast through the window and his mood swung like a saloon door from morose to excited. The frost cracked on his poncho as he moved around and he could almost feel hot coffee in his stomach already. Then a movement caught his eye and he looked out towards Fort Rankin only a few hundred yards away. "Jesus Christ a'mighty," he yelled and the disembarking passengers turned to look. There were hundreds and hundreds of Indians roiling out from behind a hill towards the fort in a mudslide of horseflesh.

The stage horses had already been led away to a corral to graze and so the obvious means of escape was gone. Hiding in the station would be hopeless, because if the Indians came their way they'd be holed up and slaughtered. The only hope was to run to the fort and get in it. Ira leapt from the stagecoach and hit the ground running, the other passengers right on his heels. Inside, Ester heard the panic and looked through the window to see everyone run like wild animals. She dropped the last plate of bacon and eggs on the table and ran herself.

As Ira and the stage passengers ran for the fort a group of the Indians peeled off from the clash with the soldiers in the hope of intercepting them. It would be close. She Wolf turned her horse and the two she was leading to follow the men heading for the stage party. Ester ran as best she could, but she was fifty-seven years old and hampered by her skirts and she fell further behind. The safety of the fort was tantalising, but she realised she wasn't going to make it. As the others ran in through the gates the first of the warriors was nearly upon her. She had a derringer in her bra and she determined to kill the first heathen bastard who came within five feet of her. As the gates closed behind him O'Brien thought he saw a lone woman swamped in a throng of warriors.

Frustrated that the soldiers had reached the fort, Half Bear pointed Wild Wind in the direction of the stage station and Julesburg where many of the warriors were now headed. Ahead of him he could see She Wolf and he tried to catch her up.

Ester's cooked breakfasts weren't wasted, although she wouldn't have been pleased to see who ate them. A party of Cheyenne burst into the station and helped themselves to the meal which was still hot. Half Bear and She Wolf were too late for a cooked breakfast but they helped themselves to what was in the warehouse. Half Bear loaded sacks of corn, flour and sugar onto the spare horses. She Wolf picked up one of hundreds of cans of meat from a shelf and asked Half Bear, *"What are these?"*

Half Bear didn't know and neither did anyone else and so the cans were left. Half Bear glanced out of the window and could see across the river to where a herd of cattle was grazing. As he watched, Cheyenne and Sioux rode gingerly across the frozen surface of the South Platte and began herding the cattle back to camp. He smiled to himself; beef would be on the menu tonight. Although the ambush of the soldiers hadn't worked as they'd planned they had killed some of them without any Cheyenne casualties and now the soldiers were hiding in their fort too afraid to come out to stop them stealing food and goods and burning the town.

She Wolf couldn't sleep. She was warm and comfortable in bed despite the snow falling gently outside and the fire flickered, crackling gently in the centre of the tipi and casting a warm glow on the buffalo-skin wall above her. Her parents snored gently on the other side of the fire, but not loud enough to disturb her. She tried to concentrate on the soporific sound of the snow pattering on the tepee wall, but she couldn't drown out the loud noise from the village. It was the sound of drums. Scalp dances had been taking place every night and all night, for days. Julesburg had burned and raids had taken place up and down the Platte. Miles of telegraph wires had been torn down and warehouses and ranches plundered of goods and livestock. Everyone now had plenty to eat and there was no sign of soldiers. The scalp dances were a celebration.

She Wolf's inability to sleep wasn't being caused by the noise however, or discomfort, or hunger, or fear; it was what was missing. Red Bird wasn't with her and it was in bed, alone at night, when the despair and longing hit hardest. She couldn't feel the heat of Red Bird's body, or the comfort of his arm around her. She couldn't whisper to him and hear him whisper back. She was only twenty –one and already a widow. Following custom, when Red Bird was killed, all his possessions were given away to people in the village, even his tipi, which was why She Wolf was back here living with her parents.

She had known Red Bird as a boy in the village all her life, but had only really been interested in of him from the age of fourteen. Since then he had courted her doggedly and then of course they'd married and it seemed now that she had had no life before Red Bird. Her world had abruptly imploded. But she still had Wild Wind to cling to and Red Bird had impressed upon her how important he thought the horse would be, although he admitted he didn't know how or why. However, Wild Wind was now Half Bear's horse and so to stay with Wild Wind she would have to follow Half Bear wherever he went. The village was in the process of splitting and so Half Bear's decisions could have a major impact on her.

The Cheyenne had moved from Cherry Creek to their winter camp on the Republican, where the chiefs had held council to decide what to do in the wake of the Sand Creek massacre. Black Kettle, still desperate for peace, spoke for going south of the Arkansas with the Southern Arapaho, Kiowas and Comanches, where the weather was milder and there were still buffalo. Nearly all the other chiefs wanted to head north into the Powder River country of modern Wyoming and Montana and join forces with the Teton Sioux and the Northern Cheyenne, with whom they would surely be invincible against the white soldiers.

Finally giving in to her insomnia, She Wolf got out of bed and got dressed. When she stepped outside the cold hit her like a slap and the dark closed tightly around her, gradually releasing its grip a little as her eyes adjusted. At least there was no wind and the snow fell benignly to earth as the sound of the drums beat through it. Her leg felt better as she tramped through the snow to find Wild Wind.

As She Wolf approached Half Bear's tipi she could see that Half Bear was outside as well and man and horse were stood conspiratorially close together. Half Bear was tying a Hudson's Bay blanket on over the top of the US Army blankets already clothing Wild Wind. Half Bear looked up and saw She Wolf approach and Wild Wind stamped his rear foot in welcome. The two humans stood either side of the horse with their hands on his neck. Half Bear wasn't entirely sure how it had happened, but he knew that Wild Wind had become talismanic for both of them.

"*Can't sleep?*" Half Bear asked.

"*No.*" She Wolf sighed and Half Bear guessed what was keeping her awake. "*Have you decided which way you will go if the village splits?*" she asked.

"*I've been thinking a lot about what to do. Red Bird was always for Black Kettle and for peace, but I don't think peace with the whites is possible anymore. They always want more of our land, or our buffalo, or the yellow metal from the ground. I think we need to make a stand against them somewhere we are strong.*"

She Wolf nodded, her face clouded in her own breath and her lips turning blue in the cold. "*So you will go to the Powder River?*" Half Bear nodded and finished tying the last of the rawhide strips under Wild Wind's belly. It was the decision she had expected and although it didn't sit well with her, she respected it and would go north with Red Bird's friend and the horse she cherished. She had no choice.

After a moment She Wolf said, "*Whenever you go on a war party I'd like to paint the red birds on Wild Wind's thighs. He came back safe last time and I think it is good medicine.*" Half Bear nodded his assent.

"*You'll need to paint him in the morning then. Some soldiers were seen at the Jackson ranch and some of us are going there tomorrow. I'll need some sleep,*" and with that Half Bear turned and ducked back into his tipi, the hide door swishing over him and hiding any trace he had ever been there. It was as if she'd just been talking to a ghost. She Wolf patted Wild Wind and went home to prepare some paint.

Bob Williams, Ted Jeffers and Zach Calhoun had all finished their stints in the Colorado Regiment and had mustered out. They'd left wearing their uniforms and taken the stage to the South Platte where Williams' brother, Jethro, had a ranch. They intended to make use of Jethro's hospitality before heading back east, where they had great stories of adventure and daring-do to tell and mementoes of the Indian war to show off to impressionable ladies of questionable repute.

The roof of the ranch house glowed as the sun rose, flooding the prairie with photons that crashed into the snow creating glinting blue-white diamonds on every surface. As the sky lightened, the twenty-seven man war party was gingerly making its way up the river on the ice, hidden from the ranch by the steep riverbanks.

Wild Wind didn't like the ice at all. His legs trembled with the effort of keeping his hooves underneath him and Half Bear could feel the horse's heart beating through his own legs. He patted the horse's neck in reassurance, recognising his efforts. The leader of the war party, Swooping Eagle, raised his hand and jabbed upwards indicating they should go up the bank. They were now adjacent to a gentle slope where the cattle obviously came down to drink and Swooping Eagle's horse bunched its thighs and darted upwards at the kick from his heels. All the horses were up and galloping at the ranch house in seconds.

Zach Calhoun had stepped outside to take a piss and was looking up at the red clouds of dawn, sighing with satisfaction, his urine carving into the snow under a wisp of steam, when the Indians burst into view, a roiling equine storm. They were barely a hundred yards away and as he fumbled himself back into his trousers three shots rang out and several arrows raced forward, hungrily seeking flesh. One bullet caught his shoulder and spun him around and an arrow whacked into his buttock, hitting bone with a force he simply couldn't believe. The Indians whooped and hollered as one as the man went down.

In seconds Swooping Eagle was leaping off his horse and running in to finish killing Calhoun, as inside the ranch everyone was clambering for their guns and heading to the windows. Swooping Eagle had taken a scalp and two others had counted coup before the first volley of bullets was fired in defence of the ranch. The Indians cantered around the building, firing bullets and arrows at the windows and yelling and screaming and blowing war whistles loud enough to be heard in the next state, or so it seemed to the five men and one woman in the ranch.

Adjacent to the ranch house was a barn full of hay and it was to this that Striking Snake ran with a buffalo horn holding coals from the campfire. Out of view of any windows and therefore immune from the hail of lead flying in other directions, Striking Snake prepared a fire. Minutes later the barn was ablaze.

By now three of the Indians had been hit and wounded and six horses badly hurt, but Half Bear was confident that She Wolf's medicine would work and that painted with red birds Wild Wind couldn't be hit. He smiled grimly as the flames spread to the house and he waited for the men to come running out like jack rabbits.

The fire raged, sending up a plume of smoke that could be seen for miles. As it ripped towards the opposite end of the house the defensive fire ceased and the Indians waited for the inevitable. A door at the gable end ripped inward and shots came out, followed by the Williams brothers, Ted Jeffers, Jethro's two teenage sons and their mother, Irene. The two teenage sons ran as fast as they could whilst the men covered them from prone positions in the grass. They each had a gun and were running to a clump of trees about three hundred yards away. Half bear could see that the plan was for the boys, being the fastest runners, to reach the trees and then cover the retreat of the others. It was a reasonable plan, but it didn't work.

The boys were cut down by arrows before they had gone half way. They had no chance with mounted men running alongside them. Williams and Jeffers then made a break. Half Bear and four others followed him. Williams was a fair runner, Half Bear thought to himself as Wild Wind cantered along, easily reeling him in. As Half Bear closed he noticed the band around Williams' hat. It was a band of flesh with pubic hair, clearly cut from a woman's body. So this man had been one of those committing the atrocities at Sand Creek. Rage flared up in Half Bear like rising magma in a volcano and he determined to make the man suffer. "*Keep him alive,*" Half Bear called to the riders with him. As he drew level he flung himself at Williams and the two of them went sprawling in the grass. Before either of them had had time to get up the other Indians had joined the fray and Williams was pinned to the ground, flat on his back, with a man sat on each of his arms and each of his legs.

Half Bear picked up Williams' hat and waved it in front of his face, pointing at the 'decoration' around it. Williams struggled and heaved, but there was no way out. Half Bear took out his knife and Williams began yelling. He began writhing with a strength that surprised the Cheyenne pinning him down, but it did him no good, as Half Bear sliced open his trousers. He then cut and pulled off the man's genitals as Williams screamed loud enough to wake the dead; loud enough at any rate to alert the dead that he would soon be joining them. Half Bear threw Williams' bloody genitals in the grass next to his face, though Williams barely registered them through the pain and the tears. He foamed at the mouth and the veins in his neck stood out like rope. Half Bear then cut open Williams' shirt and swiftly cut across his belly so that his intestines bulged out. He then took his scalp and the Indians got up and left him to his agony. Half Bear felt better that at least one white man had fully reaped what he had sown.

# CHAPTER FIVE

## Powder River
## March 1865

The four Crows had set out on foot three days ago with the intention of capturing horses and riding them home. They had been lucky with the weather so far, which had been benevolent to them as they'd travelled at night and hidden themselves during the day. It was almost two in the morning when they crested the rise and looked down on the village camped on the Powder River.

"*Fantastic,*" breathed Screeching Owl as they looked over a large herd of horses. They watched them for a few moments milling very slowly over the snow in the perpetual search for grass. There seemed to be no sign of anyone guarding them and the village itself was silent. As they were about to get up a huge, slow moving cloud rolled over the moon and it became very dark.

"*Let's go while it's dark,*" Old Buffalo commanded and they stood as one and jogged down the hill. As they got close to the horses they slowed to a walk and began looking for likely animals. Running Elk picked out a large white mare and walked up to her and jumped on. Unbeknown to the Crows, unusually the best horses were being kept in a corral near the tipis, as the camp was staying here for several weeks. Up here, loose on the prairie, were the old pack horses and the wild, unbroken animals. The mare almost exploded as Running Elk suddenly leapt aboard. She bucked wildly and the man was thrown off.

Running Elk was a good horseman and he'd managed somehow to land on his feet, but as he made contact with the snow, his left leg shot out from under him, going sideways and ripping the ligaments in his knee. He went down with a stifled scream and rolled around in agony.

Unperturbed by Running Elk's misfortune, the others tried to find horses they could ride, but soon realised that this herd was a mix of old and unbroken horses. They huddled together around Running Elk who was by now sat up in the snow.

"*Let's just bunch up a dozen good ones and drive them home,*" Old Buffalo said. Five minutes later, with the four of them in a semi-circle to the back of the select dozen captives, they set out to walk home. It would have been quite difficult to do if they'd all been fit, but Running Elk couldn't move quick enough to chivvy the horses near him when they moved out of line and had to sit down frequently due to the pain in his knee and after a mile they decided to give up trying to take the horses and to just head home.

The tipis were sprinkled in little clusters along the banks of the Powder River for about two miles, the Northern and Southern Cheyenne all mixed together with the Sioux, although they all looked the same to the raven as he glided overhead in the growing daylight, his eye fixed on something he'd seen slop out of a bowl carried by a squaw. He circled overhead while two small children hit each other with sticks in a mock war and ran about putting more footprints in the snow near his prize. A minute later the children ran off to catch up with their mother and the raven swooped.

Eagle Feather walked past the corral and headed up to the herd on the hill to check they were all okay. The low winter sun was in his face and he kept his head bowed to avoid looking straight into it. As he approached the herd he almost stood on the bow and quiver lying in the snow. He picked them up and jogged back to the village. In his haste he almost bumped into Half Bear as he stepped out of the corral after checking on Wild Wind.

"*Look at these,*" Eagle Feather said, holding the bow and quiver out for Half Bear's inspection.

"*Where did you find them?*"

"*They were lying in the snow on the way up to the herd.*" Eagle Feather panted, still feeling the exertion of his run back to camp in the snow.

"*I'm sure that's a Crow bow. They must have been here last night trying to steal horses. Are any missing?*"

"*I don't think so, but one group is separated from the rest by about half a mile.*"

"*Come on, let's go round up some bodies,*" Half Bear said, already turning towards the centre of the village. Ten minutes later twenty-five warriors were mounted and setting off in the direction of the separated horses. Half Bear and Eagle Feather were in front and it wasn't long before they found footprints mixed in amongst the sign of the horses. There was a large circle of scuffed-up snow and a direct trail of hoof prints leading out of it with accompanying footprints.

Half Bear urged Wild Wind into trot and they quickly ate up the ground, the horse eager to work on such a sunny morning. "*Here!*" Eagle feather pointed at a depression in the snow.

*"Someone sat down,"* Strong Wind said as he caught up. *"I think they tried to ride the horses and one of them got thrown off and hurt. He has to sit down to rest, so they have no horses of their own. I bet it was his bow. He probably dropped it when he was thrown and couldn't find it in the dark."*

They trotted on, filled with the excitement of the pursuit and only minutes later found another depression. At this point the hooves that belonged to the animals selected by the Crows changed direction, going back the way they had come, but the footprints went on alone. *"They gave up here,"* Half Bear said with glee. *"The horses have turned back to re-join the herd and they are heading home."*

Now the party went into canter and the snow flew up in a plume behind them, silvery-blue and glittering in the sunshine, the beauty of which was unseen by the riders, who scanned the prairie in front, filled with an all-consuming bloodlust. Two minutes later, as they crested the next rise, they could see a limping man two hundred yards ahead. They couldn't contain themselves and they whooped as one and leapt into a gallop, each trying to be first to count coup.

Half Bear pulled Wild Wind to the right slightly and let the others overtake. The Crow had lost his bow and if he'd been carrying a bow, he didn't have a rifle, but he might have a pistol and Half Bear didn't want to risk injury to Wild Wind, especially as he wasn't painted for war and so not protected by She Wolf's medicine. He was happy to spectate. It was Turtle's horse who was quickest and Turtle had brought his lance with him. As he closed in on his target Half Bear watched the lance gracefully lower as the horse pounded onwards, Turtle half standing in the stirrups. The injured man tried to jink away at the last second, but Turtle had been ready for it and his adjusted jab sent the steel tip of the lance slicing between the man's ribs and out through his back. Turtle yelled in triumph, letting go of the lance so that he wouldn't be pulled from his horse as it sped onwards.

Half Bear pulled Wild Wind to a stop and waited patiently. The horse's neck steamed gently and his breath billowed in front of his face and Half Bear watched the vapours swirling in the still air. He moved Wild Wind forward, scanning the unbroken ground ahead for any sign, as the Crow's scalp was taken. Moments later they were off again to find the rest of the Crow party. The ground started to rise into the mountains and the riders soon found themselves in a steep walled canyon. They rode in the shade and the snow became deep, untouched by the warmth of the sun and unmoved by the wind. The snow was sucking at the horses' bellies when Strong Wind signalled them to stop.

*"I just saw the barrel of a gun in the hole up there,"* Strong Wind said, pointing to the left wall of the canyon, about twenty feet above the white skirt of a scree slope that edged the cliffs. All of the men scanned the area in front intently for several minutes and then Gentle Horse spoke, *"There is another hole above the one with the gun, just below the top. I think if we start a fire there, we can maybe smoke them out."* Everyone

agreed to try Gentle Horse's plan. Five men stayed with the horses, beyond the field of fire of the gun, whilst everyone else climbed the cliff and began gathering wood for a fire. It took almost an hour to get a good fire going and once it was away the Cheyenne began stuffing burning material into the hole in the rock with long sticks and the butt of Turtle's lance. Much to their satisfaction, they could see a small smudge of blue-grey smoke emerge from the hole where the gun barrel was.

Big Horse turned to Half Bear and said, *"I'll take some branches and put them under their hole and we can smoke them from both ends. You cover me with your gun."* Half Bear nodded and floundered his way back down to the canyon floor in the deep snow. A golden eagle took to the air and called in protest at the disturbance, its huge wings shushing the air in the crystalline silence. Half Bear waved at Big Horse to signal he was ready and Big Horse jogged as fast as he could to the place underneath the Crow hidey-hole. The gun barrel moved outwards to try to bring Big Horse into its sights and as it did so, Half Bear could see the shoulder of the man holding it. Half Bear fired and the shoulder jerked back in. He fired a second and third shot to keep the man pinned inside. The gunshots rang and reverberated wildly in the confines of the canyon.

Big Horse got the fire going and began moving away. As he turned his back on the cave, a Crow leapt out, dagger in hand and sprinted hard for Big Horse's back. Half Bear's shot careened into the rocks sending a shower of chips flying harmlessly, but it alerted Big Horse to the danger. He turned just as the Crow reached him. As the Crow lunged with the knife, Big Horse threw his arms out and by luck, parried the blow. The Crow's momentum brought him crashing into Big Horse who managed to smash him full in the face with the point of his elbow. The Crow staggered, a spray of blood flying from his mouth and nose and tripped over a rock and fell heavily. Big Horse stepped in and stamped his foot on the man's head, which cracked hard against a boulder. He didn't move again.

The Cheyenne positioned themselves with ten men crowded around each of the possible exit holes. The second fire gained strength and billowed grey smoke, eagerly fed by the men who threw more fuel on as the flames grew. The Crows eventually tried to leave via the top hole, firing the gun first to try to clear the way, but they were smothered as they left the smoky tomb of rock and quickly overpowered and killed.

**Crazy Woman Fork, Powder River**
**August 1865**

It was late afternoon and still hot and the crickets were relishing it. They chirred as if their efforts could make the daylight last even longer and one could be forgiven for thinking that the shimmer above the prairie was a result of their ardent stridulations and not a product of the heat of the sun. Half Bear sat in the grass on the top of a hill looking down on the village and the village herd. He could see Wild Wind and his distinctive facial stripe amongst several thousand animals, even though he was a long way off. Half Bear admired the beauty of the horse he still cared for on behalf of Red Bird; he still couldn't think of Wild Wind as his horse, because for him, Red Bird was still walking with him. He felt a little melancholy, saddened that the horses the Cheyenne possessed had changed in their role from helpers in transport and in hunting buffalo, to weapons of war, and even though the horses always did as asked without question, he felt it unfair to abuse their trust and put them at such risk. He'd seen many horses killed and worse, horribly and fatally wounded. He'd come across a terribly crippled horse left lying on a battlefield that had eaten all the grass in the area it could reach around it and then had starved. He hoped that She Wolf's medicine would continue to work and that Wild Wind would never have to suffer.

War was becoming a way of life. There had always been skirmishing between tribes, but most of that had been about horse stealing and counting coup – really a dangerous game of tag for grown-ups, played out on the huge pitch of the prairie. With the arrival of so many greedy and aggressive white men the skirmishing and chasing was now always deadly. Half Bear had, like Red Bird and Black Kettle, craved peace and had wanted to try to live together with the whites, but since Sand Creek he had changed in his outlook and had followed the way of the warrior. Sometimes he silently asked Red Bird to forgive him.

Half Bear looked towards the village where over 8000 people were camped together at the mouth of the Crazy Woman fork of the Powder; northern and southern Cheyenne, Sioux and Arapaho. So close had they all become, that they were starting to call themselves collectively, 'The People'. Thousands more were spread over the Powder River country between the Black Hills and the Bighorns and it seemed unlikely now that the whites would dare come into this Indian stronghold. But, unbeknown to Half Bear and the rest of the Indian Nation, the soldiers were indeed daring to move into the Powder country.

General Patrick E. Connor had declared in July that Indians north of the Platte must be, "hunted like wolves." He then began to organise a raid into the Powder River country with three columns of troops. One column, under the command of Colonel Nelson Cole was to march from Columbus, Nebraska to the north of the Black Hills of Dakota, whilst another, under Colonel Samuel Walker, with six hundred men and a pack train, would go north from Fort Laramie and meet Cole after going through the Black Hills. Connor himself would lead the third column of around six hundred and seventy-five men, along the Bozeman road into Montana and then trap the Indians between his and the other two columns, which would meet him at the Rosebud River around the first of September. He gave his officers strict orders not to accept any peaceful overtures and to, "Attack and kill every male Indian over twelve years of age."

Oblivious to the machinations of the American army, Half Bear walked back down to the village. His tipi was the far side of the river, which was thronged with children playing. A party of pre-teen boys were racing each other up and down a sandbank, while more of them were yelling encouragement to the race winners and derision at the losers. Another group of smaller kids were burying two compatriots in the sand up to their necks. Groups of girls were watching the boys, or playing with a ball, or playing with dolls and a group of five were having a great time washing a horse that stood in the shallows with paternal patience. The air was alive with delighted screams and Half Bear couldn't help but smile.

He picked his way through the riffles to the far side, relishing the cold touch of the water on his hot feet and met up with a group of women and girls coming back in from a day digging up bear roots and wild turnips with their digging sticks. She Wolf was amongst them and he waved and she waved back distractedly, trying to keep up with the game in progress. Little Woman had had a poor day and her bundle of roots was small and so she had suggested a wager in the hopes of boosting her harvest. The girls were taking it in turn to throw their digging stick in the direction they were walking. Everyone else then threw their stick at the first one. Anyone who threw a stick and hit the first one won. The game was fiercely competitive and the betting frenetic. Half Bear noticed that She Wolf's bundle of roots and turnips was so big she was having difficulty carrying it. He didn't know if she'd been good at digging, or good at throwing, but knowing her, he suspected she'd done well at both.

As the game broke up Half Bear trotted to catch She Wolf. *"Hi She Wolf. I'm going to go to Black Bear's camp tomorrow,"* he said, referring to the Arapaho village on the nearby Tongue River, *"My sister, Grey Owl Woman, is getting married to Standing Bear. I think I'll be gone about four days. I'm taking Wild Wind with me. Do you want to come?"*

She Wolf put her turnips down and rolled her shoulder and as she went to pick it back up, Half Bear did it for her and they walked on together. *"Thanks. I'd like to,"* she said, *"But I'm helping Yellow Sun make a tipi, so I'd better stay here. Thanks for asking me though."*

*"Okay. I'll come and find you when we get back."*

The Arapaho camp was two hundred and fifty or so tipis high on a mesa above the river. It was a typical Indian village with children and dogs playing by the river, the women out collecting roots and berries, the men out hunting and the old folk sitting around telling stories. But what had struck Half Bear as he had arrived was the size of the horse herd corralled next to the village. There was an enormous throng of almost three thousand animals. That year Black Bear's camp was rich in horses and the horse swapping at the wedding of Grey Owl Woman and Standing Bear was a marvel to behold.

General Connor's troops had taken full advantage of the complacency that had settled over the tribes of the Powder country. No scouts had been out on the prairie to see his looming advance on Black Bear's camp. Little Horse had seen soldiers though. Little Horse was Cheyenne, but his wife was Arapaho and they were travelling with their little boy to see her relatives at Black Bear's camp. The journey was a great adventure for Little Duck who was riding a travois behind his father's horse. The landscape rolled out behind him and the horse's farting made him laugh uproariously. He was most put out when his parents began babbling about soldiers and cut free his travois, but then he found himself hauled up behind his father and they set off at a gallop. He had never been on the horse, let alone galloped at such a speed. This adventure was getting better and better, but he had to cling on for dear life and the ride became frightening.

Little Horse rode hard for camp, but it was getting dark by the time they arrived. *"Soldiers are coming, soldiers are coming,"* he yelled as they stormed into the village. A crowd gathered next to Little Horse's mount, but nobody believed him as he told of soldiers, they were incredulous and said he must have seen other Indians, or even buffalo. In frustration Little Horse left his wife and child with the reception crowd and ran to find her brother Panther. Panther was laid outside his tipi drinking tea as Little Horse ran up. *"Pack some things to leave now. Soldiers are coming. I saw them. Hurry."*

*"Little Horse there are no soldiers for hundreds of miles. You must have seen a mirage, or another tribe. Sit down and have some tea."* Panther got up and lifted the kettle from the fire, bringing a bowl with him and holding it out for Little Horse. Little Horse stared hard at his brother-in-law, hoping the severity of his demeanour would persuade him of the impending danger.

*"We're leaving Panther. There's no time for tea. Please believe me."*

Panther nodded indulgently. *"We can ride out tomorrow and have a look if you want and I'm sure we'll find an explanation. You're tired, sit down and rest."*

Little Horse struggled not to shake Panther, but he knew he didn't have time for a fight. He ran back to find his wife and son. She had persuaded the families of three of her cousins to pack up and an hour later the small party set off downriver in the gathering darkness.

For gunner Jim Butcher, getting the howitzer in place silently had been an absolute bastard of a job. Fortunately, the heathens had been having some sort of celebration all night and the drums had masked the sound of their movements. Butcher had been an artilleryman all through the Civil War, which had ended in April, and he knew what he was doing. He'd asked General Connor for his two mountain howitzers to be mounted on the bigger carriages that were pulled by two horses, rather than one, so that they were faster and he had more chance of getting them out of holes, ruts and gopher-hole collapses. It also saved a lot of grunting, heaving and swearing.

He'd been glad to get into position and to get the horses loose from the gun, as they were often more dangerous than the enemy. Once shooting started, if they were still hooked up, they could panic and pull the gun over, crushing people, or just trample and kick men as they tried to disconnect them. Horses were absolutely necessary, but an absolute pain in the ass, a lot like women in Butcher's experience.

The limber and caisson were parked beside the gun and the six-horse team that pulled them had now also gone to the rear where they were grazing and trying hard not to kill anybody. The limber was a two-wheeled cart with a box of ammunition on a shelf between the wagon wheels. It in turn, was linked to the caisson, another two wheeled vehicle with a further two ammo boxes and a spare wheel. The two together, when loaded, as they were now, weighed nearly four thousand pounds, so it wasn't an easy bit of kit to move.

Thanks to the constant background drumming they had managed to get within four hundred yards of the village outskirts and so were in range of Butcher's ammunition of choice, canister. The canister was a thin metal container filled with lead balls packed in sawdust. When fired from the howitzer, the canister broke up, releasing the lead shrapnel in much the same way as a shotgun works. It was great because it was just point and shoot and really effective close in against troops and saved the need for the accuracy necessary for shot and for messing about with fuses and the range-finding necessary for case and shells. Butcher had the howitzer pointed at the first tipi, which he intended to blow to shit as soon as this thing got started. Butcher would be the first to open fire in the Battle of the Tongue River.

As light came into the sky on the distant horizon, Butcher kept his eye on General Connor mounted on his horse. Suddenly Connor's arm went up and then flashed down in the signal to fire. Butcher responded, drowning out the sound of the bugle with his shot. At the combined howitzer and bugle blast two-hundred and fifty cavalry and eighty Pawnee scouts charged into the village from two directions. Between the two mounted pincers, riflemen fired a hail of lead into the tipis.

Within seconds the din was appalling. The wounded were screaming, the women and children were screaming, the Arapaho men were yelling instructions to each other, dogs were barking, guns firing, horses whinnying and Butcher's big-talking guns roaring.

Half Bear ran out of Grey Owl Woman's parents' tipi with his gun in hand. He sprinted hard for the horse herd where he had left Wild Wind to graze overnight. Some of the men were trying to form a skirmish line behind which the women and children could escape out into the bush, but Half Bear ran through them with some other men trying to get to the horses in order to mount up and challenge the cavalry. Half Bear's full focus was on saving Wild Wind. As he ran out of the camp, Goose Feather rode in, carrying his twin three-year-old children, one under each arm. Goose Feather rode bare-back and with no reins and yet arrowed towards the safety of the emerging skirmish line, his children's heads bobbling wildly. With only yards to go before a modicum of safety, a bullet stuck the back of his head and he lurched forward over his horse's neck, spilling his children. Half Bear didn't see the outcome for the kids, as by now they were behind him.

Up ahead, the village herders were trying to disperse the horses along the river, but the Pawnee had a huge section of the herd surrounded. For a split second, amongst the seething mass of horses, Half Bear saw Wild Wind, but then he was swallowed up in a swirl of tails and dust heading away with the Pawnee. He stopped running, his lungs heaving at the air and his legs trembling with lactic acid. A Pawnee rode at him, war club raised and Half Bear hefted his gun and shot him in the chest. He hit the earth with a satisfying crunch, but less satisfying, his horse raced away without giving Half Bear a chance to catch it.

Seeing Wild Wind's section of the herd disappearing with the Pawnee, Half Bear ran towards a loose horse a hundred yards away. When he finally caught the horse he had to stop to gather himself before mounting. His lungs were burning and his legs had nothing left. The villagers were now retreating up Wolf Creek with the soldiers chasing hard on their heels. Half bear pulled himself up onto the horse and followed. He went wide to the right of the creek in the hope of overtaking the troops and re-joining the tribe; not unlikely he thought, as the army was notorious for not looking after its horses properly, they did so much marching and carrying that they hardly had time to graze and became weak and slow.

Captain Evans ordered Butcher to get his howitzers into the village and Butcher dutifully got his men working on the task. While his men began putting the horses back in trace, he rode into the village to select good sites with elevation and good fields of fire. The village was a scene from hell. The infantry were already burning the tipis and the Indians' winter food stores and the air was thick with smoke. There were bodies everywhere, many of them children who had been caught with their mothers in front of the skirmish line. The wounded were screaming for help, but getting none from the soldiers, some of whom were shooting them. Butcher was used to war, but in the war he knew at least the enemy were all men in combat. There were two children bareley three years of age lying dead near where he stood. This was abhorrent, but still, he had his orders to follow.

Half Bear was indeed overtaking the troops. He could see them through the screen of trees along the creek, but he didn't shoot, wanting to get past them first. The column began to slow as small parties of Arapaho dismounted and waited for the troops to come on before unleashing their arrows and a rolling battle began to take shape.

After ten miles the cavalry horses were exhausted, as Half Bear had suspected would happen, and the tables turned. The soldiers couldn't just stand still, as they would get picked off, so they turned and fled back down the way they had come. The Arapaho and Half Bear chased them all the way back into the village.

Butcher had placed the howitzers on a high point in the village where they could be spun to face an attack from any direction, but for now they pointed back up Wolf Creek, as Butcher suspected that was the most likely direction a counter attack would come from. He was right. They had barely begun to relax after moving the guns when the sound of whistling, yelling and gunfire began to grow. Moments later he could see the cavalry tear-arsing back towards him and he had the gun adjusted slightly to point at them. As the cavalry veered away and the Indians emerged from the trees he fired a canister round into them. Four horses were mown down in a gout of blood by the big-talking gun and Black Bear pulled his men back into the trees. It was stalemate. The troops were too exhausted to attack and the Indians couldn't get near the big talking guns that effectively swivelled at them every time they moved and so they stayed in the trees.

At the end of the day Connor withdrew his men and the Arapaho walked back into the village to recover their wounded. Little Horse found his brother-in-law, Panther, lying dead by the remains of his burned tipi and Black Bear found his son mortally wounded. The village had lost almost everything. Two thousand of their horses had been taken by the Pawnee and Half Bear was sick to his stomach at the loss of Wild Wind.

# CHAPTER SIX

## September 1865

It was almost midnight and Running Otter sat on a buffalo-fur rug by the fire watching the flames' flickering light play over the skull of the elk. As light swirled over the empty eye sockets, it was almost as if the skull were winking at him. Certainly, the up-curved set of the teeth made it look as if it was grinning. Running Otter couldn't decide if it was a happy smile, or a malevolent grin, although the remains of the bloodstains on the bone suggested the latter. It was the skull Red Bird had gone to so much trouble to collect and it had since saved Half Bear's life by impaling the soldier through the eye socket on the bank of Sand Creek. When Red Bird had died and his possessions given away, Running Otter had made sure that he had taken custody of it.

Red Bird's vision quest had been a little out of the ordinary. Most peoples' visions had to do with themselves, they might see themselves with grey hair and so know that they wouldn't be killed in battle and live to a ripe old age, or they might see themselves with a wife or children, or they might see themselves as rich, but Running Otter had never heard of a vision about the important deeds of an animal and certainly not a specific animal. Red Bird had subsequently impressed upon Running Otter how the horse, Wild Wind, would do something of huge importance.

It had been Red Bird's conviction that the horse was so important that had pulled Running Otter away from his friend, Black Kettle, to follow Half Bear and She Wolf north into the Powder River country. Now that the horse was lost to them Running Otter was unsure if he had done the right thing, and yet, for reasons he couldn't put his finger on, he still believed in the horse's importance. The world was becoming chaotic and dangerous and he wanted to be sure that whatever this important thing was that the horse would do, was going to be a good thing for the Cheyenne. It seemed likely to Running Otter that Wild Wind would play an important part in a battle and would swing the result one way or the other. The problem was, that at the moment the horse was on the side of the soldiers. Perhaps Wild Wind could bring about the collapse of the Cheyenne way of life. If that was so, then rather than protecting the horse, they should kill it.

Running Otter needed guidance and he thought he might get it if he sought his own vision. He felt deep within himself that to get a clear picture of such an important issue he would have to go to the sacred site of Paha Sapa, the Black Hills, where communing with the Great Spirit was easier. It was getting late in the year for seeking a vision. Summer was the best time to go, because it would involve fasting and staying outside for several days, but Running Otter felt compelled to go now rather than wait.

It took him two days to make preparations to go and as he tied the last of his things to his pack horse the leaden sky released a mean drizzle. The rain almost put him off going, as it was only likely to get worse, but the importance of the questions he needed answers to, combined with the fact that he thought, as old as he was, he may never see the Black Hills again, made him grimly determined to get going. He set off with some trepidation.

The motion of riding his horse once again soothed him and as the morning wore on the rain ceased and the sun appeared. In the early afternoon he stopped by a river to eat some pemmican. He sat down, resting his back against the bole of an alder with the sun shining directly on him. On the opposite bank of the river was a huge beaver lodge, an avalanche of branches pinned to the shore, but spilling well out into the water and quite some distance up and down the river. As Running Otter's eyes lazily followed a dragonfly in its zig-zag quest for prey, his attention was suddenly caught by another movement.

Approaching the river stealthily from behind the beaver lodge, was a black bear. He trod slowly, his huge feet flipping and flopping forward, but landing silently, his head weaving side to side and his nostrils, at the end of a gingery muzzle, flared, testing the air. Running Otter sat perfectly still, his heart beating a little faster in his chest. He felt safe with the river between him and the bear and he was fascinated to see what would happen. He noted that the breeze was blowing upstream along the river and so the bear probably wouldn't smell him, or the horses and the horses wouldn't smell him and panic. They were tied up behind the trees at Running Otter's back, out of sight of the river and the bear.

As the bear neared the edge of the lodge he slowed, lowering himself to the ground and Running Otter was put in mind of the bobcats he had seen stalking gophers. He stopped where the lodge and shore met and just stood, his nose twitching and his ears swivelling. His head tilted to one side and Running Otter thought he must be listening to the movements of a beaver in the lodge. Slowly, he stood up from his stalking crouch and his back arched and then he raised his front legs clear of the ground, standing straight up. In a blur, he launched forward and both front paws smashed into the top of the lodge at an angle, sending debris flying. In a split second he was hurling twigs, his forearms blurring in a blistering dig.

Now Running Otter could hear the horses moving nervously behind him, but the bear could hear nothing over the ripping up of the lodge roof. His head shot in amongst the quicksand of wood and emerged with a beaver clamped in his jaws. The beaver squealed hideously, but the bear shook it without remorse as he heaved himself back up onto the riverbank. Running Otter could see it was a very big and therefore probably, a very old beaver. The bear jogged a few ambling paces and then began tearing up his prize.

The horses settled and Running Otter watched the bear eat the beaver. He felt privileged to have seen such a drama and he knew it was a good omen for his quest into the Black Hills, for his destination was to be the mountain known to his people as the Bear's Lair. The bear shambled away slowly and after another half an hour, Running Otter got up and resumed his journey.

The dark grey plug of solidified magma thrusting vertiginously 1,267 feet above the surrounding landscape drew Running Otter like a magnet. It had been made a long time ago when several girls were out playing away from their mothers. They were chased by a giant bear and in an effort to escape they climbed onto a rock, where they prayed to Wakan Tanka, The Great Mystery, to help them. Wakan Tanka heard them and the rock shot up from the ground, lifting them high above the bear.

When the girls got home they told their brothers of the giant bear and that it could only be killed with an arrow in the sole of its foot. The girls led the boys back to the bear at the tower of rock, where the boys made the bear think that they had climbed to the top. The bear, infuriated, tried to climb up to get them, its claws ripping vertical tears in the rock and as it scrabbled up, the boys fired arrows at its feet. Eventually, an arrow landed very close to its foot and the bear ran away.

The great tower of rock wouldn't be named by the white men until the 1875 expedition of Colonel Richard Irving Dodge named it Devils Tower, but to Running Otter, Bear's Lair was an ancient and holy place. He made his way through the great forest of ponderosa pine, the September sun bringing out the scent of turpentine, which the horses' hooves blended with the smell of the earth. In a sun-drenched clearing at the base of the Bear's Lair, Running Otter made his camp. He arranged his things methodically and slowly out of reverence and because he had already been fasting for three days in preparation for his vision quest and was beset with a heavy lethargy.

October 1865
Fort Reno, Wyoming

Wild Wind's capture by the Pawnee in August had been a terrifying ordeal that he would remember with a shudder on several occasions during the rest of his life. The herd had been stampeded wild-eyed and crazy with panic in a tight bunch in which Wild Wind saw a young horse trampled and killed. When the herd had finally settled into a nervous but still mass, he, along with a dozen others were picked out and taken by a man Wild Wind didn't feel good about. The man had an air of cruelty to him and on several occasions over the coming weeks Wild Wind's misgivings about his new master were proved justified when he was whipped for transgressions he was unaware that he had committed.

For the Pawnee scout, Limping Wolf, the horse had proven the best one he had ever had and so he was angry when Captain Stredwick told him to give it up so it could replace a lost horse in the cavalry. He watched, powerless, his blood boiling, as Private Alderson walked away with him. Wild Wind felt relief straight away, as for those few weeks with the scout he had been on edge as to when the next whipping would occur, but this new man seemed calmer.

With Private Alderson it was business as usual for Wild Wind. He was used to being led around by men and it made no difference to him if the men wore blue tunics or buckskin, as long as they were kind, for all he wanted to do was graze. Unfortunately for Wild Wind, grazing was going to be a lot harder for the coming months.

The red birds had long since washed off Wild Wind's thighs, but he was about to be marked by the white men and this time the mark wouldn't fade. A hot iron was pushed against the skin of his chest and his flesh was seared with a 'U.S.' brand. After the indignity and pain of the branding he was put into a corral in the stockade of Fort Connor where, as it turned out, he would spend much of the coming winter instead of becoming a cavalry horse proper.

General Connor's summer campaign in the Powder River country was over and he had retired from the field, leaving two companies of Galvanized Yankees in the fort that bore his name. Connor left six howitzers to help protect the fort and artilleryman Jim Butcher once again found himself stranded in another God-forsaken emplacement in the middle of nowhere.

Red Cloud studied the fort with a US Army telescope he had liberated from a deceased soldier. Not long after Connor's departure the fort was renamed Fort Reno, but that made no difference to Red Cloud, or the troops inside. Red Cloud knew that with the six big-talking guns at the fort, his warriors couldn't overpower it without very heavy loses and so he resolved to trap the men inside and to do his best to stop supplies getting into it from Fort Laramie. And so it went that by the end of that winter half of the Galvanized Yankees were dead or dying of scurvy, pneumonia and malnutrition and many of the rest had slipped away and deserted in the hope of making it home before they died or were killed.

It was the Drying Grass Moon and outside the aspen leaves had turned to gold. Inside the tipi they could hear the leaves crackle in the breeze above the popping of the fire. With their flattened petioles, the leaves moved in even the smallest breath of air and their motion and rattling throughout the summer had been so constant that it was like running water. In the silence Half Bear fleetingly thought that it wasn't for nothing that the aspen leaves were known as squaws' tongues, but he thought it best not to bring that up with She Wolf who was morose at the loss of Wild Wind and snapping at the slightest irritation.

Running Otter threw some buffalo fat on the fire and a bright crackling flame lit up the tipi like lightening. Next to him, laid on a buffalo rug, the elk skull stared accusingly at Half Bear. *"I went to the Bear's Lair of Paha-Sapa,"* Running Otter began, referring to the sacred Black Hills. *"I asked Wakan Tanka about Wild Wind. I tried for two days to reach the Great Spirit and failed, but when I tried with Red Bird's elk skull by my side I had a vision from the Great Mystery. I think this is why Red Bird was asked to bring back the skull, it brings us closer to the Spirit world. Wakan Tanka told me that this loss of the horse was a test for you two, but that Wild Wind will return to us."*

Half Bear stifled a sigh of relief. *"When will he come back?"* he asked Running Otter.

*"I don't know that. We will have to be patient, like the heron."* She Wolf stood and without a word, left Running Otter's tipi. Half Bear began to stand in order to talk with her, but Running Otter grasped his wrist and held him in place. *"Let her go. It's difficult for her. For her, the horse has Red Bird inside him. She will heal in time and I know we will get Wild Wind back. Trust me."*

Half Bear settled himself and poured some red leaf tea for them both, adding sugar that had been taken from the warehouse at Julesburg. It was much easier to take the sweetener from a warehouse than it was to distil it from the sap of the box elder, but Half Bear knew he preferred the happier days of making box elder sweetener in the time when hardly anyone had ever seen a white man.

**June 1866**

The winter had passed slowly, inevitably and without incident, but by spring the white men were out on the plains trying to bring in the Cheyenne, Sioux and

Arapaho chiefs to make new treaties to allow the improvement of the Bozeman Trail across Wyoming and into Montana and to build protective forts along it. At the same time Colonel Henry B. Carrington left Fort Kearney in Nebraska with orders to build those protective forts along the Bozeman. He had seven hundred men of the 18th Infantry with two hundred wagons filled with mowing machines, shingle and brick machines, wooden doors, window sashes, locks, nails, musical instruments for a twenty-five piece band, rocking chairs, canned goods, churns, vegetable seed, ammunition and gunpowder. The expedition was set to be of such a permanent nature that many of the men brought their wives and children and even pets and servants. Although the 18th Infantry was poorly armed with largely obsolete muzzle loaders and a few Spencer carbines they also had four pieces of artillery.

Red Cloud and many of the other plains chiefs did eventually come in to Fort Laramie to hear the army proposals for a new treaty. They assembled on the 5th of June, but Red Cloud asked for the negotiations to wait until more of the Teton Sioux could join them. It was agreed that the hearings would begin on June 13th. Unfortunately for the whites, Colonel Carrington arrived near the fort that very day with his colossal wagon train and when Red Cloud learned that he was here to improve and protect the Bozeman Trail, regardless of anything the Sioux might have had to say, the Indians withdrew from the fort and vowed to fight any white incursions into the Powder River country.

Carrington proceeded with his convoy of wagons to Fort Reno. The afternoon of June 28th was glorious, there was blue sky, but a gentle breeze meant it wasn't too hot. At the head of the column Carrington was musing that the day had gone well with no breakdowns, or any of the myriad other minor catastrophes that seemed to strike a column this big with such a diversity of people and beasts. In the distance he could see Fort Reno and he looked forward to resting in a comfortable chair and passing the time of day with the commanding officers at the fort.

Carrington was very much a people man. He had graduated from Yale in 1845 and had become professor of natural science and Greek at the Irving Institute of Tarrytown, New York in 1846. He'd then gone on to study law at Yale. He was ardently anti-slavery and had helped set up the Republican Party. He'd organised regiments for the civil war and had been commissioned Colonel of the 18th Infantry in 1861. He'd found it was always good to talk to new people and he was sure he would hear some interesting tales on his arrival at Fort Reno.

As they got closer to the fort things didn't look right. There was no sign of life and despite the fact that the column must have been visible for miles, nobody had come out to greet them. The only movement Carrington could see was the United States flag flapping limply in the breeze and a red tailed hawk doing slow circuits above and beyond the buildings. Eventually, when they were less than a mile away, a group of ten horsemen trotted out from the fort and headed in their direction followed by a rooster tail of dust. Carrington halted the column as the horsemen approached.

"Good afternoon sir," the leading horseman announced, "Captain George Bailey, commanding officer of C and D companies Fifth United States Volunteer Infantry, Fort Reno, at your service." He snapped a salute which Carrington returned, but he was absolutely aghast at the state of the men in front of him. They looked to a man, as if they had been dragged behind a horse for a mile and they looked thin as rails with unnervingly red eyes as a result of scurvy. It looked as if it was taking all their effort to remain in their saddles.

"Colonel Henry Carrington, Eighteenth United States Infantry and you will be pleased to hear, your relief. Let's get settled at the fort and then I'd like to hear what's been going on here."

"Absolutely sir." Bailey wheeled his horse around and the party set off back to the fort.

That evening after feeding the garrison who ate like wolves, Bailey told Carrington of the siege they had been under throughout the winter and spring led by Red Cloud. The previous commander, Captain Williford, had died of illness on the twenty- ninth of April. For months most of their supplies had been ransacked or driven off by the Indians and they had hardly dared to leave the confines of the fort. Carrington was appalled that the US Army hadn't done more to get supplies in to the men, but he diplomatically kept that to himself.

"You can take your men back to Fort Kearney and muster out at your convenience," Carrington told Bailey, who visibly sagged with relief. "I'm going to leave two companies here and I'm then going to build a new fort north of here on the Bozeman trail. You have confirmed what I already knew – there are a lot of hostile Indians here. I have artillery with me, but some of my gunners are raw recruits, do you have any experienced artillery men here?"

"I do. Butcher is a veteran of the Civil War and an excellent man. He was a great help to General Connor on the Tongue River. Do you wish to speak with him?"

"I would be grateful."

Jim Butcher subsequently found himself a part of the 18th Infantry. He'd been asked and he'd acceded, passing up the chance to muster out. He wanted away from the confines of Fort Reno, but he didn't want to traipse back eastward with a few poorly armed men in a country seething with hostile Indians. He figured that if he did a job for Carrington, he'd be better off in the end.

Carrington's column set off again on July 9th with Jim Butcher riding beside a mountain howitzer, on a horse with a distinctive kink in the blaze on its face. As the column snaked its way across the prairie, it was watched by hundreds of warriors. Finally, on the 13th of July the column halted at the junction of Little Piney and Big

Piney Creeks. Close by were the pine forests of the Bighorn Mountains and the surrounding grassland was lush. These were the best hunting grounds of the plains Indians and it was here that Carrington decided to build Fort Phil Kearney.

Half Bear watched a village of tents spring up next to the rivers like mushrooms in the autumn rain. The soldiers scurried about like ants, silent at this range up in the hills, but Half Bear could imagine the chatter. He shifted position in his saddle and Red Cloud looked his way. Red Cloud was pleased that warriors like Half Bear were joining him all the time. The Indians felt that enough was enough and the only way to win was to all come together as one. Emissaries had even been sent to the Crows, traditional enemies of the Cheyenne and Sioux, to try to persuade some of them to join in the effort against the whites.

As the tents went up several wagons began moving in their direction, towards the wooded slopes of the Bighorns. Twenty or so mounted soldiers came with the wagons and the warriors waited to see what they were up to. On reaching the trees they began cutting them and it was apparent that they were harvesting logs to build a stockade. Red Cloud nodded. He had seen enough.

As the party of Indians turned away, Half Bear glanced back and his eyes were caught by the glint of metal on a gun carriage. He felt a flutter of excitement, as there, next to the big-talking gun he was certain he could see Wild Wind. He felt a wave of euphoria flood through him. Miraculously the horse was back within reach and surely Running Otter had been right predicting his return. Here was a glorious chance to reclaim Red Bird's horse.

Three days after the canvas mushrooms appeared, Two Moon, Black Horse and Dull Knife rode out to the troops with almost a hundred warriors under a white flag of truce. With the help of an old trapper, Jim Bridger, who had married an Indian woman and who was now guiding Carrington's expedition, the two sides could parley. Carrington cheerfully invited forty of the warriors and chiefs into the encampment and welcomed them with stirring music from the military band. The Cheyenne watched and listened, amused at Carrington's attempts to impress them and get them on side. The instruments were impressive and the sun glinted off the brass as if the instruments had captured the sun, but what the chiefs were really watching, was the movement around them. They were assessing with keen eyes, the troops and the weaponry available to Carrington.

Carrington was no fool and he made a display of the howitzers he had. He arranged for Butcher to fire a case round at a nearby hill, which he did, shredding a patch of aspen with shrapnel and duly impressing the Indians with the gun's power. The parley ended amongst smiles and waves and the troops hoped that they had kept the Indians friendly, or had at least made them afraid to attack them and their big talking guns.

The Cheyenne left and within hours the warriors along the Tongue and Powder rivers knew that the fort was too strong for frontal attack and so they would have to attack the troops when they came out.

It was still dark the following morning when the band of Oglalas snuck up along a gully towards the soldiers' horse herd. "*Spread out here,*" Bloody Knife told the twelve men with him. The plan was simple, the thirteen of them would rush up and get the horses moving towards the slope behind them, where mounted warriors were hidden and who would then drive the herd away. The warriors spread themselves about ten yards apart and watched again for troops. They had only seen one herder with the horses so far and he was stood close to where Bloody Knife now lay. Bloody Knife got to one knee and drew back the arrow in his bow. As he let fly, he hooted an owl call and the rest of them leapt up as one. The arrow struck the soldier in the kidney, his back arching and knees crumpling as Bloody Knife cut his throat.

The horses stampeded as planned and were picked up by White Mountain and his mounted warriors. They had captured one hundred and seventy-five horses at a stroke and Red Cloud watched, delighted at the first action against the new invaders.

The soldiers came out of the camp like bees from a disturbed nest and gave chase to White Mountain. There were twenty of them, riding hard and Red Cloud let them go, allowing them to get a good distance between themselves and safety. White Mountain rode easily. His horses were good, fat on spring grass, whilst those of the troops were tired from marching and from having little time to graze, but he didn't pull away, he wanted to give the soldiers hope of catching him so they would keep coming. He patted his horse's neck. She wasn't even properly sweating yet, he looked back over his shoulder with glee. They were right behind him.

Half Bear lay in the gully with a mixed party of Oglalas and Cheyenne. As the loose horses sped past he scanned them for any sign of Wild Wind, but he didn't see him. That would have been too easy he thought. As White Mountain followed, driving the river of horseflesh in front of him, with the furious soldiers behind, he readied himself. He had to smile at White Mountain who was laughing his head off as he galloped past. Half Bear aimed at the third soldier. His gun would be the signal to fire. He let the barrel smoothly follow his target and then the rifle erupted, kicking his shoulder and making his ears ring. The soldier flew out of his saddle as the bullet slammed into his shoulder. He would have survived the wound had he not landed on his head, breaking his neck.

A flurry of arrows leapt from the gully and four other men were unseated. The soldiers halted their charge and whirled around to help those on the ground, turning into the teeth of a gale of arrows. With confusion and panic taking hold, forty mounted warriors erupted from a stand of pine with war whistles screaming and a rout commenced. The soldiers were chased all the way back to where they had come from. Over the several miles back only one more soldier was unseated, but the Indians were delighted, they had inflicted casualties and stolen horses. It was a sign of things to come.

That summer Carrington found himself on the receiving end of a guerrilla war. It seemed every man and his dog was using the Bozeman Trail to get to the new goldfields in Idaho and Montana and nearly everyone found themselves harassed by Red Cloud's men. The troops were constantly out trying to escort the wagons safely, but they were spread too thinly and they were in constant fear of ambush. Their nerves were worn to shreds. It was even worse for those soldiers selected to bring in the logs needed to build the fort walls and buildings, as they had to go to the forest where ambush was even easier.

Butcher suggested to Carrington that he send out mounted sentries into the hills and that if they saw a group of Indians they should signal the fort and he would try to hit them with case rounds. Carrington, glad of any suggestion, tried it and they had some success. Butcher could indeed break up clusters of Indians if they were identified, but the Indians became adept at hiding their movements and took delight in trying to kill the artillery observers. As the summer wore on Carrington's officers became frustrated with him as they thought he didn't act aggressively enough. The feeling amongst junior officers was that they should send out bigger forces to actively hunt Indians, instead of just reacting all the time.

Red Cloud's warriors grew in number. The Arapaho chief Black Bear, whose village had been destroyed by Connor on the Tongue River, heard of Red Cloud's war and he brought his warriors to join the effort, as did another Arapaho, Sorrel Horse. Sitting Bull brought his warriors and a young Oglala known as Crazy Horse joined the fray. By the end of the summer there were over three thousand warriors keen to see the destruction of Fort Phil Kearney.

Wild Wind was saddled up and ready to go. He stood relaxed and still, free from the agitation of flies around his ears now that there had been several nights of frost. The lumps and bumps of bites on his chest and belly still itched a bit, but as he chewed the last remnants of hay he'd pulled from the stable, he was content. Corporal Mulgrave wasn't though. It was his turn to escort the wood-cutting team into the hills. The stockade around the fort was at last complete. It was eight feet high and enclosed seventeen acres and had needed over eight thousand logs. Now they were harvesting for the remaining planking needed for the buildings, for which they had already made over one hundred thousand adobe bricks. The building work seemed interminable and Mulgrave couldn't wait until it was finished so he could sit behind the log walls and be safe from these crazy fucking Indians.

Mulgrave put his foot in the stirrup and jumped up into the saddle. He leaned over and pulled the girth in tighter and then he raised his arm and whistled. The gates to the fort swung open and the four wagons and the twelve wood-cutters in them started forward with the twenty mounted escort. Mulgrave put his hand on the rifle in its scabbard and then on the pistol at his belt and felt the dread build in him like a summer thunder cloud.

Half Bear hauled himself out of the river where he had been having his morning swim. He jogged back to the tipi carrying his clothes so that he could dry himself by the fire. He stopped briefly to watch two ducks fly overhead. They whistled through the air, their wings and bodies undulating with the effort of flight, but their heads remained still. He was always fascinated by this and he admired their grace. Today was an auspicious day he thought.

Mulgrave rode out ahead with Carmichael, who for some mysterious reason was whistling cheerfully. 'Idiot', Mulgrave thought. "Carmichael, if you don't stop that whistling I might have to shoot you myself."
"Sorry sir."
By now they were in a vast area littered with tree stumps, but up ahead, the haulage road was swallowed by the trees and Mulgrave's eyes swept back and forth, searching every twig for movement. There was a crash and as his belly flipped and his hand went for his gun, he saw the tail of a deer spring over a shrub and disappear.
"That made me jump," Carmichael beamed, looking like he was enjoying a holiday. Mulgrave wanted to slap him. Five minutes later they entered the trees and the sunshine dimmed and the temperature dropped. The track was summer-hard, but Mulgrave could see it might be a nightmare of mud if there was much rain before the winter freeze. As the second wagon entered the trees somebody at the rear shouted, "Sir!" just as there was huge boom from the direction of the fort. 'Howitzer', Mulgrave thought as he pulled Wild Wind around and spurred him on to the rear, where the noise was. As he left the trees and looked right there were twenty-plus riders galloping on the plain towards them. The howitzer had obviously tried to hit them, to no avail. They were closing fast, the horse' nostrils flaring and their heads nodding with the effort.
All Mulgrave's troops were now by the last wagon and the wood-cutters were dismounting to join them, getting ready to shoot at the targets moving closer and closer and still temptingly out in the open. "Hold your fire until they get within fifty yards!" Mulgrave shouted, but Carmichael fired anyway. Mulgrave wasn't sure if Carmichael had fired from a twitch, or deliberately to piss him off. Either way, he bellowed, "Carmichael, hold your fire!"

The horses on the first wagon were prancing with fear and when the Indians rushed in from their hiding places in the trees on both sides they were bolting even before Half Bear whacked one with the butt of his gun. They turned in a panic, somehow managing to keep from trampling each other, but the wagon was pulled over and began disintegrating as it was ripped out onto the prairie. The wood-cutters turned at the commotion and Half Bear, still running, fired from the hip at the nearest man as arrows flew.

The horses on the second wagon wanted away from the charging Indians as well, but they bolted into the trees where the shattered remains of the wagon got stuck. Yellow Eagle raced in and cut the horses free before they did serious injury to themselves, touching each as he went and thereby claiming them as his own.

Beyond the trees the galloping Indians now veered away, whooping and yelling as another howitzer round exploded nearer to the soldiers than the Indians. "Jesus Christ," Mulgrave exhaled through gritted teeth as his horse went up on its back legs. Half Bear continued his run through the wood cutters, dropping his gun, and pulling his knife. As Wild Wind turned pirouette on his hind legs and came back to earth, Half Bear leapt, bringing his knife down in Mulgrave's thigh with his left hand and grabbing his tunic with his right. Gravity brought them down together in a crumpled heap.

Wild Wind was almost overcome with panic. The gunfire was cacophonous and suddenly the very earth exploded in fire and smoke, though he had no comprehension that it was caused by a howitzer round impacting. It was the last straw and he reared up, adrenaline surging through his veins like liquid fire.

His forefeet were inches from returning to the ground when he saw Half Bear. He had a flash of recognition, which distracted him from the violence around him. The man he knew approached him, not calmly with soothing words as he always had done before, but at a full run. Not only that, but he then collided with his flank and began to fight with the man sat on top of him. He knew the men were fighting, physical blows were exchanged just as if he was squabbling with another horse over patchy forage, or access to a mare in heat. Wild Wind had no clue as to why the fight was taking place over his body and the fog of confusion raced back over him. As the men fell away from him his instinct told him to find safety in the herd and so he galloped hard in an effort to catch the retreating cavalry horses.

Carmichael saw Mulgrave pulled off his horse and leapt down off his own. As he ran over he took out his revolver and held it by the barrel. He couldn't shoot for fear of hitting Mulgrave. He swung at the Indian's head and clipped him, sending him sprawling in the grass. He grabbed Mulgrave's tunic and hauled him upright as

Thompson pulled up next to them and between them they hauled Mulgrave up behind Thompson, who then took off for the fort.

Four of the wood cutters had been killed, but guarded by the mounted men, the rest of them and Carmichael disengaged from the Indians and jumped into the two remaining wagons and they too headed back to the fort, chased half-heartedly by the mounted Indians.

Half Bear hauled himself up, his vision still blurred and blood pouring from the wound in his scalp. As his sight cleared, he watched Wild Wind, still rider-less, join the back of the fleeing wood-cutting detail, understandably following his instinct to stick with the herd. Half Bear bent over double in frustration. He watched blood drip into the dirt and rued his bad luck. He had been so close.

It was December. All through the summer and autumn Mulgrave's woodcutting details had been plagued by skirmishing Indians. Red Cloud and his forces moved their camp to the headwaters of the Tongue River, within striking distance of Fort Phil Kearney. He had watched the bluecoats all summer and seen how they had reacted to the taunting of the Indians. Crazy Horse, High Backbone and Yellow Eagle especially, had sent them crazy, inducing them into several reckless chases and it was this characteristic of wanting to chase, that got Red Cloud and the other chiefs thinking that if they could get a big number of men to come out of the fort and get involved in a chase, even armed with only bows, they could trap them and kill them all.

The snow was falling thickly outside the tipi as Half Bear packed enough pemmican for several days into a bag he would strap onto his pack horse. He pulled on thick leggings and then high-topped buffalo-fur moccasins. Over his tunic he wrapped himself in a buffalo robe, fur side in. Outside, where morning looked like evening under the snow clouds, he strapped the pemmican and his rifle to his pack horse and mounted him, keeping hold of his war horse by a lariat. The thickening snow muffled the sound of the two thousand warriors making the same preparations.

A gray jay watched with interest as the men and horses trudged in silence over the watershed and into the valley of Peno Creek. A party of three mule deer bounded stiff legged through the woods ahead of the men, anticipating trouble and wanting no part of it. They were now only about ten miles from the fort and it was here that Red Cloud decided to make temporary camp. Three circles were set up, one for each of the Sioux, Cheyenne and Arapaho.

The morning of the 21st of December started winter-grey, but as the morning gathered strength, the sky became bright and clear. A small war party set off for the wood haul road to wait for the wagons of the wood cutters. Ten warriors led by Crazy Horse, Hump and Little Wolf rode up to Lodge Trail Ridge where they dismounted and hid amongst the trees on the slope facing the fort.

The other two thousand warriors, including Half Bear, followed down the Bozeman Trail to the point where it narrowed on its way down to Peno Creek. The warriors split and the Cheyenne and Arapaho hid on the west side of the trail, the Sioux on the east. Most of the warriors dismounted and hid their horses in the trees out of sight and then hid themselves in the trees close to the trail, or laid in the long grass at the trail's edge. Others remained mounted, but hidden behind two rocky outcrops.

The snow crunched under Half Bear's feet as he looked for a position in the grass. There was a dwarf birch growing very close to the trail and under its leafless, but shrubby canopy there was almost no snow. It looked to Half Bear a good place to lie in wait without getting too wet. He spread his robe on the ground, covered the edges of it in snow for added camouflage and lay down on his belly, pulling the branches of the birch over him. He checked over his rifle for a final time and looked to his left, where at the top end of the ambush he could see Little Horse setting himself in behind a tree. It had been Little Horse who had tried to warn the Arapaho of Connor's impending attack on the Tongue the year before and now he was being given the honour of giving the signal to attack. Half Bear smiled to himself and settled in to wait for Wild Wind to come back to him.

Corporal Mulgrave found himself leading out the wood wagons again and Carmichael was with him and whistling again. Mulgrave didn't mention the whistling, as after all the irritating bugger had saved his life. He looked over at Carmichael, who winked at him. Maybe he should slap him after all he thought, although Mulgrave smiled despite himself. His leg had taken a long time to recover from the stab wound, but it was finally just about healed. At the moment it was his freezing hands that were of greater concern. His head snapped around at the noise of the war whistles, which went through him like fingernails on a blackboard. "Fuck. Not again!"

Sixteen mounted warriors streaked past the rear of the column, sending a volley of arrows into the rear wagon. Fortunately, nobody was hit and the soldiers replied with a volley of gunfire, which was similarly fruitless. As the riders sped on and then began a wide turn in a spray of grass clods and snow to come back for a second pass, the gates of the fort opened and mounted troops poured out with infantry behind. The Indians were half way through their turn, when a howitzer round came whistling over and exploded behind them. The last Indian horse was caught by shrapnel and it fell in a spray of blood, one of its hind legs cut off at the hock. The rider threw himself clear as the horse rolled. Mulgrave was amazed to see him land on his feet, stagger and then start running. The horse screamed like a banshee, thrashing in wild tight circles until somebody shot it out of mercy.

The Indians did a second pass, all except one, who had spun around to pick up the runner, and then they all headed away, back to hell, or wherever it was they had come from, leaving the column rattled but unhurt. As they left, Crazy Horse and his nine other decoys showed themselves on the slope by the fort. They ran towards it yelling and screaming and a few seconds later the howitzer barked in their direction and the bluecoats, now back in-bound for the fort, swung around to chase them.

The charge was led by Captain William Fetterman who had spent two minutes pleading the lily-livered Carrington to let him command the rescue detail. As soon as it had been apparent that the wood cutters were under fire, Carrington had ordered Captain Powell to take out a force to protect the wagons and drive the Indians back. Fetterman, sick of seeing Carrington let the Indians get away with murder, wanted to get out and punish them and so argued that as Powell's senior, he should go. Carrington gave in, but gave him strict orders not to chase the Indians beyond the ridge.

As Fetterman raced up the hill towards Crazy Horse, the Indians got on their horses and rode up towards the ridge top. When they reached the top they galloped backwards and forwards yelling at Fetterman and his men. Fetterman slowed and as he did so Crazy Horse got off his mount and ran around yelling. The troops unleashed a hail of lead in his direction, splintering trees and knocking snow off branches, but Crazy Horse didn't even duck, he just yelled and gesticulated at Fetterman, who completely lost his cool. Here he was with eighty men armed with guns and there were only ten Indians, armed at best with bows and this guy was running around mocking them. The bastard had even flashed his ass at them. If ever there was a time to punish Indians, this was it. "Let's kill that bastard," Fetterman yelled, digging his heels into his horse's flanks. Delighted at the reaction, Crazy Horse sprang back on his horse and galloped over the ridge, heading for Peno Creek.

Half Bear lay in the snow shivering, but concentrating on the sound of the battle beyond the ridge. The shooting had steadily got louder and in the last minute it increased in intensity. Suddenly Crazy Horse and the others burst through the trees at the top of the ridge and came careening down the other side, the horses rocking backwards in an effort to stay on their feet. The snow was crazily kicked up in front of them and the riders bounced in their saddles looking anything but in control. Their yelling echoed amongst the timber disturbing two crows who swooped down from the trees and swept away, low over the frozen surface of the creek.

Seconds later a swarm of bluecoats were racing over the ridge and crashing down the slope towards the creek. Many of them were infantry who had caught up with the cavalry when they had paused to shoot several times on the way up. The Indian decoys took their mounts across the creek, splintering ice and hurling diamonds of water into the air. The troops were now all encircled within the trap and Little Horse stepped out from behind a tree and raised his lance. All hell broke loose.

The mounted warriors were amongst the troops in seconds, the ground vibrating as if undergoing an earthquake in response to their hooves. Those on foot raced into the infantry and a whirlwind of savage hand-to-hand fighting broke out. Arrows flew as thick as summer insects.

For the first few seconds Half Bear just raised himself to one knee and began firing the rifle. He hit three men and then the two sides were so intermingled he couldn't fire without hitting one of his own. He stood and tried to see Wild Wind. He was with the cavalry at the far end of the battle and Half Bear began jogging in that direction. Already the fighting with the infantry was lessening as most of them had already been killed.

The cavalry had begun trying to extricate themselves from the melee. They were working their way up a slope at the top of which, was a large area of boulders offering refuge. As they reached the boulders the men were dismounting and finding cover. As they found shelter the firing from the cavalry became intense and the Indians became pinned down. Despite lead flying like wind- driven sleet, Little Horse bounded from rock to rock as though he were a big horn sheep, the tip of his lance sniffing out targets ahead of him. As he crested a boulder, a gun was fired at him almost point blank, but somehow missed and Little Horse stabbed the soldier's face with the lance, shattering bone.

White Bull also ran up the rocks impervious to bullets and closed in on a soldier who fired at him until an arrow from White Bull's bow hit him square in the chest. As the man went down White Bull smashed his head with the butt of his lance and so counted coup. Others weren't so lucky in their advances and many were cut down until both sides were pinned. As Limping Elk stood to move a soldier popped up to shoot at him. Limping Elk ducked and shouted, *"Next time I move and the soldier pops up, shoot him. Are you ready?"*

*"We're ready,"* came a shouted reply. Limping Elk jumped up and as the soldier raised his gun a flock of arrows took off and two hit their mark. At the top of the boulders a soldier got up and ran for the ridge, but Half Bear was ready and his third shot hit the man in the back of his knee. Half Bear continued upwards towards a group of horses milling between the boulders and the trees. There, still unhurt, was Wild Wind. Half Bear ran up to him and touched his rump with his hand, making his claim, which was registered by the men below him.

As Half Bear squatted for a moment catching his breath, the Indians, as one, made a rush at the boulders and finished off the last of the cavalry. Eighty-one blue coats were dead. There were no survivors of what the white history writers would call the Fetterman Massacre.

Half bear swung himself up into Wild Wind's saddle and raised his gun in triumph. Red Bird's prophesy could now come true.

# CHAPTER SEVEN

## Tongue River, Wyoming Spring 1867

The seasons were turning again. In the first light of the day, as he left the tipi for a swim in the river, the ice on the trees was dripping diamonds in the new-born sunshine, telling Half Bear of the coming of spring. A platinum swirl of mist rolled listlessly on the far shore as he waded out up to his knees, pushing aside a flotilla of tiny icebergs. Though the water was freezing, he still dived in without further prevarication. The cold took his breath away and trip-hammered his heart, but he relished the sensation of it. A dog sat on the bank and watched him, shaking its head as though even it thought Half Bear was completely nuts.

She Wolf came down to the water's edge to find Half Bear, holding a steaming cup of red leaf tea for him. *"Isn't it too cold to swim?"* she asked him.

*"No. It always feels this cold. It's cold in summer, but at least then it's warm when I get out,"* he said, wrapping himself in a buffalo rug. She Wolf shook her head, in total agreement with the dog.

*"I want to ask you a favour,"* she said, passing over the tea.

*"Go ahead."*

*"My sister, Shining Star, is due to have a baby soon. I'd like to go and see her, but she is with her husband, Wounded Elk, who is one of the Dog Soldiers with Roman Nose. Would you come with me? There is no-one else I could really ask and I'd also like to stay close to Wild Wind."*

Half Bear nodded. Roman Nose, although not a chief, was a great warrior and many of the dog soldiers were following him now, rather than chief Black Kettle, who they thought was wrong to still seek peace with the whites when they were so murderous and dishonest, with their endlessly changing treaties. Both Black Kettle and Roman Nose had left the Powder River Country and gone back south, but then they had split, with Roman Nose going back into Kansas to hunt buffalo along the

Smoky Hill, in defiance of the treaty signed between Black Kettle and the whites. Black Kettle had taken his followers south of the Arkansas.

*"Well I have nothing planned and I'm happy to see what fate may have in store for us on the Smoky Hill,"* Half Bear said, relishing the warmth of the tea.

General Winfield Scott Hancock rode over the plains with a column of 1400 men and artillery looking for Cheyenne chiefs with whom to make yet another treaty. Chiefs Tall Bull, White Horse, Gray Beard and Bull Bear had responded to requests to meet Hancock and had parleyed with him at Fort Larned, where Hancock had demonstrated his power by showing off his new 7th Cavalry, led by George Armstrong Custer and by firing cannons. It was this eagerness to fire cannons that led to him being named Old Man of the Thunder by the Indians.

Hancock made it plain that he wanted Roman Nose at any talks, wrongly believing him to be a powerful chief. As Roman Nose hadn't come in to talk with the other chiefs, he determined to find him and took his column of troops towards Pawnee Fork. Many of the Indian treaty delegates left the day before Hancock and rode to Pawnee Fork to warn Roman Nose of the troop movement and impending arrival.

When Half Bear and She Wolf arrived at the camp on Pawnee Fork early morning, on the fourteenth of April, it was in a state of ferment and warriors were painting their horses and themselves for war. They found Wounded Elk at his tipi, painting black stars on his white stallion. Eschewing the normal greetings, Half Bear asked bluntly, *"What's going on?"*

Wounded Elk continued his painting as he talked, *" Old Man of the Thunder wants to see Roman Nose to make a treaty and he's marching towards us with over a thousand infantry and cavalry and big talking guns,"* the stallion shied away when Wounded Elk went to dab paint on his cheek and Wounded Elk had to pull hard on the lariat to finish the job, *"I doubt Roman Nose will agree to a treaty, especially now we've heard of Red Cloud's victories, so we are getting ready for our own. We've been burning the prairie so Old Man of the Thunder couldn't camp too close to our women and children, but it seems he's coming anyway. The women are being sent north, but I doubt they'll be able to outrun him because our horses are still winter-weak."*

As Wounded Elk was talking, She Wolf was already unpacking the load on the pack horses and digging out paint. Without waiting for Half Bear to suggest it, she began painting red birds on Wild Wind. Less than an hour later, with red cardinals flashing on his thighs, Wild Wind trotted out from the camp carrying Half Bear amongst three hundred other warriors, led by Roman Nose and Bull Bear.

The air near the village was filled with smoke as they left to scout the troop column and it followed them, a haunting spirit portending harm, for miles. As the last of the smoke cleared, the Indians could see the troops. Roman Nose was livid at the incursion of the army and before setting off had told Bull Bear that he would kill Old Man of the Thunder right in front of his own troops, but Bull Bear pleaded with him not to, so that the women and children might have a chance to get away.

As soon as the troops saw the Indians coming they spread out in a line, the cavalry prancing forward with sabres drawn. *"They are ready to fight,"* Half bear said to Wounded Elk, the wind whipping his voice away before it could travel to the man riding next to Wounded Elk. By now the Indians had also formed a line and were spread for almost a mile. The feathers and cloth on upright lances and headdresses cracked in the wind, adding to the perpetual motion of the horses' manes and tails. Roman Nose raised his white flag of truce. The two lines were now stilled only a hundred and fifty yards apart. For a few minutes there was a standoff.

To Major Wynkoop, riding close to General Hancock, the situation had all the hallmarks of an impending disaster. He knew many of the Indians before him personally from his time as commander at Forts Lyon and Riley and he was now the Indian Agent for the southern Cheyenne and Arapaho. He knew the appearance of the Indians spread in a line gave the impression of imminent attack to the troops and he was sure that the way the cavalry had just lined up would have filled the Indians with distrust over their intentions. Something had to be done to calm this down. "Permission to ride forward and talk to them sir?" Wynkoop suddenly asked.

"You may go," Hancock replied gruffly. Wynkoop nodded at Edmond Guerrier, employed by Hancock as interpreter, to join him. They rode out between the two lines of men.

*"It's Tall Chief Wynkoop,"* Bull Bear said as the two mounted men came forward and at that Bull Bear, Roman Nose, Tall Bull and Gray Beard rode forward to meet Major Wynkoop.

Half Bear watched the two groups meet and suddenly realised that he was holding his breath. The horses in the tiny gathering danced around each other and nothing bad was happening, in fact he could see hand shaking and back slapping, and so Half Bear let his breath go in a huge sigh of relief. The group of horses now turned towards the soldiers and began trotting in their direction. A small group, led by General Hancock, then broke from the ranks of the cavalry to go to meet them. Hancock and his officers pulled up again as Wynkoop and the Indians approached. Roman Nose rode right up to Hancock and stared hard into his eyes, saying nothing. Hancock was enraged at the sight of this arrogant Indian calmly sitting there wearing an officer's blue tunic and glaring at him with defiance in his eyes.

"Do you want peace or war?" Hancock asked without introduction. Guerrier quickly translated.

*"We do not want war. If we did, we wouldn't have stood out here in front of your men and your big talking guns."* Guerrier tried to take the sarcasm out of Roman Nose's reply, but it wasn't lost on Hancock.

"Why didn't you come to the council at Fort Larned with the other chiefs?" Hancock asked, barely keeping a lid on his temper as Roman Nose continued to stare at him as if he were a specimen in a jar.

*"My horses are tired and weak from the winter and everyone I speak to has a different idea of your intentions for us."* As Hancock considered this, Bull Bear spoke.

*"Our women and children are frightened at the news of so many soldiers advancing on our village. They are running away."*

"Why should they be running?"

Roman Nose, still staring directly at Hancock said in a menacing voice, *"Have you not heard of Sand Creek?"*

"You must get them back, otherwise it is an act of treachery," Hancock replied. Bull Bear turned his horse, about to ride away in frustration and disgust, when Roman Nose pulled next to him and said softly,

*"Go back to the line. I am going to kill Hancock."* Bull Bear leaned out and grabbed the bridal on Roman Nose's horse. He pushed his own horse on, pulling Roman Nose with him.

*"Don't do that. There are five times more of them than us and they have guns, whilst most of us have bows. Their horses are fresh with grain and ours are weak. They have big talking guns. I don't want our wives and children slaughtered because of your temper,"* and with that he pushed the bridal away from him.

The wind was blowing hard by now and it was difficult for the men to hear each other. Hancock was frustrated and shouted, "This meeting is at an end. I will speak to you at your village with your women and children." With that he wheeled away and he and the other officers returned to their line. The Indians too, wheeled about and all three hundred galloped back towards the village.

By the time the warriors began catching up with the women and children, the sun was slanting across the prairie setting the grass gold and burnishing the flying insects so that they gleamed. Half Bear and Wounded Elk could see Shining Star and She Wolf in the distance, but as they watched, Shining Star dismounted her horse in a half-fall and She Wolf leapt off hers to help Shining Star lower herself to sit on the ground. As one, the two men urged their horses forward and within two minutes they were dismounted with the women.

*"What's wrong?"* Wounded Elk asked Shining Star, but all she could do in reply was grimace and groan with pain. Wounded Elk looked questioningly at She Wolf.

*"Her water has just broken. She's going to have the baby."*

*"The soldiers are probably following us. Can you ride?"* Wounded Elk asked Shining Star, who nodded.

*"Yes, for now,"* she said, as the pain from the contraction eased.

"*We need to find somewhere to hide, because the contractions will get closer together and she can't give birth on a horse,*" She Wolf said, as she and Wounded Elk helped Shining Star back to her feet and got her back on her horse.

Half bear swung back up onto Wild Wind, "*I know where there is a big cavity in the bank of Beaver Creek that we could hide in. We'll follow the rest of the tribe for a few miles and then when we turn off for the creek, the soldiers will follow the main trail left by the village and they may not come for us.*"

She Wolf nodded, "*That's fine, but what will we do with the horses, because we can't hide them.*"

"*We just let them go,*" Wounded Elk said, with eyebrows raised, surprised at the question with so obvious an answer.

She Wolf was quick to reply, "*No we can't. Half Bear's horse means a lot to us and we can't lose him.*"

Wounded Elk was slightly taken aback at the forcefulness of She Wolf and his eyebrows were called into play again. Half Bear didn't want to get into the significance of Wild Wind right now and instead said, "*Okay once we get to Beaver Creek I'll come back towards the village with the horses. I'll swing wide of our trail so I don't bump into pursuing soldiers and if it looks like they're coming your way, I'll do a killdeer and draw them off,*" referring to the bird that acts like it has a broken wing and attracts predators to it and thus away from its nest or chicks on the ground.

"*Okay. Let's go.*" Wounded Elk urged, keen to get his wife to somewhere safer than where they were right now.

The short journey to the creek was fraught. Although Shining Star's labour had only just begun and her contractions had no regular pattern yet, some of them were hitting her less than ten minutes apart and each time they did she needed support to stay on her horse. It was a huge relief to find the cavity in the riverbank where they could hide. With a roof of soil and tree roots above them and a soft sandy floor beneath them and drinking water within reach, it was the best they could ever have hoped for as a shelter.

Shining Star lay down, her hair already lank with sweat and her breathing raggedly tired. Half Bear turned to Wounded Elk, "*You take my gun and stay here. I'll go back and watch for soldiers. Wait for me for three days. After that, if you've not heard from me do what you think is best, okay?*"

Wounded Elk nodded, trying not to let his fear for his wife show.

Half Bear headed back towards the village with the horses in tow behind Wild Wind. He went wide of the tracks that the retreating Cheyenne had made and tried to keep to higher ground to watch for soldiers, without making a silhouette of himself on a ridge top. Most of his journey was through the night, illuminated by the moon in a clear sky.

By mid-morning there had still been no sign of troops, which seemed odd, but was a pleasant surprise, although Half Bear alternately worried that he had somehow bypassed them and then chastised himself for having self-doubt. His worry over missing pursuers was dispelled when he saw a vast pall of smoke on the horizon ahead. As he neared the crest of a hill, which he knew was very close to the village, he dismounted, picketed the horses and jogged up to the top to see what was happening.

He lay in the grass and looked downslope to see all of Old Man of the Thunder's men still there. They were burning all two hundred and fifty-one of the village tipis. They had obviously been through and inventoried all the village possessions, as piles of clothing, buffalo robes and all the accoutrements of living were also piled up in bonfires. Over four hundred saddles were burning in a huge inferno which blotted out the sun as its smoke gyrated in the air, a sick, black ghoul. Half Bear felt ill, everything Roman Nose's people owned except the clothes they had on and the horses they rode was being destroyed and for what? Not for harming anyone, but for running away from an army that had recently slaughtered women and children at Sand Creek. There was no justice with the white man. Half Bear knew that once Roman Nose found out about this latest attempt to destroy the Cheyenne way of life, he would take the fight to the whites like never before and that would then in turn, spur yet another punitive expedition. The only positive in the inferno below him, was that in being so thorough in their destruction, the troops were allowing the people themselves time to escape.

Over the next twenty-four hours Half Bear rode big loops with the horses, watching the movement of the troops. After burning the village they finally set off on the trail of Roman Nose's people and they stayed on it beyond the point where She Wolf, Shining Star, Wounded Elk and himself had turned off for the creek. It seemed that they would be safe and indeed everyone else would be safe, as the marching infantry were too slow to catch people on horses.

Yvette Cooper hadn't had a letter from her brother John in over two years. The post from the frontier was bad, she knew, but this was something more than a missing, or delayed, letter or two. This was something serious. She suspected that this was probably something terminal; but she couldn't be sure and that's what troubled her. Whilst John Keller had been the eternal optimist and a fastidious letter writer, Yvette, as pessimistic as John was optimistic, had been resigned to his death ever since he had left to go west.

She went to her desk and picked up the bundle of letters John had sent to her. She re-read them, making notes of the towns he mentioned and anything else that may give her a rough idea of where to begin looking for his cabin in the mountains. Not that she would be looking for it herself, she was going to hire someone else to do that. She had no husband to send on a search and rescue mission, as he had died of an illness the doctors couldn't identify, only three months after John's wife had died. She had another brother, but Stuart wasn't the sort of rugged man one could send west on a man-hunt in hostile Indian country; he was a tailor in Boston and could only really be described as a simpering dandy. However, he knew a lot of people, including many Civil War veterans and she was sure that Stuart would find her the right man for the job.

As it turned out, Stuart did find the man for the job. Dale Jackson was fifty-two years old and had been a frontiersman all his life. He was six-foot three-inches tall and strong as a bull. His thick grey hair was pulled back in a pony-tail and there were probably birds lost in his beard whilst trying to roost in it. He had come back to the family home in Boston on hearing of his mother's serious illness. He had gone to meet the tailor to get a suit for the likely funeral and had got chatting to him. The tailor had told him of a widow, his sister, who was willing to pay someone to find news of her other brother in the mountains of Colorado. That was a mission that suited Jackson just fine, because as soon as his familial duties were over, that was where he was headed as, in his opinion, the city was a hateful, crawling cesspit of humanity.

Jackson's willingness to look for Keller was bolstered even further when he went to meet Yvette Cooper. Yvette decided within seconds that this huge man, with a startling beard and skin veined black with dirt that would never come out, was the right man for the job. As an added incentive to him, she told him, truthfully, that Keller had described to her where he had buried his gold in relation to the cabin and that if he could find the cabin and any evidence of Keller's whereabouts, or demise, he could have half of the gold, or all of it, depending on how honest he was. Mrs Cooper told him that she trusted him and that she believed most people were basically good in spite of herself. Jackson wasn't so sure of that, but thought he would at least send back some of the gold.

The first golden rays of the morning sun pulled the rattlesnake out from underneath her rock. She lay in a coil, basking in solar glory and using the photons' energy to incubate the eggs within her. She was close to term and replete with the montane vole she had eaten the previous afternoon. Still sluggish in the morning chill and looking into the sun with the wind behind her, she didn't register the approach of the man until it was almost too late.

Half Bear had dismounted Wild Wind to take a piss. He wandered about fifty yards away from the horses, stretching his legs and trying to get the circulation restored in his backside. As he stepped over a rock, his foot was halted in mid-air by the rattle of a snake. The snake was a big one, right where his foot was due to land. He wrenched himself backward and as he went, his foot went into an old marmot burrow and his ankle twisted with a twang of ligament and he fell heavily, clawing futilely at the air as he went. His back slammed into the dirt and his head whipped back onto a rock with a sickening crunch only the snake heard. He was knocked out cold. The rattler, recognising the impossibility of swallowing Half Bear, instead slithered up onto his upturned belly to make use of the man's body heat. Heated from above and below, she was the reptilian filling in a thermal sandwich.

Five minutes after Half Bear's fall Dale Jackson rode up to a gaggle of unaccompanied horses. "What's going on here, U.S?" he asked the army branded horse. Jackson raised himself in his saddle and looked all around him for the missing rider. "Quite the conundrum, eh, U.S?" The branded horse was a fine looking beast to be sure, with what looked like three Indian ponies tied to it. It would be unusual indeed to have one soldier with three other horses way out here. Jackson took his rifle from its scabbard and began a wide circle around the horses, figuring to expand the circle a few times and if he found nobody, then he'd take the army horse and cut the others loose.

Within two minutes he'd spotted the prone body of the Indian, with a snake sat on his belly, of all things. "Jesus Christ. I've seen it all now," he muttered. He sat stock-still in his saddle, trying to figure out if the Indian was still breathing or not, but he couldn't tell. He could shoot him to make sure, but the sound of a shot carried a long way and there might be more of the devils nearby. He could get off his horse and stab him, but in Jackson's experience, these Indians were like animals and were even more dangerous when wounded. He didn't want to risk getting stabbed himself, especially as he could just turn around and take a good horse now, without a major risk.

Jackson hadn't got into his fifties living in dangerous places by taking big risks and so he opted for caution. He turned around and roped his horse to Wild Wind, cutting loose the others. U.S had a fine army saddle and bridle and, all-in-all, this had been a good little encounter. He had no idea what was going on with the Indian, but he didn't really give a shit, he now had a good horse and his tired steed was about to get a rest.

When Half Bear woke up, his head was being crushed underneath the weight of a buffalo, or so it seemed and his vision was obscured by a red fog. A moment later his agonised brain told him of the snake lying on his belly. He lifted his head to try to see it, but something exploded in his skull and his neck pulsated with a searing pain. He lowered his head back down and in the absence of any physical ability, determined to drive the snake away by willing it to go.

Five minutes later the snake finally slithered away and as the snake left him, Half Bear turned on his side and vomited. He stayed on his side and gave himself up to drowsiness, trusting that the horses would be fine if he took a short nap to get rid of the crippling headache. By the time he awoke again it was mid-afternoon. He still had a headache, but it was just desperately bad rather than cataclysmic. What added to the pain was the realisation that he had lost Wild Wind again. Someone had taken him, as the other horses had been untied and were milling around close to where he'd left them, which Wild Wind would surely have done as well. He was in no condition to chase horse thieves though and anyway, Wounded Elk had his gun. He decided to find She Wolf, Shining Star and Wounded Elk and then take things from there. His depression at losing the horse again was even greater than the crushing pain in his head and the whiplash in his neck combined.

Shining Star's labour had been a gruelling twenty–one hours. It was a test of endurance she thought she would not see the end of. She had grunted, heaved and sweated as her body tried to turn itself inside-out. Wounded Elk had escaped sight of the trauma by making a lookout post in a nearby cottonwood, but he couldn't avoid the agonised crying of his wife. Labour, something normally undergone away from men, had proved a more worrying experience than battle, where at least one had the chance to do something to improve the situation; during this all he could do was hope and beseech The Great Mystery for all to turn out well.

At last, with her eyes closed in exhaustion and pain, Shining Star heard a baby cry. She Wolf cut the umbilical cord close to the baby's belly and bathed it in river water. She dried it and dusted it with the spores of a prairie puffball so its skin wouldn't chafe and then wrapped it in a cloth which Shining Star had brought with her. Then she gave the baby to Shining Star to hold and Shining Star's world came back into kilter.

"*It's a girl,*" She Wolf said, "*and she looks healthy.*"

It was only early afternoon, but Jackson was already desperate to find Keller's cabin. It had been raining non-stop for the last forty-eight hours and it was thoroughly demoralising. It hammered down on Jackson's hat, which had long ago given up any pretence at being waterproof, and it oozed icily down his neck and into his clothing. He was freezing and every move brought fresh cold, chaffing, misery.

Wild Wind didn't look too chipper either. His coat was soaked and rain dripped from his eyelashes and trickled down into his ears, making him shake his head every few minutes. He was walking uphill and so was warm enough, steam floating gently from his shoulders and rump, but he was also tired and hungry. They were well up into the mountains now and river beside them was a steep-sided raging torrent. With the roar of the river next to him and the drumming on his head, Jackson couldn't even hear Wild Wind's footfalls. The moose didn't hear them either.

They turned to follow the kink in the river, pushing through a scrubby alder and almost bumped face to face into the moose. Jackson nearly jumped out of his skin, but didn't move a muscle that might have spurred Wild Wind into flight. Wild Wind was equally startled by the behemoth in front of him, but trusted the man, who made no move to flee. Unfortunately, Jackson's own horse leapt up onto her hind legs in surprise and the lariat holding her to Wild Wind's pommel snapped. She turned and bolted.

The moose was stunned into stillness for all of a tenth of a second and then it spun on its heels and crashed off into the trees. "Dammit!" Jackson cursed. He'd now have to turn around and find Bess, the comfort of the fire-warmed cabin of his imagination, receding rapidly into the distance.

Fortunately, Bess hadn't gone far and an hour later they were back where the moose had been. According to Mrs Cooper's letters there should be a fork in the river coming soon and if they followed it, there would be a pair of ponds adjacent to each other. If he carried on upstream past the way-marking ponds, then he would quickly reach a meadow and the cabin.

As afternoon merged into evening and Jackson's bones yearned for a rest, the trio finally reached the meadow and Keller's cabin. The rain had eased to a mist and a small patch of eggshell blue sky had appeared as Jackson dismounted and walked to the door to the longed-for shelter in squelching boots. Just stepping inside, where there was an absence of rain and wind, felt like entering heaven and near the stove was the unbelievable nirvana of a pile of dry wood and kindling. In minutes Jackson had a fire going, with coffee on and the horses brought inside for a break from the wet. The world was once again a beautiful place.

It wasn't just Jackson that felt comfort and relief, as at the other end of the cabin Wild Wind relaxed in a safe haven he recognised. The cabin brought back good memories of times with Keller and as they replayed slowly in his mind's eye his eyes closed and he savoured the absence of wind and rain. He leaned his shoulder against Bess and stamped his foot.

With a tin cup of hot coffee in his hands, Jackson wiped condensation off the window and peered out into the gloom and across the meadow. In front of a dark army of conifers he could see a huge rock, almost ten feet long and four feet tall, beneath which was possibly a small fortune in gold. Tomorrow he would dig and find out.

The following morning Jackson awoke to find that summer had deigned to arrive. The sun was high in the sky already, although Jackson had the suspicion he had slept rather late, and it was sucking the rain from the ground in a vaporous mist and making the air muggy. He put the horses out and within minutes they were grazing close together, seemingly happy in each other's company. Jackson put his boots outside in the sun, partly to get them dried and partly to remove the stench from the cabin. He peeled his socks off revealing two basically white, but very dirty, wrinkled appendages that reminded him of dead fish. He laid his socks in the grass, pitying any creepy crawly that might accidentally stumble across them and in bare feet he pulled a chair outside and had coffee al fresco, the sun massaging his skin and staining the inside of his bliss-closed eyelids red.

Being pissed off by the rain aside, Jackson loved being outdoors. He'd grown up on a ranch in Kentucky and when he wasn't helping his father with cattle, he was out hunting or fishing. What he really liked, was his horse and the associated freedom of movement. He would ride for hours just to see what would come next. Nobody was surprised when he left to go west aged only nineteen. There were those that were surprised it had taken him so long to go. He'd been moving ever since and had hunted, trapped, prospected and cow-handed to keep the wolf from the door. He was honest and able to handle himself and a gun and so in his mid-thirties he had done a stint as sheriff in a small Kansas town, but had given it up when it felt like he was settling down and the days were becoming all the same. His job keeping bar in a saloon near the railroad went for the same reason. No job had managed to tie him down and neither had any woman, though several had tried and two had almost succeeded.

He saw the bone when he got up to get another coffee. It was settled deep in the grass by the cabin wall. He pulled it free of the vegetation and held it out in the sun. He was no physician, so he didn't know if it was part of an arm or a leg, or even for definite if it was human, although that doubt was dispelled two minutes later when he found the majority of the skull. It seemed reasonable to assume that the bones were the remains of Keller. It was apparent that he hadn't been buried and that animals has scattered his remains. Jackson couldn't begin to guess what had killed him, although the cabin hadn't seemed ransacked as if it had been robbed and it obviously wasn't burned, as the Indians might have done if they'd killed him. Maybe he'd just got sick and got so bad he couldn't leave.

For half an hour Jackson scoured the ground around the cabin in his bare feet collecting bones. In addition to the first bone and the skull, he found the pelvis, almost intact about twenty yards away, three bits he presumed were backbones, another long bone and three ribs. He gathered them into a pile and determined to bury them later in the day.

Unperturbed by handling the remains of a body, Jackson made himself a brunch of fried duck and wild onion. He then put on a pair of knee-length winter moccasins that were in the cabin and left his stinking boots to pollute the pure mountain air. He took Keller's shovel and walked over to the rock where the gold might be. U.S and Bess followed him, nosing his shoulders out of interest to see what he'd do. It was so long since Keller had buried his gold that there was no sign whatsoever of where he had dug, so Jackson decided to dig at one corner and do a trench all the way around until he found it; if it was there to find.

He dug down two feet and had started trenching when his shovel hit a wooden box. He uncovered it quickly, scraping off soil to reveal a box two feet by a foot, or thereabouts. Inside the box were thirty-seven carefully folded paper packets containing a mix of gold dust, flakes and nuggets. Jackson was suddenly rich. Sat on the chair in front of the cabin, watching the horses flick at flies with their tails and listening to two gray jays getting mad at each other, Jackson contemplated what to do. Being that rare breed, an honest man, he decided he would get half of the gold back to Mrs Cooper, but he wasn't sure how to do that. He really wanted to go west and it was a long way to ride back east to Mrs Cooper. He couldn't trust it to the post and he doubted he could find anyone else honest enough to take it for him.

As he pondered in the sunshine he became distracted by the view around him. With a snow capped peak above him and lush grass and forest around him he thought that this was undoubtedly one of the most beautiful places he had ever seen and it seemed a shame to leave it so soon. Perhaps he should spend the summer here, he could run a trap line, and then who knows what might happen. What might happen, he thought out of nowhere, would be that the Central Pacific Railroad out of California would get closer to meeting the Union Pacific Railroad out of Council Bluffs and a complete railroad from California to the east would be closer. They'd been building for years already. It couldn't take much longer, although the Indians weren't making it easy. Summer here, head west, see the Pacific and then go back to Mrs Cooper on the completed railroad. Then perhaps choose somewhere to become an old man. "Brilliant", he said aloud and U.S whinnied in agreement.

Jackson set up a trap line, although he wasn't too bothered he if he caught things or not. If he did, it would be extra money, if he didn't, he got to spend a pleasant day riding without any work to do. Wild Wind had a delightful summer. The sun was warm, the grass lush and he had an equine companion. Even the flies weren't too bad. He and Bess took it in turns to take Jackson along his trap line and that was hardly work. It was a far cry from the fear and toil of warfare.

By mid-summer Jackson had decided to extend his stay and overwinter and he began preparing for it. He wrote to Mrs Cooper to tell her that he had found Keller. Sparing her the details, he told her he was buried in a beautiful spot in the Rocky Mountains. He also told her he'd recovered Keller's gold and that once he had wintered where Keller had lived, he would begin a journey back to her with it. He dismantled his snares and began gathering, cutting and splitting firewood. He cut a crop of hay, such as it was from a marginal mountain pasture and rode out to ranches and towns buying in feed for the horses and himself. By the time the fireweed by the cabin flowered at the top, signalling the end of summer, Jackson felt ready for winter.

The fluffy seed from the fireweed dispersed on the wind, the aspen turned gold, then the frosts arrived and the aspen reluctantly disrobed. It was November when Jackson noticed the swelling of Bess' belly. At first he wasn't sure if she was just fat, but as December came and Wild Wind was starting to thin for lack of grass, Jackson was sure that Bess's belly had grown larger. He got a rope and measured her and then made a habit of re-measuring her every few days. There was no doubt about it, she was pregnant.

As Keller had done before him, Jackson got into a routine of horse care and feeding himself and the fire. The temperature plummeted and the snow fell. Jackson loved watching the snow fall. It was never the same. It could fall slowly or fast, in huge flakes, or tiny, in a howling gale, a gentle swirl, or in dead calm. It built up over the window so that he had to go out and clear it with the shovel to keep enjoying the spectacle. After one of the best Christmas' he'd ever had, the days got imperceptibly longer, but the temperature fell lower and the snow kept coming. The trees cracked and popped as sap within them froze, expanded and split the wood. Choruses of wolves rent the air both day and night and a great horned owl seemed to question Jackson's every move. Jackson, for the most part ensconced by the fire, loved it.

Spring, when it finally came, arrived in a great rush. For a few short weeks the ground was saturated with snow-melt and the grass and wildflowers in the meadow exploded into life and colour. Ever since his youth, Jackson had been amazed at the changing of the seasons and how staggeringly different they were and up here in the mountains the change seemed all the more startling.

In mid-May Jackson noticed that Bess' teats had swollen and were starting to ooze a yellow, sticky fluid and he knew from a lifetime with horses that the birth would only be a fortnight away. Twelve days later, on the twenty-sixth of May, Jackson got out of bed and peered out of the window to see a beautiful sunrise. The few clouds that there were had turned pink and high above them the sky was an azure blue. A raven was kronking a hallelujah at the heavens from the top of the aspen and Jackson watched him, amused by his effort. His eyes dropped to the meadow and he noticed Bess' belly with a jolt. It had sagged almost to the ground. The foal inside her had turned to position itself for birth. It was coming today.

Jackson pulled his boots on and jogged outside, grabbing a bridle and rope as he went. He led Bess inside, watched by an only mildly interested Wild Wind, who looked long enough to see where Bess was headed and then put his head back in the grass. He was obviously unperturbed by the prospect of fatherhood. Bess was already breathing heavily as Jackson led her in and she paced around the small space like a caged lion. She continually checked her sides with her muzzle and the whites of her eyes kept flashing in the dingy light. There was nothing Jackson could do for now except try to reassure Bess with gentle words. He'd cleaned the worst of the grime from his hands and arms and equipped himself with a rope in case he had to intervene in a complicated birth, but for now he worried as if he were the expectant father. Bess pawed the floor and began a restless pattern of lying down and getting up again. She sweated and fretted and Jackson wondered if she knew what all the pain was. Did she know she was about to become a mother, or would the arrival of the foal be a complete surprise that she would take in her stride.

In the early afternoon Bess lay down and this time didn't get straight back up again. A bulging amniotic sac made an appearance from under her tail and Jackson could see the foal's two front feet within it. His worries over a complicated birth were dispelled and he blew out a sigh of relief. The sac burst, gushing fluid into the dirt floor and a minute later the whole foal emerged, eyes closed and bedraggled in slime. Bess began licking her infant male offspring and he responded by opening his eyes and wriggling in an effort to stand.

# CHAPTER EIGHT

## Colorado
## June 1868

Jackson was admiring his feet. Whilst they weren't exactly clean and didn't smell of roses, they were far from the smelly wet fish that he had extracted from his boots in this exact same spot last summer. Now they were firm and dry and were even tanned, as he'd taken to walking around the environs of the cabin barefoot with his trouser legs, as they were now, rolled up high on his calves. He spread his toes to feel the breeze between them. Out of the corner of his eye he noticed all three horses' heads go up in the air in unison and he looked to his right to see a white man on a grey horse emerging from the trees. He wore a greyish shirt that had probably once been white, grey trousers, black boots and, incongruously, an army hat. 'Militia', Jackson thought.

Bess' foal trotted a few steps towards the newcomers, interested to see a strange horse. Jackson admired him briefly. He'd named him 'Mountain', for want of anything better, as he had been born in the mountains and in the lee of a snow-capped peak. It would do as a name for now. Mountain stopped and just watched, nostrils flaring and ears twitching. Bess walked protectively up to her foal and stood against his shoulder.

The stranger watched Jackson for a second, saw no hostility and waved a greeting. Jackson waved back and motioned the man to come forward. "Howdy," the man said as he dismounted to the sound of creaking saddle leather. "My name's Walt Henderson. I'm looking for Dale Jackson."

"You found him," Jackson replied nonchalantly, hiding his surprise that anyone would have come this far from the rest of the world to look for him. "What's up?"

"There's a Major Forsyth at Fort Hays putting together a group of frontiersmen like yourself and he's heard of you and asked me to come to see if you'd be willing to join his group."

"Why's he want frontiersmen and what's his interest in me?" Jackson asked, flattered and cautiously interested already.

"He needs men who can track Indians. Every time the army chases a big group of 'em, they peel off in small groups where the ground is hard, or in water, or whatever, and the trail gets smaller and smaller until its gone and the Indians have vanished. He wants to get on the trail of big groups of hostile Indians and catch 'em all."

"Uh huh. And how's he know me?"

"He's heard of you from your lawman days in Kansas. Knows you've been out in the boonies your whole life and he thinks you'd be a good man to have along." Henderson winced and flexed his legs out one after the other. "Mind if I sit down?"

"Sure," Jackson said, hiking a thumb back in the direction of inside the cabin, "Sorry 'bout my manners, grab a chair from in the there."

Henderson came back out of the cabin and settled himself on a rough stool Jackson had carved from a log. He'd carved it for want of something to do over the winter, not really expecting a guest to come and use it, but now, he was pleased to see his efforts being appreciated.

"And this venture will pay, I presume?"

"It will. Major Forsyth is offering good money, five times regular army pay."

"Could I leave my mare and her foal at Fort Hays while we go on this Indian hunt?"

"I'm sure that would be fine."

"Okay. When is this merry band due to leave Fort Hays?" Jackson asked.

"End of August."

"Okay. I'll come and have a chat with Major Forsyth, but I'm probably in for one last adventure before I settle down."


At Fort Hays, Kansas, on the morning of the twenty-ninth of August, Dale Jackson mounted his horse, U.S, and glanced over at the corral where Bess and Mountain were pacing with about twenty other horses. They looked fine and Jackson was sure that they would be well looked after. The dust was rising rapidly in a choking cloud as the other fifty- three men of the Forsyth Scouts mounted their horses and the mules carrying the expedition's supplies added their scuffing feet to the dust storm.

For a few moments the horses and men milled like smoke particles in a gentle breeze, but gradually pairs began to form up and a column coalesced and oozed forward, away from the fort blockhouse, led by Major George A. Forsyth and Lieutenant Fred Beecher. Although it was still early morning, the sun was hot in a perfectly blue sky and the lack of breeze had everyone sweating already. It would be a long day as the column headed out towards the Republican River in the search for hostile Indians.

The 'hostile' Indians were camped on the Arikaree Fork of the Republican River. Roman Nose was there with the Cheyenne Dog Soldier leaders, Tall Bull and White Horse. There were also two camps of Sioux under Pawnee Killer and some Arapaho. Roman Nose was a great war leader and incredibly brave in battle. He had the advantage of knowing that no white man's bullet could kill him whilst he wore his feathered war bonnet. It had been made for him by his friend, Ice. On either side of the headdress was a row of eagle feathers that trailed almost to the ground. One of these rows was red and the other, white. A single buffalo horn at the front, over the brow, gave the wearer great strength and behind the horn was the stuffed skin of a kingfisher. This would give Roman Nose great powers of recovery if hit by a bullet, because when the kingfisher dives into the river the water closes up immediately behind him. On the right side of the headdress was a hawk skin, because Ice had had a vision in which a hawk had held a gun and a sabre in its talons. The skin of a barn swallow at the back would make the wearer as evasive and difficult to hit as the bird when it jinks low to the ground when hunting. Also near the back, where the feathers were red, was the skin of bat, so that the person wearing it could hunt well at night. Elaborate ceremonies had been performed over the headdress to give it its power, but to maintain that power, strict rules had to be followed and those rules were about to be inadvertently broken.

It was the night of September the fourteenth and outside it had gone cold and a brisk wind was blowing across the prairie. Not that Half Bear minded, as he was inside a tipi feasting with Roman Nose and several other Cheyenne and their Sioux hosts. As he ate some delicious fried bread Half Bear was mesmerised for a few moments by the flames dancing in the fire in the centre of the tipi. Waves of bright red rippled over a log as the fire went this way and that, pulled by the wind above the smoke hole. The walls of the tipi rippled in sympathy. Eight Horns broke the spell the fire had cast over Half Bear. He nudged Half Bear at his right and Roman Nose at his left.

"*That Sioux woman is using an iron fork to lift the bread out of the frying pan,*" he said. The significance of this hit Half Bear with a jolt.

"*That breaks my medicine,*" Roman Nose murmured with a resigned sigh, "*If I'd known, I wouldn't have eaten the bread.*"

The men close to Roman Nose knew that his food mustn't be served with iron implements, only wooden ones, otherwise the ceremonies performed to give his war bonnet its invincibility would be broken. Unfortunately, their Sioux hosts were unaware of this taboo. Tall Bull, sitting to Half Bear's right, looked up and noticed something wrong with the three men to his left. He called over to Roman Nose.

*"What's wrong?"*

*"The Sioux woman used an iron fork for serving the bread. It has broken my medicine,"* Roman Nose replied, leaning across Half Bear.

*"You must begin the ceremonies tomorrow to regain it. These are uncertain times. We may need you at any minute to lead a battle."*

Roman Nose nodded, annoyed with himself that he hadn't been more careful and slightly depressed at the lengths he would now have to go to to restore his medicine. It would take three days of ceremony to repair the damage.

It was early morning of the fifteenth of September. The prairie sparkled with dew and watery diamonds were splashed sideways as Wild Wind walked through the grass. Jackson looked back over his shoulder and could see where the horses had left wakes in the dew like ships' passage on the ocean. Jackson felt good, but he was beginning to wonder if he'd made the right choice in joining the Forsyth Scouts. Perhaps he should have just headed west to Oregon. They were over two weeks into this venture and no contact had been made with hostile Indians; or so he thought. On the far side of the hill to his left, a small war party of Sioux had seen them. Without showing themselves, they rode back to the Arikaree River to warn the village that soldiers were coming to attack them.

The village crier roved through the camp exhorting the men to gather their horses and to paint themselves for war. Young boys raced out to the prairie to gather in the war horses. White Horse and Tall Bull made their way over to the Sioux camp to tell them of developments and to urge them to make ready so that the Sioux, Cheyenne and Arapaho could all attack as one.

Half Bear checked his gun and pushed it back into the scabbard on his horse's saddle. Only a handful of men amongst the Sioux, Cheyenne and Arapaho on the Arikaree had guns and his was the only modern one, all the rest being virtually obsolete muzzle-loaders. As he painted his face, the crier yelled out an instruction to start out with the Sioux and not to wait for Roman Nose, who would follow on when he was ready.

Almost six-hundred Indians cantered away from the Arikaree River hoping to intercept the white soldiers. Major Forsyth was totally unaware that there was a huge camp of Indians nearby and rather than head towards them for an engagement as the Indians assumed he was doing, he was inadvertently moving directly away from them.

By late morning the Indians were advancing at a walk with scouts ahead of them, anticipating bumping into oncoming soldiers at any time. The day wore on and the sun set, leaving White Horse and Tall Bull perplexed. Rather than blunder about in the dark they decided to make temporary camp and look for the soldiers in the morning.

It was well after midnight and Jackson couldn't sleep. He lay on his back under a thick blanket and watched the cloud scudding under the moon. It was amazing how bright the moon was. It cast shadows of the cottonwood he was under whenever the cloud moved away and he remembered his teacher telling him that the moon's glow was sunlight reflected back from the moon surface. It seemed pretty amazing that the sun could light the earth at night by bouncing off the moon. Earnshaw, lying five feet to his left, was oblivious to such celestial wonders. He was fast asleep, yet snoring and farting loud enough to make the horses feel inadequate in their emissions.

Jackson could hear the horses shuffling about, but he didn't raise himself to look up, as doing so would have exposed him to the wind. They were fine, he told himself, they were tied to picket pins and wouldn't move unless they were stampeded by something and if that happened he'd know about it.

An owl hooted and another replied. A split second later adrenaline flooded into Jackson's bloodstream. Owls hooted when they were perched. They weren't perched in this cottonwood and there wasn't another tree for a long way. People were communicating with each other and trying to disguise it! As Jackson reached for his gun there was an outbreak of yelling. The moon reappeared and Jackson saw Indians running through the horses waving blankets and slapping those they passed close to. Crouched on one knee, Jackson took a bead on an Indian as he ran through the herd. He began squeezing the trigger just as Earnshaw sat bolt upright right in front of his gun. The target jinked away.

"Shit!" Jackson exhaled.

"What the hell's going on?" Earnshaw asked, still groggy with sleep.

"Indians stealing our horses. Get up."

A rifle cracked and then again a second later, but by now the Indians had run through the herd and were away, taking, as it turned out, only seven horses that had broken free of their pickets. The rest had remained tethered. To Jackson's great relief, U.S was still where he had left him.

Lieutenant Beecher jogged past, "Pack your gear Jackson. They might be back. We'll move out when everyone is ready," he growled. Light was coming into the sky when the scouts were finally ready to move. They assembled on the bank of the dry river and had just begun to move when they saw a glint in the distance. It was the infant sun striking the top of a Cheyenne lance. Jackson watched for a second as hundreds of Indians charged, line abreast, kicking up a storm of dust. They were over two miles away but closing fast.

"Get in cover on that island!" Major Forsyth yelled, pointing at the grassy island in the flat of the riverbed. All fifty men whirled about as one and headed to the island less than two hundred yards away. It was only small, maybe a hundred yards long and it wasn't in the centre of the river, being much closer to the right bank, but the grass would offer places for concealment and the Indians would have to approach across the exposed flat of the riverbed.

Jackson and Earnshaw dismounted on the island and began digging in the sandy soil to make a trench and breastwork. Earnshaw kept looking up to report on the progress of the approaching riders. "Stop watching them and dig a damn hole, Earnshaw!" Jackson berated him. Seconds later the shooting began from both sides.

The Indians swarmed into the riverbed, screaming and yelling with war whistles screeching. A solid tidal-bore of horses surged along the riverbed towards the island. Forsyth's men opened fire, putting out a sleet of lead, but amazingly no-one seemed hit.

Half Bear was riding hard just behind Bad Heart as the island exploded with gunfire. They had intended to overrun it, but now, unable to see any targets and racing into a storm of lead that was tearing open the very fabric of the air, that didn't seem such a good idea. Half Bear could sense that the charge would split and flow either side of the island. He could also sense that Bad Heart wasn't going to pull out. Bad Heart had balls. Just as Half Bear had decided to pull left and leave Bad Heart to his headlong charge, he saw Wild Wind turn to face him above the chest-deep grass at the high point of the island. Half Bear couldn't believe it. He let out a whoop.

Bad Heart's horse leapt up the bank and onto the island. Half Bear followed. He knew he would only have one shot at this and if he failed, they would both probably die. The horses were the only things that the Indians could see amongst the grass and they would all soon be killed. Bad Heart blew past Wild Wind, startling him so that he began to trot away. Half bear urged his horse on and pulled level with Wild Wind. He kicked his feet clear of his stirrups, pushed his hands down on the saddle and ripped his legs upwards so that his feet landed on the saddle and then he dived out and landed, sprawling across Wild Wind's back. He felt a burning impact across his left buttock and knew he'd been shot, but he couldn't tell how bad it was. Wild Wind was now galloping back to the riverbed and it was all Half Bear could do to hold on. He swung his legs up just as Wild Wind leapt down to the river. Half Bear was smashed upwards on landing, the breath driven out of him, but the impact helped seat him.

"Son of a bitch!" Jackson yelled. "Bastard stole my horse." He fired at Half Bear, just as Half Bear leaned forward and down over the horse's neck to retch. The bullet went high and Half Bear galloped on towards the hill at the bend in the river. Out of range of the guns he reined Wild Wind in and stood watching the battle a moment to regain his breath and his wits. Bad Heart had already turned and was charging back over the island in a staggering display of bravery. The rest of the warriors were now riding around the island shooting arrows into the grass in the hope of hitting someone.

Half Bear watched as Weasel Bear charged at the island, yelling and shaking his shield high above his head. A bullet hit his hip and was deflected up, exiting through his back near his neck in a spray of blood Half Bear could see, even from as far away as he was. Weasel Bear fell from his horse and landed in a thick patch of grass near the bank. Weasel Bear's nephew, White Thunder, also saw his uncle fall and raced in to help him. He leapt from his horse and lifted Weasel Bear by the shoulders just as a bullet hit his own shoulder and ripped out above his waist. Both men were soon dead.

Half Bear had been elated by recovering Wild Wind, but his joy was being dampened by the developing battle in the riverbed. The warriors were being killed and they couldn't even see their killers. They didn't have guns and now Half Bear had lost his rifle as it was in the scabbard on his other horse, which, as he watched, was struck in the neck by an arrow and collapsed. At least the wound in his backside wasn't bad. It was a deep scratch and would sting for days, but he'd be all right. The bleeding had almost stopped already.

Runners had been sent back to implore Roman Nose to come and in the end, abandoning the ceremony he had begun to restore his medicine, he rode out to a hill above the island. Half Bear watched as the battle petered out. Everyone was waiting to follow Roman Nose's lead. For a time Roman Nose sat on the ground with Tangle Hair and several others and a deep discussion took place, but Half Bear couldn't hear it from his position down near the riverbank. After a few minutes the meeting broke up and Roman Nose painted his face, shook out his war bonnet and placed it on his head. He mounted his horse and began trotting down to the riverbed. Almost a hundred others followed his lead and a charge began. As the yelling of the warriors reached a crescendo and the attackers swept past Half Bear's position, Forsyth's men unleashed concentrated fire into the charging warriors. Roman Nose was hit just above his hips and thrown from his horse. He landed hard in long grass not far from Half Bear who heard his breath driven from him explosively on impact. Half Bear launched Wild Wind downslope to pick him up.

The firing had almost stopped again as Half Bear wrestled Roman Nose onto Wild Wind's back and led them at a run to safety behind a hill. He lay Roman Nose on the ground and pushed some soft earth under his head. Roman Nose's eyes were closed in pain, but he was conscious and his hands opened and closed as fists in time with his ragged breathing. Half Bear didn't bother to examine the wound, he could see it was fatal. The bullet had gone right through and the grass underneath Roman Nose was staining with dark blood.

Half Bear sat with Roman Nose throughout the afternoon. The battle had virtually stopped in a standoff with Forsyth's men hidden on the island and the Indians surrounding them. Only the occasional shot rang out. *"Can you turn me a little so I can see the sunset?"* Half Bear jumped at the sound of Roman Nose's voice.

*"Of course."* With the help of two others, Half Bear gently lifted Roman Nose and laid him back down with his head and shoulders propped up to see the western horizon.

*"This will be my last sunset. Half Bear, watch all the sunsets you can and revel in each dawn. You might never know which will be your last,"* Roman Nose said softly. Gradually the sun sank and the sky turned pale blue and gradually yellow and then deep red, the undersides of the clouds turning pink. *"It's a good one,"* Roman Nose said and smiled. He closed his eyes and passed away.

Half Bear squeezed Roman Nose's hand in a final goodbye. He was heartsick at the loss of such a great man and at the loss of the other warriors during the day. He had no interest now in seeing how the battle would end. With others already making preparations to prepare Roman Nose's body for its final journey, Half Bear mounted Wild Wind and headed back to the village to find She Wolf and Running Otter.

There was a cold bite in the wind as it rippled through the grass and pulled at She Wolf's hair. She was sheltered from the worst of it, sat as she was on a buffalo robe in the lee of Running Otter's tipi. Half Bear and Running Otter were sat with her, each of them sipping at red leaf tea with blankets wrapped around their shoulders.

*"I don't know what to do anymore,"* Half Bear said, *"I thought it would be right to join with leaders that wanted to resist the white men, but that hasn't worked out so well. Maybe I should have stayed with Black Kettle all along."*

*"Don't be hard on yourself,"* Running Otter replied, *"None of us can ever really know what the future holds. You did what you thought was best and we were happy to follow you."* She Wolf nodded in agreement, but Half Bear didn't feel reassured.

*"What do you think we should do now?"* Half Bear asked, directing his question at Running Otter. For a split second Running Otter thought he heard dogs barking and then he realised that it was geese. They all looked up to see a loose 'U' formation of nearly eighty snow geese flying towards them. Their bodies undulated as they flapped languidly at the air and their honking voices filled the heavens.

Running Otter raised a finger to point at the geese, *"Perhaps we should do as they are doing and go south. Black Kettle is camped to the south on the Washita River. He is my friend and I miss him."* He paused to watch the geese pass over and head for the southern horizon. *"Whether we are friendly or hostile seems to matter little to the white man. He treats us well, or badly, on a whim. I would like to see Black Kettle."*

*"That is fine with me"* Half Bear sighed. *"We'll take Wild Wind and head for the Washita tomorrow."*

# CHAPTER NINE

## Washita River, Oklahoma
## November 1868

It was bitterly cold outside. The fifty-one lodges of Black Kettle's band of Cheyenne hunkered down against the wind on the bank of the Washita River. The snow glittered under the moonlight, mirroring the icy stars overhead, but the fire sparkling within the winter shroud gave no comforting heat. Inside his tipi, Running Otter put another log and some buffalo chips onto the fire and sat back, gratified at the brief shower of sparks racing up like hornets from a disturbed nest.

As the fire settled back down to a steady glow, Running Otter's sense of unease crept back. He had no idea why he felt so worried, but he couldn't dismiss it. All should be well, or as well as it could be. Black Kettle had told him that General Hazen at Fort Cobb had reassured him that if he stayed here on the Washita the village would be safe from the soldiers, although in a contradiction to his promise of safety, Hazen had denied him permission to move the village closer to the fort. Still, Black Kettle had been given sugar, coffee and tobacco and a promise of protection. Running Otter ruminated on the white man's promises. At Medicine Lodge they had been promised food and clothing in return for living here, but now they found themselves desperately short of food. Running Otter ruminated and the question that rolled around his head was, *'why hadn't Hazen allowed them to move down to the fort?'*

Outside it had begun snowing again. George Armstrong Custer's black horse, stark against the white snow, kicked its way through the two-foot-deep blanket, sending white sprays out in front of it and leaving a furrow behind. The Seventh Cavalry laboured in Custer's wake, vaporous breaths mingling with the swirling snowflakes. The Osage scouts riding with the cavalry were following the easily read trail of Bear Shield and his small war party and Custer was almost beside himself at the prospect of catching the Indians and punishing them.

She Wolf couldn't sleep. Her parents were snoring gently as she got up and dressed in the light of the fire's embers. Uneasy, and fearing something bad happening, she had decided five minutes ago to repaint the red birds on Wild Wind to protect him. She dressed quickly, gathered her paint, and stepped out into the whirling snow. It was so cold now that the snow squeaked underfoot like the polystyrene chips of a later age. It seeped through her clothes and probed for her bones and she jogged towards Wild Wind to keep warm.

Wild Wind too, was feeling the cold, but overriding that sensation was the itch under the blankets tied on his back. He lay down and rolled over on a patch of stony ground and flailed his legs as his back wriggled side to side. He felt glorious relief from the itch as the stones abraded him. To top it off, he saw the woman approach through the dark and the whirling snow. He greeted her cheerfully with a whinney and a stamp of the foot and she in turn spoke soft words.

She Wolf then put her arms around his neck and held him for over a minute and he felt her warmth seep into his winter coat. He almost forgot it was snowing. The woman slipped a bridal over his head and led him to her tipi where she began to brush his thighs, cleaning off the muck in preparation for painting. Wild Wind closed his eyes and stood in peaceful bliss as the woman groomed him.

Crow Neck's horse was almost exhausted. They had reached the Washita and there couldn't be far to go to the village, but the horse desperately needed rest. Up ahead Bear Shield had stopped for some reason and Crow Neck took the opportunity to dismount and shift the saddle over onto his spare horse. *"I'll come back for you tomorrow,"* he said to the exhausted animal as he pushed her to a patch of brown grass blown clear of snow by the scouring wind. The tiny column of men and horses advanced again and Crow Neck mounted his spare horse and looked back to see his best warhorse bend her head to graze. *'She won't go far'*, he tried to reassure himself and reluctantly he rode away.

Major Joel Elliot was freezing, but he was grimly determined to forge on in the experimental winter campaign with Custer. They had been given orders from General Sheridan to head south from the Antelope Hills towards the Washita, where the hostile Indians were camped for winter and to destroy the villages and horses, kill or hang all warriors and to take prisoner all women and children. Sheridan had been convinced that if they attacked in winter it would mean that if a village was destroyed, the women and children would surely have to come in to a fort and surrender, as they wouldn't survive out in the cold. With their families in captivity, the warriors would be powerless. Elliot thought it was a good idea and was also hoping to grab some glory in a major victory against the savages.

Dawn came and went, unnoticed under a leaden sky. There was daylight by the time She Wolf had finished painting Wild Wind, but it was a washed out, low wattage gloom in which the grey sky blended with the grey horizon. She Wolf marvelled at Wild Wind's patience. He had stood still the whole time she had painted him and he seemed to enjoy the attention. She held the velvet of his muzzle, feeling his breath and rested her forehead against his, sharing his warmth. She was still resting with the horse when Running Otter walked over to her.

"*You're up early,*" Running Otter said, noticing the new red birds on Wild Wind's thighs and knowing that She Wolf must have started painting in the dark.

"*I couldn't sleep and had a bad feeling.*"

"*A bad feeling about what?*" Running Otter asked, jolted that someone else might have felt the same thing he had.

"*I don't know, but I wanted to paint Wild Wind to keep him safe.*"

"*I couldn't sleep either,*" Running Otter said. "*I think the whites may betray us again. I'm worried that we weren't allowed to move down to Fort Cobb.*" She Wolf said nothing, not wanting to think about white men and instead ran her hand along Wild Wind's neck, feeling the solid mass of his muscles. '*Such beauty and such power,*' she marvelled.

The deer was struggling. There were eighty-two other white-tails in the yard, but she was the slowest. Despite her peers compacting the snow into wide trails, it was still sapping her strength. The tiny little slips with seemingly every step, required constant corrective muscle twitches and she was near the end of her tether. She stopped to rest, her nostrils flaring out to smell the frigid air and her mouth agape in an effort to keep cool, for even though it was cold, the effort of walking, combined with the infection coursing through her, was making her hot.

The injury had at first seemed minor. She had stood on a branch and a sharp twig had gone up between the cloven halves of the hoof of her right rear foot. The stab wound had become infected and now gangrene had taken hold.

The rest of the yard were moving away from her now, heading towards a patch of willow offering forage and she listened as their footsteps receded. Behind her, the three wolves were closing in. They loped easily over the compacted snow, silent winter wraiths with smiling mouths and lolling tongues. They had been following the trail all night, encouraged by the gangrenous smell in the snow that promised a weak, exhausted individual in the herd. The lead wolf stopped for a second and lifted her head to smell the breeze, her yearling son and daughter doing the same. They were close. As if in confirmation, a raven circled just ahead of them and let out a 'kronk' of encouragement.

It was mid-afternoon by the time Crow Neck set off to retrieve his horse. The sky was dark grey and it was snowing again, big flakes that fell straight down and nestled on the mane of the horse he was riding. He pulled his blanket tightly around himself in an effort to stop his body heat flowing out of it. He was already cold and wishing he'd forced his horse on last night so that he didn't have to do this now, but as soon as he thought it, he chastised himself knowing he'd done the right thing. He'd done what he always did and put the needs of his animal before his own.

'It couldn't be far now,' he told himself, 'probably just over this next rise'. As they climbed higher Crow Neck stared ahead and saw movement. It wasn't his horse, it was a lot of horses, or possibly a herd of buffalo. 'Is that buffalo, or soldiers on horses?' The bad light, distance and falling snow made it impossible to tell, but Crow Neck was doubtful it was buffalo, by the way the column moved. He was almost certain it was soldiers and adrenaline sparked his heart to urgency. His resting horse could rest a bit longer, he had to get back and warn people that soldiers were coming.

She Wolf was riding in the same snow-fall as Crow Neck. Wild Wind's mane had a white crust of snow over it and the sleeves over She Wolf's forearms were becoming similarly decorated. She shook each one in turn and brushed the snow from her thighs then looked back up to see a white-tailed deer stood in a trail in the snow. With a barely perceptible pull on the reins she brought Wild Wind to a stop. The deer seemed totally unfazed by their presence and just stood stock-still.

She Wolf caught her breath when she saw the wolves. They were only a hundred yards behind the deer and had just seen it. The first wolf squatted and urinated. It was a she-wolf. She took two further steps and then all three wolves exploded into a run. Wild Wind skittered nervously and turned side-on to the deer, eyes wide and nostrils flaring, but She Wolf held him in place.

The deer saw death coming, but made no move to avoid it. Rooster-tails of snow flew back from the wolves' feet, their bodies undulating with powerful strides, tails trailing in their wake. The young male slammed into the rump of the deer, partially turning it sideways. A split second later his mother crashed into the deer's throat and her daughter tore into the belly. The deer collapsed as if shot and was dead seconds later.

She Wolf was awe-struck. One could live a long life and never see such a drama played out. She felt honoured, but the death of the deer orchestrated by the she-wolf was surely a sign of some sort. She Wolf turned Wild Wind and pushed him to a trot as the raven landed in a willow and settled down to wait for a banquet.

She Wolf headed towards the village for five minutes and then stopped. Perhaps the death of the deer, flagged for her attention by the presence of the she wolf, was a sign of something bad happening in the village. She could race back to warn them, but if it was already too late, what could she do? On the other hand, she could turn down-river and travel two miles to the Arapaho village and raise the alarm with them and bring a rescue party to Black Kettle. Convinced catastrophe was already underway, she galloped downriver for help.

Crow Neck dismounted outside Bad Man's tipi in fading light and a dwindling snow-fall. Bad Man emerged and seeing Crow Neck's countenance asked, "*What's wrong Crow Neck?*"

"*I think I saw soldiers coming this way.*"

"*Think you saw?*"

"*Well they were a long way off and it was dark and snowing much harder than it is now. I thought they might be buffalo, but I don't think so.*"

"*I bet it was buffalo. You are a worrier, Crow Neck. Squaws worry less than you.*"

"*No, I think it was soldiers. You would do well to bring your horses in close just in case.*"

Bad Man sighed and shrugged, but gathered his coat and went to round up his horses in case Crow Neck was right, after all he had to be right one of these days.

Private Samuel Poundstone sat on his horse and watched as Custer conferred with the Osage scouts and his officers. They squatted in a circular huddle, the scouts pointing this way and that and Custer's head nodding. As far as Poundstone was concerned, Custer was a total dumbass. He'd been given command of the Seventh in the fall and for no good reason Poundstone could see, had decided to separate the men from the horses they had had for the last year. He'd then given companies horses of all the same colour! Four companies got the bays, three companies were given sorrels, one company got chestnuts, one got browns, another blacks, another greys and the rest, that Custer called brindles, were given to the company with the most junior officer. Poundstone was devastated. His horse, Texas, was now in G Company. He'd loved that horse and he was his friend. Texas always did as he had wanted and now he had a crazy son-of-a-bitch mare called Gypsy, who did what the hell she wanted.

On top of taking his horse from him, Custer had told them that they were going to hunt Indians in the winter! The last few days had been hell. They had left the fort in such a thick blizzard that they couldn't see a thing and had blindly followed Custer, who himself was just following a compass. The following day had been so bright and sunny that they were in real danger of snow blindness. They had smeared gunpowder around their eyes to cut down the glare, but in the end, Poundstone had cut eye slits in his bandana and tied that around his head as a mask. One day it was so cold that to sit still in the saddle would have risked frostbite and so to keep from freezing they had all walked by their horses' sides. At night they had kept the horses bits in their coats to stop them freezing. It was all taking army bullshit to a whole new level.

The pow-wow with Custer and his officers broke up and Major Elliot walked past telling the men to eat supper and then to prepare themselves for a night march. From the state of the trail the scouts thought Black Kettle's camp was close now and if they moved overnight they could attack it at dawn. 'A night march! Sweet Jesus, I've heard it all now,' Poundstone muttered to himself.

She Wolf had raised a rescue party who had charged into Black Kettle's camp to find all was well. Feeling stupid, she had ridden back with the Arapaho and paid a visit on her friend Calling Jay. They stayed up late by the fire and She Wolf was given a bed in Calling Jay's tipi. She woke up in the middle of the night. Calling Jay and her husband were fast asleep as she crept out of the tipi and into a crystalline silence. There wasn't a breath of wind and the stars were beautiful. She wondered what they were, but her thoughts were interrupted by an owl hooting and Wild Wind giving a soft nicker in reply. He was picketed outside the tipi, as She Wolf hadn't wanted to leave him too far away. She hugged his neck and admired the red birds still painted on his hips. Reassured all was well she went back to bed and fell asleep within minutes.

The seven hundred men of the Seventh Cavalry halted just before dawn. It was still clear, but down by the river there was a thick, low fog. The troops were surrounded by a profound silence. Poundstone had mounted Gypsy and as she moved around from foot to foot, her hooves crunched the crust of hard-frozen snow. To Poundstone it sounded like gunfire and he inwardly cursed her for the hundredth time. From down in the village the troops heard a baby cry.

Custer split his force into four. They would attack from four directions at the same time. He would take companies K, C, A and D on the most direct route across the river. Poundstone mustered with Major Elliot, fervently hoping the battle would be swift and that they could end this bullshit.

Black Kettle stepped outside his tipi just as dawn was lightening the sky. It looked as though it would be a clear blue winter day once the fog left the river valley. He smiled, but seconds later the smile was gone when a woman screamed out, "*Soldiers.*"

He jumped back inside, picked up his rifle and jumped out again. He fired a shot straight up into the blue heavens, jolting the village awake. On the other side of the river Custer yelled the order to charge and bugles flared and the band played 'Gary Owen', as per pre-battle orders. The horses thundered to the river and splashed across in seconds.

Black Kettle jumped on his horse, pulling his wife up behind him to keep her safe. He charged towards the river intent on meeting the advance and reassuring the troops they were good Indians. As he raced for the river he was dismayed to realise that there were troops converging from several directions. Custer flew past him, knocking down his good friend Bad Leg and racing on through the village. Black Kettle raised his hand in peace as the bullet tore into his stomach. His horse whirled in fear and another bullet hit his back. As he fell his wife was hit with three more bullets and she splashed into the river beside him. The cavalry continued to charge through the shallows, rocking the bodies in the violent water like corks on an ocean swell.

The gunshot ripped its way through the fog and rolled over the Arapaho camp, jolting She Wolf instantly awake. She had slept in her dress and so it only took moments to pull on winter moccasins and a coat and then she was freeing Wild Wind from his picket. Even though she had been quick off the mark, warriors were mounting horses all around her and some had already galloped off, heading towards Black Kettle's camp.

Despite her worry, She Wolf couldn't help but be exhilarated by Wild Wind's gallop. It was smooth and rhythmical and so fast it was frightening. He gained on the horses in front, their tails flying out behind them like the taunting capes of matadors, drawing him on even faster. He overtook three together and showed no sign of slowing down. They would be there in minutes. She Wolf was fearful for Running Otter, he was old and wouldn't be able to run away from whatever was happening.

Up ahead was a meander in the river and She Wolf could see women and children emerging from the water and cutting across its neck. Behind them were some cavalry and the shooting now was a rolling barrage of sound. The leading warriors began to clash with the troops and their pursuit of the women slowed. She Wolf thought that the little group she could see would make it now and so she galloped onwards.

Custer had driven through the village in minutes. Exhilarated, he raced on up a small hill and spun around. He could see the whole village from here and to his left Captain Benteen's unit was engaged in a shootout with a handful of warriors. It would be over in minutes. First Lieutenant Edward Godfrey charged up to Custer, the wind pushing his long black beard back under his chin and the tops of his cheeks flushed with the sun, or the excitement, Custer couldn't tell.

"Sir, there is another much bigger village just downstream about two miles and there are hundreds of Indians riding this way," Godfrey shouted above the gunfire. "There was a lot of shooting that way. I think Major Elliot may be down there, he set off on a chase."

Custer sat back in his saddle and blew air out through pursed lips, "No, Elliot's fine. We need to get the horse herd destroyed and I want every tipi burned." As Custer gave his orders the firing had lessened and Captain Benteen was already driving the horse herd in towards the village. There were over seven hundred horses to kill and it would take some time.

Captain Benteen's second in command, Lieutenant Gibson, raced up to the command post. His horse slipped near the crest, its front legs splaying and head smashing into the snow. Gibson was thrown over its head and landed on his face in the snow. Unhurt, he gathered himself and stood with snow falling from his face. "Well done Gibson, that was an artful master class in the dismount," Custer smiled.

Unperturbed by Custer's sarcasm Gibson barked, "Sir, Captain Benteen has the horse herd and will begin destroying it. He also has about fifty women and children prisoner."

Major Elliot saw a large group of Indians fleeing east and he determined to catch and kill them. With a wave of his hand he shouted, "Here goes for a brevet or a coffin!" and he spurred his horse on. He was confident he would gain the brevet, the Indians were far too primitive to put him in a coffin. Most of them didn't even have guns, just bows and arrows. He smiled to himself, pleased to have shouted out a quote which would read well in the after-action report and his biography.

Elliot had nineteen men with him and they thundered through the snow in pursuit of a group of women. He could see three men amongst the women and as he closed in the men turned and two of them loosed arrows, the third fired a musket.

Private Poundstone, riding just behind Major Elliot, thought he was about to die. The arrow seemed destined for him, but Gypsy ran into a rut and dropped to the left and the arrow tore through the right sleeve of Poundstone's jacket. Cheered that fate was on his side, he aimed Gypsy at the Indian who had fired the arrow with the intent of running him over with half a ton of horse. Something glinted to his right and Poundstone looked to see hundreds of warriors lining the crest of the hills. Something was spinning lazily in the wind from the tip of a lance, catching the sun as it went. "Jesus Christ!" Poundstone exhaled. He reined in Gypsy and began a turn, only to come face to face with a line of warriors racing at him on foot from the riverbank on the left.

Major Elliot saw the problem a tenth of a second after Poundstone. He halted the charge and got the men to dismount. They were on a flat area near the river, where the wind had kept the long grass relatively free of snow. "Take cover!" he yelled, throwing himself prone in the turf. The Indians surged towards them like the tide coming in around a rock. The terrified troopers lay prone, not daring to raise their heads. They held their guns up and fired without taking aim, in the hopes of driving the savages back. It wasn't going to work. With arrows flying thick and fast Elliot got to his knee, took aim and fired at a charging warrior. The bullet slammed into the Indian's shoulder, spinning him around and thumping him into the grass on his back. Elliot lay prone again and jacked another round into his carbine.

"Take aim!" Elliot yelled at his men. He got up again, an example to the troops and took aim just as an arrow hit his larynx and sliced between his third and fourth cervical vertebrae. When Elliot had been six years old his mother had given him five eggs to carry out from the barn. As he'd stepped outside, he'd tripped and the eggs had landed in the gravel with a wet crack. It was the exact same sound the arrow made as it hit him. He fell back, flat on his back. He couldn't move. He knew his spine had been severed and he blinked, just to make sure he could still move something. He thought of his mother rolling her eyes as the eggs broke and for a split second he was six years old. His throat was filling with blood and he couldn't seem to cough to clear it. His airway blocked, his eyes fluttered and he thought that perhaps arrows weren't so primitive after all. A second later he was dead.

She Wolf rode past Elliot's men pinned in the grass knowing that they would have only minutes before they would all be dead.

Poundstone, lying in the grass and trying to blend in with the earth, saw a squaw riding towards him on a course to pass only yards to his right. She was riding a magnificent horse with lifelike cardinals painted on its sides and a U.S brand on its chest. He readied himself, seeing a chance to escape the mess he was in. As she came level with where he was, he sprang up and grabbed for her ankle, intent on pulling her off and escaping on the horse.

When the man leapt up from the grass and grabbed her, She Wolf pulled Half Bear's pistol from the back of her waistband, pushed it down on the top of the man's head and fired. It was the last bullet in the gun. It blew through the top of Poundstone's skull and exited through his jaw, taking the majority of his brain with it. She Wolf rode on towards Running Otter, the sound of the battle diminishing behind her.

When the first shot of the morning had been fired by Black Kettle, Running Otter had been sat on blankets underneath an aspen with the horse herd laid out before him. He'd woken well before dawn and had gone to sit with the animals, the company of whom he often preferred to people. The horses were beautiful creatures that shared their lives with the Cheyenne so that they could live well, hunt buffalo and travel. They were a gift from the Great Spirit.

Running Otter was on higher ground, to the east of where, in minutes, Custer would establish his command post. He watched in horror as the soldiers attacked the village from four directions. He was helpless to do anything. He was an unarmed, old man and the best he could do would be to try to survive the storm. Beyond the reach of the tree, the snow was about eighteen inches deep and Running Otter could see an opportunity for concealment. He got up and trampled a trench in the snow, then lined the bottom with a blanket. He then wrapped himself in the rest of the blankets and lay down in the trench. He pulled snow over himself until only his head was exposed. Unless anyone passed very close, Running Otter thought his head would just look like a rock on the snow. Here he decided to wait and see how things played out.

Running Otter watched as many of the villagers managed to escape eastwards along and in the river towards the Arapaho camp. Distressingly though, a group of forty or fifty women and children were gathered in a group below where the army officers were collecting on a small hill. Whilst the group of women prisoners milled in a small area under guard another group of soldiers corralled the horses and began shooting into the herd. The scene that unfolded was the most horrifying Running Otter had seen in his seven decades.

As they were shot many of the horses called out with human-like cries. Running Otter could see the panic and fear in the horses and many of those that collapsed were trampled by their panicked peers. The barbarity of the act wrenched his heart and guts. Running Otter's own seventeen horses were in the herd and he cried and sobbed, tears streaking his face and burning into the snow. It was like murdering children. The horses were intelligent, thinking individuals, with their own unique characters and Running Otter felt their fear and confusion. His heart breaking he buried his face in the snow, but his ears continued to torture his heart.

It took a long time to kill seven hundred horses. Whilst the slaughter went on other soldiers tore down tipis and piled them up for burning. All food, possessions, saddles, guns and powder were thrown on the heap. When it was lit a huge black pall of smoke roiled upwards and every so often there was an explosion as a bag of gunpowder exploded.

She Wolf sat on Wild Wind and watched her village burn. She had joined a group of over two hundred men on a hillock to the east of Custer, their rage as hot as the fire below them. After a few moments She Wolf's eyes began to wander and she thought she saw a rock below them move. She did. It moved again. As she stared intently she began to think it was a human head. "*Hey,*" she said to the warrior next to her, "*I think someone is buried in the snow down there. Will you help me pick him up?*"

Black Coyote nodded and She Wolf began to trot downslope with Black Coyote and four other men. As they got closer, She Wolf could see that it was a human head and not only that, but it was Running Otter's head. Running Otter turned to see the horses approach and he was relieved to see She Wolf in front. He pushed himself up and out of the snow and staggered slightly as he stood. She Wolf was appalled at Running Otter's appearance. He was twenty years older and his face puffed as if he'd been beaten, but she hid her concern as she held out a hand to him. He was too weak to pull himself up and Black Coyote dismounted and lifted the old man up behind She Wolf.

"*Take me away from here,*" Running Otter's voice pleaded. "*My heart is broken.*" His head collapsed against She Wolf's shoulder and she felt his tears falling.

When Black Kettle fired his rifle into the air, Half Bear had been sat on a boulder at the edge of the river. He'd woken up early, before dawn, in a worried sweat, although the source of his fear eluded him. Worry seemed to be a contagion at the moment and he had caught it from She Wolf the day before when she had asked to ride Wild Wind and borrow his revolver, which he gave her, though it only had one bullet left.

The sound of the river rushing over the shallows had halted him as he'd walked along and he'd sat down to remember Red Bird who had loved that same sound. A belted kingfisher had flown close by and dived into the water in an explosion of crystal, but wrenched itself free of the river with nothing to show for its effort.

Half Bear leapt to his feet at the gunshot and scrambled ashore. As he reached the first of the tipis he could see the cavalry erupt over the river. He grabbed his bow from his tipi and ran hard for the horse herd. She Wolf had Wild Wind, so he intended on taking someone else's. He didn't need to go far because as he passed Bad Man's tipi, there were four horses there. Bad Man was tying the girth on a horse and he pointed to a pile of saddles and bridles on the ground by the tipi. "*Take one,*" Bad Man said, meaning the saddles and the horses.

The village was in chaos. There were gunshots, men yelling, women screaming, children crying, dogs barking, horses whinnying and yet, even through all of the turmoil, Half Bear could hear a white man's army band. It was surreal.

Once mounted, Half Bear thought he had two options, attack soldiers, or go with the fleeing women and try to cover their retreat. In a split second he chose the latter. He put his bow over his shoulder and head so that it nestled across his back and he turned the horse around and galloped east, where the women were running towards the safety of the Arapaho camp. He caught up with the women in seconds. One woman was struggling trying to carry two toddlers. He saw that she could barely breathe now with the effort of running and she could hardly see through tears. Half Bear rode to her and she handed the children to him.

"*Save them for me please,*" she begged.

"*Climb up behind me,*" Half Bear shouted as he took the toddlers, the sound of a bugle blaring loud behind them. The horse shifted sideways slightly, but Half Bear managed to hold him, despite having a toddler under each arm. The woman finally managed to scramble up and Half Bear urged the horse on. Two hundred yards ahead a swarm of warriors was approaching and Half Bear aimed for the centre of the mass. Once in amongst the charging Arapaho, Half Bear dropped the woman and her children and turned back towards the soldiers.

Major Elliott and his men were in front of him now and were dismounting in panic at the wave of warriors crashing in their direction. Half Bear urged the horse on but it was struck in the chest by a bullet. Its front legs buckled and in a full tilt gallop, its rear end shot up and over in a summersault. It happened so fast, Half Bear couldn't react, but by chance he was thrown clear. He had a brief glimpse of sky and then he landed on his back with a breathtakingly massive impact. He lay stunned for a few moments unable to breathe. As his breath whooshed back in, he flexed his fingers and limbs to check all were unbroken and then he rolled to a kneeling position.

He could see nothing in front of him except a huge patch of brown grass, but the sound of gunfire was exploding out from amongst it and he saw a muzzle flash. He took his bow off his back and loaded an arrow from the parfleche at his side. As he drew back the bowstring, an officer popped up out of the grass and fired, ducking down again too quick to fire on, but Half Bear brought the arrow to bear on the spot where he had been. The officer shouted something and popped back up, bringing his carbine level to sight. Half Bear let fly. The arrow hit the man in throat and he went down.

Half Bear made a move to stand, intending to count coup and possibly take possession of the man's gun, but his legs collapsed from underneath him and concussion robbed him of consciousness.

# CHAPTER TEN

## Washita River, Oklahoma
## November 1868

The darkness was a dense, living thing and the air was brittle with cold. Outside the tipi Wild Wind browsed quietly on willow twigs, the blanket draped over his back silvered with frost. Inside, Running Otter lay on his back under a buffalo robe by the fire. Although he was still, expressionless and made no sound to portray his emotions, every few minutes a tear would well out from the corner of an eye and run unchecked into the grey hair at his temples. She Wolf held his hand in an effort to comfort him and monitor him, as Limping Bear and his wife, Calling Owl Woman, moved their possessions around to make space to accommodate their three guests. All the remaining inhabitants of Black Kettle's village had fled here to the Arapaho camp in the aftermath of the attack on the banks of the Washita.

*"We can't live like this,"* Half Bear said, as the firelight played over the bumps and hollows of his face. *"I think we should move north again to the Powder River country and join Red Cloud who has pushed out the whites."*

*"I think you are right Half Bear,"* Running Otter spoke up in a hoarse whisper. A moment later he continued, *"I'm dying,"* the statement causing even the fire to momentarily dampen in shock before recovering its vigour.

*"What do you mean?"* She Wolf asked.

*"I've been having pain in my back and bowels since the end of summer. It's getting worse. Something bad is inside me. I can feel it growing and it's going to kill me."* He closed his eyes and squeezed gently on She Wolf's hand. *"I think you both should join Red Cloud's people,"* he began again, *"but will you take me to Paha Sapa first? I want to go there one last time. I want to ask The Great Spirit why the white man has been sent to destroy us. If we can find the reason, then perhaps we can make amends and prevent the end of The People."*

*"Of course,"* Half Bear replied. *"When do you want to go?"*

"*Soon.*" Running Otter whispered, his eyes closed again in drowsiness, or pain, She Wolf couldn't tell.

"*Soon? Do you mean going in the winter? You can't seek a vision in the winter,*" Half Bear said.

"*I'm going to try. I have nothing to lose and everything to gain.*" Running Otter closed his eyes again and fell asleep.

"*Do you think he can travel?*" Half Bear asked She Wolf.

"*Well, he can't ride, but we need a travois to carry a tipi anyway, so he could travel on that. We just need to borrow another horse.*"

It was only midday, but the sky was black with rage, the sun nowhere to be seen and certainly not felt; it was crushingly cold. She Wolf thought it wouldn't be long before the snow came down hard. The only saving grace was that it wasn't windy. Ten yards in front of her, Running Otter lay on the travois looking back in her direction. He was buried in buffalo robes so that only his eyes and nose were exposed to the elements. Although she could see his eyes, She Wolf had no idea how Running Otter was, he appeared barely conscious most of the time, but then his eyes might suddenly crinkle in a smile as if this were a summer day in his youth.

Two minutes after She Wolf had thought that it would snow, fat snowflakes began to flow steadily down to earth, tiny victims of gravity. Half Bear turned in his saddle and called to her over Running Otter's head, "*We need to camp. I can see a river up ahead. We'll cross it now and camp on the far side.*"

"Okay," she replied, bending her head down to keep the snow out of her eyes. Travelling in this was madness she thought. At this rate Running Otter wouldn't live to see the Paha Sapa, never mind survive a vision quest there. As she thought it, Wild Wind's head nodded in telepathic agreement and she patted his shoulder with a rue smile.

Half Bear's horse suddenly dropped down into the scar cut by the river. A moment later Running Otter also dropped, his eyes widening in surprise as the end of the travois dropped over the edge of the bank and he was gone from view. The river was a solid mass of ice and Half Bear thought it looked frozen almost down to its bed. Without hesitation he nudged his horse out onto the ice. The horse kept his footing well, as the surface was covered in tiny lumps that his hooves could grab and a thin layer of wind-blown snow took off the slippery sheen. Half Bear turned right to look for somewhere they could climb back out. He couldn't tell if he was going upstream or down, as he couldn't see the water beneath the ice. The snow was now coming down so thick he could barely see the ground.

Now twenty yards behind Half Bear, Wild Wind stepped out onto the river and the ice groaned a complaint. She Wolf's heart fluttered, but the ice held and it looked thick enough to support dozens of horses and so she relaxed a bit. She looked up to see the travois pull past a massive boulder on the far shore and then Half Bear began to rise above the river for the climb out.

It happened near the boulder. The huge rock had finally been pushed from the riverbank only yesterday by expanding ice in the cracks beneath it. It had been sitting in the same spot since the end of the last ice age and it had waited with serenity as the river had edged closer to it and gouged the soil beneath it. It really was a cruel twist of fate to fall the day before Wild Wind was going to walk past it. It hadn't fallen far, but its sheer mass had sent fissures skittering across the river's surface. Those cracks had closed rapidly in the cold, but they were like very poor welds in steel and they were about to be tested.

Wild Wind stepped out onto a pancake of ice some fifteen feet in diameter. The welds at its edges broke and the pancake flipped. Wild Wind's rear end went down into the river as if sucked into a black hole whilst his front end shot skyward, launched from a catapult. She Wolf had no chance and was thrown backwards into the water just as Wild Wind's rear hooves touched bottom.

The world began to run in slow motion as she left Wild Wind's saddle. Her breath was smashed out of her as her back crashed into the water and she was momentarily paralysed. She felt the smooth hard stones of the riverbed push into her back and then she was lifted enough by the water to stay in only intermittent contact with them. She was swept bumpily in the current between Wild Wind's thrashing feet, which miraculously didn't strike her. Then she was jammed, her back on the riverbed and her face against the underside of the ice.

This was ridiculous. She was now in water only waist deep. She could easily have stood up in it, but instead she was going to die in it. Her limbs were paralysed and in any case the current was swift and merciless. She couldn't get out. Through the semi-opaque ice she could see Wild Wind begin to scramble up the riverbank to safety and she was pleased about that at least. He might live to fulfil his destiny. They had already shared quite some adventure.

He was coming back! She saw him turn and suddenly hooves exploded through the ice around her and she rose to the surface like a grain of rice in a boiling pan. As she hit the air she grabbed wildly and caught a chunk of Wild Wind's tail. A second later she was half in and half out of the river, but Half Bear was grabbing her and getting her out. Half Bear had heard the ice give with a thunderclap. He'd turned to see Wild Wind rear up and She Wolf thrown back into the water. He was racing to reach her as Wild Wind began to lurch up the bank to safety, but the horse didn't make it. His hooves slipped on frozen soil and the precipitous slope threw him back onto the river where he splintered the roof of She Wolf's tomb. She erupted from the water aided by the animal she had done so much to try to protect.

Half Bear got She Wolf standing, but she was catatonic with the cold. He bent at the waist and lifted her onto his shoulder and jogged as best he could back to the travois. He stripped her of her wet clothes and pushed her under the buffalo robes with Running Otter.

"*Sorry about this,*" he said to Running Otter as the cold, wet woman invaded his space.

"*No problem. It's a long time since I was under blankets with a naked squaw,*" Running Otter said with a smile.

"*Yeah, well don't get any ideas. Just keep her warm while I put up the tipi and get a fire going,*" Half Bear said, already jogging away in a search for firewood, his feet crunching in the snow.

Darkness had swallowed the landscape by the time the tipi was up and a fire was burning within it. She Wolf was asleep, swaddled in blankets by the fire. Half Bear touched her cheek and announced to Running Otter, "*She seems warm enough.*"

"*Of course she is. She was rescued by my hot blood,*" Running Otter grinned and Half Bear laughed, both at Running Otter's joke and with relief.

"*Are you hungry?*" Half Bear asked Running Otter as he watched the fire. There was no response to his question and Half Bear looked up, the same question on his lips until his eyes met Running Otter. The old man had gone grey and sweat beaded his top lip and forehead and his eyes seemed to bulge outwards, the veins in his forehead looking like worms in a puddle after rain.

Half Bear skipped over She Wolf and knelt beside Running Otter, holding his hand, which was now as light and as delicate as a small bird. "*What's wrong?*"

Running Otter couldn't reply. He sucked raggedly for air, but couldn't seem to get any. Half Bear's stomach flipped. He'd seen three old people die like this and Running Otter looked awful.

"*Wild Wind….is….important,*" Running Otter managed to gasp in a whisper. Half Bear nodded.

"*Yes I know. I'll look after him,*" he said, trying to reassure and calm the old man. Running Otter sighed with relief, his message understood, and his eyes closed. Half Bear hesitated and then shook Running Otter by the shoulders. There was no response, so he held his cheek down to Running Otter's mouth to feel for breath. He knew there'd be none, and he was right. With tears in his eyes, Half Bear sat back and looked up at the smoke swirling up and disappearing out of the tipi's smoke-hole, in tandem with Running Otter's spirit.

They had built a scaffold of aspen poles, wrapped Running Otter's body in a blanket and lifted him onto the platform where he was high above the river. A squirrel watched proceedings with interest, wondering if there was any food in the package that the people were leaving behind. By the time it was done, it was too late to leave and so they had watched the sunset together and then eaten a duck that Half Bear had killed with his bow. Although Running Otter's spirit would likely be following the footprints of those who had passed before him to the milky way, they didn't want to linger too long in case they attracted his ghost back to them. They had left after dawn the following day, but no longer heading to the Black Hills. There was now no point, Running Otter would never have his vision, so instead they turned towards the Powder River Country and Red Cloud's people.

### Powder River, May 1869

Under a hot May sun She Wolf's near drowning and Running Otter's death seemed a lifetime ago. The snow and violence of winter had gone, replaced with a summer of sunshine and a peace that had broken out across the plains. Half Bear swung an axe at the base of a young aspen tree, sending woodchips flying and renting the air with rhythmical 'whacks'. He was bare chested and sweating heavily, but enjoying the physicality of the exercise. She Wolf sat on the pole Half Bear had already cut, with Wild Wind stood just behind her, close enough that every so often his swishing tail crashed over her head, but she didn't mind and didn't move. She enjoyed the proximity of the horse, his constant presence a reassurance.

*"Watch out,"* Half Bear said, standing up straight and stepping away from the tree as it slowly began to lean forward. It accelerated into the ground with a crash, its leaves shaking and crackling with the shock of its demise. With deft swings Half Bear worked along the trunk, taking off branches and leaving just the straight pole, which he attached to Wild Wind with a rope, along with She Wolf's perch.

She Wolf slipped a rope bridle over Wild Wind's head and jumped up onto his back. With a small kick of her heels they moved off, hauling the poles which would be used to finish marking out the racecourse. She Wolf was excited at the thought of the forthcoming race. They had been working for a few days on the team and its tactics. The course would be a circuit of about a mile and a half with a short river crossing and a run through a stand of trees where further poles had been stacked as jumps. It would be very, very tough to win and the triumphant rider would not only have to be a skilled horseman with good horses, but lucky as well. It was always the case that many riders wouldn't finish.

Half Bear walked along at Wild Wind's head, his axe over his shoulder and deep in thought. He had recruited two of his biggest friends, Black Buffalo and Sitting Coyote, to act as catchers and now he just had to decide which order to run his horses. Each horse would do a lap and at the end of the lap the riders had to jump off and mount a new horse. There would be chaos at the changeovers and it was the catchers' job to gather up the spent horses to keep loose steeds from adding to that chaos. It was a dangerous job and someone nearly always got run over, so being big helped.

Half Bear's decision on which horse to run where wasn't too onerous, as since they had arrived here last winter with two horses they had only accumulated two more between them. Wild Wind was the best horse and it was tempting to run him last for the glory of finishing first, but Half Bear wasn't going to be sucked into sentimentality. The most important thing would be to arrive amongst the leaders at the first changeover and so avoid the worst of the unpredictability. His next best horse, Dragonfly, would run the next leg for the same reason and the slowest of the three, Rain, would go last.

"*I hope Running Otter will see Wild Wind run tomorrow,*" She Wolf said, breaking Half Bear's reverie.

He smiled, "*I'm sure he will.*"

The sky was an unbroken blue and over a thousand people sat underneath it on the hillside facing the course. The start-line was already a seething mass of skittering horses, wild-eyed and frothy mouthed from the excitement that was building and feeding itself in a positive feedback of frenzy. Despite recent rain and lush grass, a storm of dust was rising as thirty-two riders and ninety-six horses barely controlled themselves.

All eyes turned to the hill as the starter, Limping Badger, raised a lance. Its point glinted in the sun and the red ribbon attached below the point flowed smoothly and sinuously in the breeze. Moments later the lance arced downwards and the horses exploded forward. The crowd cheered as the ground thundered below the erupting herd.

Half Bear hadn't seen the lance either rise or fall and had been unprepared for the start. Black Buffalo, holding Dragonfly, had been barged in the back by a horse, knocking him down. He'd held onto the lariat holding Dragonfly, but had been dragged three yards and another horse had barely missed trampling him. Half Bear watched hooves skip across his friend with his heart in his mouth, hoping Black Buffalo wouldn't be hurt and, more importantly, that Dragonfly would be waiting for him at the end of the first lap. Although Half Bear was distracted at the race start, Wild Wind wasn't. He launched forward with the other horses and Half Bear's head was snapped back with a cruel whiplash.

Half Bear recovered his senses quickly, despite being sat astride an out-of-control missile. The starting area was wide, but still horses drifted into each other and riders clashed legs, arms and shoulders and for a split second Half Bear's left knee was squashed between Wild Wind and the rump of the horse next to them. As the two separated Half Bear kicked Wild Wind on to greater effort in an attempt to reach the pole marking the turn in amongst the leaders.

Wild Wind had been getting increasingly excited since the horses had begun to gather at the start line. At first he'd been anxious, not knowing if the men were mustering for a battle, but the mood was all wrong for that. He could sense that the men were happy and excited themselves. This was to be something else.

By the time everyone was ready at the start line, Wild Wind was sweating and his heart was beating hard. Suddenly the horses around him exploded into life and he leapt forward with the herd. Seconds later they were barging other horses and he felt the command from his rider to go faster. He knew now that he wasn't being asked just to run, but to race and he felt pure joy just from the excitement and the physicality of the competition.

They hit the turn in third place and the wildness of it made Half Bear whoop with exhilaration. Wild Wind seemed to respond by going even faster. On the hill, She Wolf leapt up and down with delight as she watched Wild Wind go into second place, the red bird on his rump alive with the muscular movement beneath the paint. In a flash they were in amongst the trees and they jumped the fence. In the corner of his eye, Half Bear saw the leading rider fly forwards over his horse's neck, but he whooshed out of peripheral vision literally, in the blink of an eye, so Half Bear had no idea of his fate. It was Broken Hand that had fallen and he landed on his back with a shattering crunch that broke two of his ribs, yet he was up in a flash, unable to breath, but his legs pumping to get him clear of the landing zone, as horses began to rain down all around him. In a few days, when the pain had subsided a little, he'd laugh about it, tentatively.

Half Bear laughed maniacally, the speed and the adrenaline were intoxicating, both for him and Wild Wind. Half Bear's vision had closed down to Wild Wind's bouncing ears and flowing mane and the ground rushing beneath them. They hurtled around the next pole and headed for the river. The slope leading to it was gentle, with sandy soil and Wild Wind raced down without a break of stride. They crashed into the water, temporarily blinding both of them and the deceleration threw Half Bear against the horse's neck, but he righted himself as he was lurched backwards coming up again on the far bank. Behind them it was carnage. Six riders fell in the water and their horses hampered the progress of several others. The water boiled with horses.

They turned again. Half Bear's plan was working so far. They were in front with the first changeover flying towards them. He could see Black Buffalo trying to hold Dragonfly still and in front of them Sitting Coyote was waiting to catch Wild Wind 'Good luck with that,' Half Bear thought to himself. He waited until the last moment then heaved back on the reins, but Wild Wind didn't want to stop. He slowed to a fast canter and Half Bear pushed his hands down on the horse's back, lifted his backside clear and flung his legs out to the left, trying to throw the reins to the right for Sitting Coyote to catch. He ran as hard as he could as he hit the ground, but his first few steps were giant staggers that almost ended with him laid out using his face for a brake, but he managed to recover and get into a full sprint.

Dragonfly was placed perfectly with her backside pointed straight at him. Half Bear launched himself up, placing his hands on her rump and 'leap frogged' onto her back. He flew straight into a riding position, grabbed the reins from Black Buffalo and was away with a 'whoop'! It wasn't so easy for Sitting Coyote. He tried to stop Wild Wind, but the horse slewed across the line of approach for the coming field and he high stepped, nostrils flaring, into the path of a jet black horse. The collision was monumental and lifted Sitting Coyote off the ground on the end of the rope. Even in mid-air his concern was for the horse and not his own safety. He needn't have worried about the horses, as they proved to be fine. He should have been concerned for his landing though, as he broke his left ankle when he returned to earth.

Half Bear and Dragonfly were away, leaving a fearful mess in the changeover area behind them. It was a place only for the brave and the mad. It was difficult to assess the lead they had as Half Bear focused on racing onwards. They hit the first turn in the clear, but Half Bear could sense hoof-beats close behind. She Wolf was almost apoplectic shouting them on, but couldn't be heard in the din. Dragonfly staggered at the jump in the woods and a horse overtook them. Two more overtook in the river. She was a good horse, but she wasn't fast enough.

Half Bear readied himself for the changeover. The leader leapt off his mount only to run face-first into the cheek of a horse that swung its head to look his way. At the moment of impact his head came to an abrupt halt, but his feet carried on, running up into the air until he was almost horizontal and gravity took him down. He was out cold even before he hit the grass. A split second later the man in second place dismounted, only to stagger with a ligament-wrenching twist of the knee. His catcher gave up on the horse and raced in to help the rider. The loose horse wandered into the path of the rider in third place, sending him veering off and ruining his smooth changeover.

Half Bear dismounted in first place once more. Rain was sideways on to him but he leapt up, scissoring his legs and getting on quickly, Black Buffalo getting knocked onto his butt by Rain's shoulder in the process. Rain's top speed wasn't exceptional, but he could hold it. It would be close. He took the jump well and Half Bear yelled with excitement. It was the river where it all went wrong. As they emerged from the crashing tidal wave of entry, Rain lost his footing and his right shoulder shot downwards and his rump reared up. Half Bear was thrown up and forward and landed briefly astride Rain's neck, his testicles cushioning the blow for the rest of his body. The pain was so bad that he barely noticed slamming into the water, which at that point was only eight inches deep over sand and gravel.

Oblivious to having no rider, Rain continued his quest for glory, leaving Half Bear floundering in the shallows and wondering what exactly it was that he loved so much about horses. She Wolf saw Half Bear's demise in the river and was disappointed for him, but she couldn't help feeling a much greater excitement for Wild Wind, who had won his lap.

She Wolf was helping to prepare buffalo hides that would be sewn together to make a tipi. It was an arduous task. The hides were staked out in the grass and bone scrapers were used to carefully remove all traces of flesh from them. When that was done the leather would be rubbed with the brains of the buffalo to keep it soft. She Wolf rocked back and forth on her knees, rubbing, rubbing, rubbing with the bone, her sweat dripping steadily onto the leather. Still, despite her concentration on the task at hand, she saw Half Bear leave his tipi and hobble off towards the river for his daily swim. Watching him walk, in obvious pain, she couldn't believe he still wanted to swim. It was five days since the horse race and large areas of the right side of Half Bear's body had swollen and turned alarming shades of blue, black and yellow with bruising after the fall into the river. She Wolf was amazed at the sight of Half Bear's bruises, but it wasn't Half Bear's physical injuries that concerned her, it was his mood. After the race he had been elated by it all and had recounted his race to anyone who would listen, but now, four days later, he was sullen.

Butterfly Robe Woman appeared from her tipi and caught She Wolf's eye. The two women smiled at each other and She Wolf beckoned her over with a sideways nod of her head. "Can you take over for a few moments, while I catch Half Bear?" she asked.

"Of course." She Wolf handed the scraper over and as Butterfly Robe Woman settled herself to begin the task, She Wolf stood, dizzy for a second after being knelt down for so long, and then jogged after Half Bear. She found him sat on a boulder by the water's edge, knees drawn up and supporting his elbows, head in hands, staring at the river burbling through a gravelly riffle.

"Half Bear, what's wrong, you've seemed to be upset for a few days?" she asked. Half Bear blew air out though pursed lips and flicked a small twig out into the current, where it whirled in an aquatic cyclone for a moment and then raced away, in a hurry to reach the ocean.

"Red Cloud signed a new treaty at Fort Laramie to keep the peace," he said, not taking his eyes from the water.

"Well, that's a good thing isn't it? My father says Red Cloud drove a hard bargain and that the whites have guaranteed him that we can have Paha Sapa forever." Half Bear nodded slowly.

"That's true. They also said we can carry on hunting buffalo in the Powder River country. But in return, Red Cloud has to take his people onto a reservation. I don't want to live on a reservation. I don't want to end up farming like a white man. I also don't trust the whites to keep the treaty promises. They have broken so many already and they continue to punish us and others for things we haven't even done.

*"And apart from that, I don't think Wild Wind can fulfil Red Bird's vision from on a reservation."*

She Wolf turned her gaze away from Half Bear, the movement of a leaf spinning in the current capturing her attention. *"Maybe we've read too much into Red Bird's vision. He said Wild Wind would do something of great importance by a river. Perhaps he's done that already by rescuing me from the ice?"*

Half Bear turned to look at her. *"I don't think so."*

*"Why not? It might not seem important to most people, but saving my life would have been hugely important to Red Bird."*

*"That's true, but Red Bird was definite that whatever Wild Wind would do, it would be of massive importance. I want Wild Wind to fulfil his destiny and I don't want to be a reservation Indian. I think we need to move again and join Sitting Bull on the Rosebud River."*

# CHAPTER ELEVEN

## Black Hills, South Dakota
## May 1873

The eleven warriors and the squaw rode sedately on a seemingly endless ocean of grass. The wind blew through it causing ripples that chased each other, as if the surface of the land was an emerald-green sheet of silk. Despite the beauty of the long-grass prairie under an azure sky, Half Bear's frustration and sense of injustice was burning him so badly it blinded him to his surroundings. Even his companions had faded from his consciousness as the desire to hurt the white miners consumed him. Even though Half Bear had known all along that this day would come, it still beggared his belief. The whites were appalling. Red Cloud and other chiefs had signed the treaty at Fort Laramie in good faith and the whites had promised, promised, that the Black Hills would be left for the The People and that no whites would be allowed to enter it. Yet now, five years later, the Black Hills were infested with madmen craving yellow metal. It wasn't even as if five years had passed before the invasion had begun, they had come in small groups almost before the ink had dried on the agreement. The whites' treaties meant nothing and Half Bear had decided to kill some.

She Wolf shifted in her saddle and moved Dragonfly over to the left, giving Rain following on behind at the end of the lariat, more room. She looked ahead to Half Bear who was riding Falling Leaf with Wild Wind behind him. Even from behind, She Wolf could tell that Half Bear was brooding. She herself wasn't consumed with any overriding emotion, but the sense of the loss of Red Bird was still, even almost nine years since his death, a constant ache, like small, ceaseless waves lapping on the shoreline of her soul. She still wanted to be with the horse Red Bird had loved and foreseen great things for, in order to keep that filamentous connection to him alive. So She Wolf would follow Half Bear and Wild Wind to the end of the earth. She smiled as she watched them, the red birds painted on Wild Wind's hips were beautiful.

As the afternoon wore on, the scant clouds of the morning coalesced and grew tall. By late afternoon they were huge dark grey thunderheads flexing their meteorological muscles and menacingly preparing to demonstrate their power. By the time the wind had begun to blow the horses' forelocks up into a dance, the war party were galloping for the river, where the banks and trees would offer protection. The afternoon sky turned to midnight, briefly lit by a flash of lightning, which was followed by an explosion of thunder so loud that She Wolf felt it in her chest. They raced into the cottonwoods as hail came down in a roaring, defoliating blast and the wind whipped the trees into gyrating dervishes.

Ten minutes later it was over and the sky began to clear. The horses were picketed whilst temporary war lodges were built of branches, sod and buffalo hides. A fire was started, pemmican heated for a meal and water boiled for red leaf tea, all done virtually without a word spoken amongst the party, all of whom knew what must be done before they could enjoy a smoke and a rest.

As the sun sank below the horizon behind him, Half Bear waded across the shin-deep river and climbed the far bank. The land was lit in the golden light of the setting sun and in the near distance a group of ten or so pronghorn antelope grazed contentedly. Half Bear could see four very young fawns in the group and he found his mood lifted watching the circle of life continue. He stood watching them for a few moments, the last rays of the sun warming his back under his sleeveless buckskin shirt. His arms grew goose pimples around the wounds on his biceps.

Before setting off, the war party had entered the sweat-lodge with Black Hawk, the medicine man. They had sat in a circle around the fire and Half Bear had spoken, "*Black Hawk, we wish to go to war,*" and he had handed Black Hawk a pipe. The old man took the pipe, lit it and smoked for a minute. The bowl glowed and hissed and Black Hawk's eyes closed as smoke emerged from his nostrils. Gently he began to hum and then sing a medicine war-song, his voice deep and rich, belying his age, his shoulders rocking to and fro with the rhythm.

"*It is well,*" he said, "*You will find your enemies. They will come to you on your second day in the Black Hills. Have no fear of them. Pass me your bow Half Bear.*" Half Bear reached around the edge of the fire and gave Black Hawk his bow. Black Hawk prayed for several minutes and then handed back the bow. "*You will not be hit by an arrow, or a bullet, as long as you carry this bow, but each of you must sacrifice four pieces of flesh and leave them here.*"

Half Bear nodded his assent and Black Hawk stood and drew his knife. He pinched up a section of flesh on Half Bear's upper arm and quickly sliced it off. He took off another slice below the first and took two more on the other arm. Quickly and with no fuss or spoken word he worked around the circle of warriors and took their sacrificial skin.

Back in the here and now, Half Bear couldn't decide if the breeze was soothing, or irritating his wounds. In the distance he could see the dark shape of the timbered Black Hills. They would reach them tomorrow and he would set out to drive the whites away from their slopes.

The heat of mid-afternoon lifted the scent of pine resin into the air. Half Bear loved the smell of it because it reminded him of boyhood elk hunts here with his father. As he walked back to where Falling Leaf and Wild Wind were tied his footsteps reverberated with the hollow thump that they always had when walking over the ancient accumulation of needles and tree roots. Nine of the other members of the war party milled in a quiet group beneath a huge ponderosa pine, enjoying the shade and the rest. A squirrel chirred loudly, annoyed at the intrusion of the humans.

Screaming Badger and Scar had gone up ahead on foot to look over the brow of the hill. As Half Bear leaned on Falling Leaf's shoulder and the horse leaned companionably back, Screaming Badger and Scar came running back down the hill, the shells and stone arrowheads they had tied in their hair flying and clacking together as they took giant, heavy, downhill strides.

"There is a big canvass tent with a stove-pipe at the bottom of the hill, on the far side of a small stream," Scar panted. Half Bear nodded. Of course there was, this was day two in the hills and Black Hawk had predicted this.

"Did you see anyone?" Half Bear asked. Both scouts said, "No," in unison.

Screaming Badger continued, "There were six mules in a corral, but no horses."

"Okay, we'll leave the horses here with She Wolf and we'll go to the top," Half Bear tilted his chin up in the direction of the hillcrest, "We'll form a line and go down the other side until we reach the tent. Yes?" Everybody nodded and they set off at a jog. As they crested the rise each man began to move downhill using the trees as cover between each short downward dash. Suddenly, at the far left of the line, Bad Heart issued an owl call warning. Two white men on two horses were moving up the stream towards the tent. They were on course to pass only twenty yards below the line of warriors, all of whom lay flat, or melted against tree trunks. The silence was complete and the air still, rich with pine scent. The sun glinted off the water and a dragonfly hawked in sharp zig-zags, egged on to greater effort by the calls of a gray jay. Beyond the water the mules contentedly ate grass, ears flicking, but this soporific pastoral beauty was about to be marred by bloodshed.

Joe Crenshaw had met Kurt Westermaier on the Missouri riverboat. They'd struck up an immediate friendship, partly because Joe was the exact opposite of Kurt. Joe was what his teacher had politely called, 'outgoing', whereas as an adult, some people had called him a brash blabbermouth. He wasn't bothered what people thought though. He was happy in himself and he knew what he wanted in life and that was adventure and to become rich.

Kurt, on the other hand, was shy and his reluctance to get involved in conversations was exacerbated by his relatively poor grasp of English. He'd left Aachen in Germany two years ago barely able to say, 'My name is Kurt,' but that hadn't stopped him following his dream to live in the American west. He couldn't believe the life he was now living. The mountains were beautiful, a far cry from the contour-less land on the Belgian border and the wildlife was amazing. He couldn't get over the immensity of the buffalo herds he'd seen and he'd also watched bears on two separate occasions, creatures long since vanished from Western Europe.

Joe liked Kurt, not just because he was easy to get on with, but because he was great at planning stuff, like how to get all their supplies and other crap up here, and importantly, the dames absolutely loved to hear him talk. They loved his accent and he often drew a crowd and then he reeled them in like the Pied Piper and once Kurt had broken the ice it was easy going from there. On top of all that, three weeks ago Kurt had found placer gold in the creek to the west of their camp. It looked like the two of them were going to be very rich.

Half Bear drew back his bow and blew out a scream from his war whistle. He let his arrow go at the second rider and for the tiniest split second his heart was in his mouth as the arrow flew low. Half Bear was afraid it was going to hit the horse, which he was hoping they'd capture. With an intake of breath to restart the breathing he hadn't realised he'd stopped, the arrow whacked into the rider's thigh, just as another hit his bicep, though it was only the arrow that shattered his cheek which Kurt actually felt.

Joe turned in his saddle to talk to Kurt behind him, just as the arrows let fly. His chest became a relatively huge target and to his delight, Scar hit it flush in the middle. Joe flew out of the saddle as if hit by a wrecking ball. Both horses bolted at the sudden attack, but Kurt held on even though he was only semi-conscious. He bounced in the saddle like a wood-limbed marionette as his horse charged towards the tent.

The Indians raced downhill as one, whooping and screaming and sending the gray jay away in panic. The dragonfly continued to hawk, unconcerned at the noise and the blur of motion close by. Realising he was too slow and too far away and that he wasn't going to be quick enough to count coup on the dismounted man, Half Bear altered his run to follow the injured rider. The horse raced past the tent and into the trees.

Kurt's vision was blurred, but he saw the branch coming and he got his arm up just in time to take the impact before his face did. Both the radius and ulna of his forearm fractured and he was pushed off the horse, landing on his back. He blacked out.

Half Bear ran hard, pulling his knife out as he went, intending to scalp the prospector. He saw the man hit a branch and dismounted almost two hundred metres in front of him. In the rough grass and tangle of berry bushes it seemed to take an age to close the distance. He ran jumping and knees high-stepping, arms out for balance.

In the time it took for Half Bear to close the distance to ten yards, Kurt came around. The pain in his face was monumental, but it woke him up to the danger he was in. He drew his pistol, rolled over and got onto one knee. He raised the gun with Half Bear only five yards from reaching him. He fired.

As the gun came up Half Bear thought of jinking right, but then he realised that the bow was still in his right hand. He couldn't be killed by a bullet whilst he held the bow and so he ran on. The gun fired and the bullet whipped through his hair. A split second later the two men collided, the first point of impact was Half Bear's knife and Kurt's chest. Kurt never even realised his shot had missed. Half Bear yelled in triumph at his victory against the white man and with delight in the power of Black Hawk's medicine.

Twenty minutes later the war party was reunited with She Wolf. They had two new horses, two rifles and a revolver with ammunition and two scalps. Half Bear had also relieved Kurt's body of a small bag of yellow metal. He'd decided to take it, not because it was any use to him, but because it seemed to have such vast importance to white men.

The accident happened three days later. It could have happened to any one of them, but it happened to Half Bear. They were heading down a gently graded scree slope on a gloriously sunny afternoon. Runs With A Limp was leading, Scar and She Wolf followed, with Half Bear next and the rest of the war party strung out behind. Half Bear was riding Dragonfly, who seemed to be managing the slope with aplomb, until she stepped on the loose rock. It squirted out from under her and she stumbled forward, her front legs buckled and she pitched Half Bear almost over her head. As rocks cascaded away in a dusty, racing, avalanche with Dragonfly's foreleg amongst them, she hit something solid and her reflexes launched her back upright, throwing an already mid-air Half Bear, sideways and off. As Half Bear turned in flight, Dragonfly's feet went from under her again and she too began to fall. Half Bear hit the rocks hard, but recovered and began to scramble upright when Dragonfly fell on him.

The collision was pulverising. The horse's flank landed on Half Bear and she rolled onto her back and then over to the other flank, getting to her feet like a tumbling gymnast. Half Bear lay still as Runs With A Limp, She Wolf and Stone Heart leapt off their mounts to go to his aid. *"Get a blanket,"* Stone Heart called as he reached Half Bear. Scar pulled a blanket from the pack behind his saddle and raced down to where Half Bear was now laid on his side, groaning in agony. Stone Heart spread the blanket out behind Half Bear, *"We'll roll him onto it and carry him down to the grass."*

Walking slowly so as not to fall in the loose rock, Runs With A Limp, Stone Heart, Scar and Poor Bear took a corner of blanket each and carried Half Bear down to the grassy area below the scree. She Wolf walked with them holding Half Bear's hand, which felt cool, as if death was stalking him already. When they'd laid him out on the flattest bit of ground in the immediate area, Stone Heart asked Half Bear where it hurt. *"Hips,"* Half Bear groaned. Stone Heart put his hands on either side of Half Bear's pelvis and gently pushed. Half Bear grimaced as Stone Heart's hands moved in different directions and he felt bone grating in response to his touch. Stone Heart untied the drawstring on Half Bear's leggings and looked at his belly, which was swelling ominously.

Stone Heart sat back on his haunches. *"He's broken his hips and I think he might be bleeding inside,"* he said. Without further word from anyone, the horses were picketed to graze, a camp was set up and a fire started to keep Half Bear warm. She Wolf sat with him as activity swirled gently around them and the sun began to dip behind the mountains. As the sky turned pink and red, Half Bear looked increasingly ashen. He squeezed She Wolf's hand to get her attention.

*"I came to live with Sitting Bull because I didn't want to live on a reservation, waiting for hand-outs that never come. I still don't. I've been thinking recently that if Sitting Bull is defeated, I would take myself across the Shining Mountains. Perhaps you should do that, She Wolf. Cross the mountains if things go bad. Not everything about the white man's ways are bad. I think many of them live a good life. Perhaps if you took what is good about the white way of life and combined it with ours you could have a good life. Maybe you could live life as a rancher, independent and free from trouble... What do you think?"*

*"I don't know Half Bear, perhaps I could, but it might not come to that."*

*"But it might. Take the bag of yellow metal I got from the prospector and keep it. It seems incredibly valuable to the whites and you might be able to use it."* Half Bear shook his head gently and took a deep breath, then he began again, *"Don't kill a horse to come with me to the afterlife, especially not Wild Wind. I'm sure there will be horses where I'm going and I want Wild Wind to stay here and fulfil the destiny Red Bird foretold. It was years ago now and Wild Wind is getting old, but I still believe it. He will do something special. Truly."*

Tears rolled down She Wolf's cheeks, but she made no effort to brush them away. *"You'll be fine Half Bear. Stop this talk of death."*

*"I'm going to die. I feel really bad inside. It's much more than broken bones."*

*"If you die and if you see Red Bird, will you tell him that I love him?"*

Half bear smiled, *"I'm sure he already knows that, but yes, I'll tell him."*

At that moment a chorus of wolf howls washed over them from across the other side of the valley. Their ululating cries overlapped and mingled so that it was impossible to tell how many there were. Half Bear smiled again. *"Brother Wolf is calling for me. I might run with him for a time. It'll be fun."* He closed his eyes and still with a wry smile on his face, he slipped away.

# CHAPTER TWELVE

## Eastern Oregon
## June 1876

Dale Jackson sat in a rocker on his porch with a coffee in his hand and leaned back to watch the evening sky turn pink and red above the 'Hell and Back' ranch. Behind him the Wallowa Mountains of Eastern Oregon reached upwards to catch the last golden rays. He could hear some of his cattle lowing gently in the pasture nearby and out in front of him, he could see Mountain and Bess grazing together. Mountain picked his head up and snorted and whipped his tail up between his legs with a swish that Jackson heard, to his surprise, as Mountain looked a good long way off. The horse reminded him again, as he often did, of U.S. It was almost eight years now since he and U.S. had parted company at the Battle of Beecher Island. His eyes were drawn to the steam rising off his coffee and they lost focus as the memory of that fight washed over him, as unstoppable as the sunset.

The excitement of the pre-dawn horse raid by the Indians jolted through him, not unpleasantly, but then the memories of the following eight day siege surged around him with probing fingers of dread. He and Earnshaw and the rest of the Forsyth Scouts were still desperately digging into the sand as at least five hundred warriors swarmed along the riverbed towards them, with murder on their minds. As they'd come within range, all fifty of the scouts had thrown themselves flat in the long grass and put out a terrific wall of fire. It seemed incredible that anyone could survive riding into it, but all of them did, although four hundred and ninety-eight of them were put off from overrunning the island by the savagery of that salvo. As the tide of riders had parted around the island, Jackson had watched in absolute awe as two Indians had continued their charge up onto the higher ground right beside them. He was absolutely dumbfounded when one of those Indians leapt off his horse and onto U.S. and rode off with him. It was easily the most surprising event of his life. For a full three seconds Jackson had stood watching U.S. disappear and then he had suddenly realised that he was stood up in a growing blizzard of arrows. He came to his senses and hit the dirt.

He and Earnshaw had dug themselves further into the sand every time there was a lull in the battle. The Indians had ridden around the island whooping and screaming and making ears-splitting whistling noises all day. They had fired thousands of arrows, but it seemed that everyone was by now well hidden and the Indians were shooting blind. Fortunately, very few of the warriors had guns and those that did, only had old single-shot muskets, otherwise things would have been a lot worse. Even so, twenty of the Forsyth Scouts would be killed over the coming days.

Even with the last rays of the sun slanting onto the porch, warming the decking planks and his skin, Jackson felt the cold fear and knotted stomach of the siege. He had lain in the cold sand watching grass blades move out in front of him, as the Indians tried to crawl to his position unseen. Every time the grass had moved he and Earnshaw had taken it in turns to shoot. The pair of them had hardly moved for four days as the Indians had harassed them. On the third night it had rained steadily all night, making them even more miserable than they had ever thought possible, but at least they managed to collect some water to drink.

For another four days the Indians kept their distance, probably hoping that the defenders would die of thirst, or try to break out and expose themselves, but they held fast, drinking rain water and eating their dead horses. Such was their misery, Jackson seriously began to doubt that there was a god in heaven. The wounded had a terrible time and Doctor Mooers was shot in the head and died on the fourth day, making their untended suffering all the greater. Jackson's faith never really recovered, even after the arrival of a rescue party brought by Trudeau and Stillwell, who Colonel Forsyth had sent off to try to get to Fort Wallace after the first day of the fight.

Susan clattered some plates in the kitchen and the sound brought Jackson back to the present. His dog, Cur, sauntered over from a successful foraging expedition in the brush, the crusty skin of a long-dead jackrabbit dangling out of his mouth. "Jesus, Cur, that's disgusting. That skin is older than I am. I bet it makes you puke." Cur took little notice, his eyebrows lifting alternately as his head turned and he kept an eye on Jackson in case he seemed inclined to take the skin from him. Satisfied he was safe, he lay down on the porch to chew on his sun-dried jackrabbit.

Cur was no particular breed, but a mix of what, Jackson couldn't tell. His ears stood up like a wolf, but he was half the size of one and he was chocolate brown with a huge bushy tail like a fox. Despite his doubtful ancestry and poor taste in food, Jackson reckoned the dog had taught him a thing or two about loyalty and perseverance. It occurred to him then that mixed breed people had taught him a lot as well.

Susan was half European and half Cheyenne. They'd met almost seven years ago whilst travelling west on the Union Pacific Railroad. Jackson had been back east to deliver in person Keller's gold to his sister, Yvette Cooper. He'd been honest and taken all the gold he'd found. He'd been a little less honest when he'd told Mrs Cooper what he'd found at Keller's cabin, but he was comfortable with what he classed as 'white lies'. He'd told Mrs Cooper that he didn't know the cause of Keller's death, which was true, but in order to spare her further distress, he'd told her that Keller had been given a Christian burial. That was partially true, in that he had interred part of what he took to be Keller, but he omitted the fact that the burial was years after the death and only a fraction of the body had ended up in a grave. However, Mrs Cooper seemed put at rest by this story and true to her word she had given him half of the gold.

Until he'd met Susan, Jackson had always thought of the Indians as godless heathens standing in the way of progress. He had been shocked to learn that the Cheyenne were probably more spiritual than anyone he'd ever known. She'd also told him how the westward migration of the whites into land settled by the Cheyenne and Sioux had appeared to her. Indians had been forcibly removed from areas, often killed in the process. When Indians defended themselves and killed whites, the whites would seek out Indians to punish, but the easiest ones to find, were the ones living at 'peace', often those closest to the white settlements and so innocents would be killed in a vicious cycle. Promises of food, clothing and weapons to hunt buffalo were made to get the Indians onto reservations and then the promises broken, time and time again. Dale Jackson now thoroughly regretted his part in the wars against the Indians, but he was philosophical enough to know that there was nothing in the past that could be changed. Instead, he had decided to help Indians wherever they crossed his path.

A movement to his left caught his eye and he strained into the growing gloom to make it out. As he watched he realised that it was a horse and rider walking in towards the ranch. He hauled himself out of his chair to go and put more coffee on. When he came back out, a man was dismounting near the gate to the horse's corral. In the dark he was in silhouette, but Jackson could tell it was Tom Eagle Feather. Tom walked towards him carrying his saddle, bridle and bags, his spurs chinking gently with each step. Tom had been away since April to visit brothers living as Cheyenne, whom he hadn't seen for four years.

"Howdy, Tom," Jackson said, holding out a mug of coffee.

"Good evening, Dale," was the response, accompanied with a grateful smile for the coffee. Jackson had insisted all his employees called him by his Christian name, there would be none of that 'Mr Jackson, sir' servitude on his ranch. Tom dumped his saddle and bags over the rail of the porch and sat down, taking the coffee from Jackson's hand.

"You eaten, or do want some bread and stew?" Jackson asked.

"Ahh. Stew would be fantastic. Thanks."

"Coming up. Don't move." Jackson went back inside to ask Susan to reheat the leftovers for Tom. When he came back out he slumped back into his chair and asked, "How're your brothers?"

"Well, they're still alive, despite the best efforts of you white folk. But things ain't lookin' too good."

"Sounds like you have a tale to tell me?"

"Uh-huh, I do." Tom blew on the coffee and took a sip. "I got this story from my brothers who are with Wooden Leg's village and I got the whites' view of it from stage drivers, agents and newspapers. I wouldn't want to give you some half-assed, one-sided fairy story."

Jackson nodded sagely. "''ppreciate that."

"Okay. I'll assume that, as you now live as a hermit to the west of The Shining Mountains that you will be ignorant as to events of recent years, so I will give you a little history."

"Okay. Not unreasonable," Jackson concurred.

"Okay. So, despite the fact that the Black Hills were given to us," Tom thought of himself as Indian, with an unfortunate and un-asked for streak of white, "General Custer took an expedition there two years ago, without our consent. Red Cloud, for one, wasn't happy, but that is by-the by. Whilst there, prospectors with him found a lot of gold. There was then a gold rush. Prior to this, to be fair, President Grant had said that the prospectors should get out and last year he sent General Crook to tell the miners to get out. But the miners refused to go and there were so many whites wanting in, he needed a new approach, because otherwise it would have ended with the army fighting whites to get them out. So he sent a commission to try to buy the Black Hills from the Indians.

"Not surprisingly, the Indians wouldn't sell and a lot of them got so mad they wanted a fight. Red Cloud lost his warriors to Sitting Bull and Crazy Horse 'coz they had had enough of trying to talk to white folk. So, President Grant then says he's buying the Hills anyway and in December, runners went out to tell all non-agency Indians to come in to agencies by January thirty-first, or be classed as hostiles. Of course the snow was so deep and the weather so bad, that a lot of the messengers didn't even reach who they were supposed to until after the deadline. Even if they made it they were told by the Indians that people couldn't travel in those weather conditions. You can't march women and children through blizzards for days and weeks. Sitting Bull said he would consider coming in when the weather warmed. Crazy Horse said it was too cold to move and anyway, he was in his own country and doing nobody any harm.

"It turns out if they'd come in, they would have starved, because a lot of agency Indians left in March to go hunt because they were starving. Anyway, everyone expected trouble in the spring 'coz they hadn't come in, but Colonel Reynolds attacked Wooden Leg's village, where my brothers are, on March seventeenth. He burned all their tipis, pemmican and saddles and stole all their fifteen hundred horses. Fortunately, Reynolds is a dumbass and when they all went to sleep that night, the Indians stole the horses back.

"Wooden Leg moved his village to join Crazy Horse and a lot of villages are joining up with him and Sitting Bull to avoid bad conditions on reservations and to stay safe. There is now a huge number of Indians in the Powder River country minding their own business, but the whites are classing them as hostile. There is going to be big trouble." Tom took a swig of coffee. Jackson nodded and looked off into the night.

As they sat in the stillness a herd of twelve elk walked close by the house. They stopped to graze and the two men sat in silence and watched them. Cur's head came up, but Jackson waved his hand down to command the dog to lie still. Jackson liked to watch the elk. He knew other ranchers shot them for competing with the cattle for grass, but Jackson didn't mind, there was enough grass for all. He thought that the elk had been here before he had and it seemed unfair to stop them going where they always had, much like the Indians he suddenly thought.

### Little Bighorn River, Montana
### June 1876

It was already a very hot day, nudging ninety degrees and it wasn't even midday. She Wolf had been digging for wild turnips, but had given up. It was too hot and she was too irritated, with sweat running down her back and chest and dripping off her nose. Her back was aching, so she was going to drop the turnips at the tipi and take Wild Wind down to the river for a swim. It sounded like the river was already full of horses and kids playing as their laughing, screaming and splashing carried up to her through the still air and made her smile.

Walking back to the Cheyenne end of the village she was impressed once again with how big it was. It was almost two miles long and a quarter of a mile wide, with over a thousand tipis. There were probably eight to ten thousand people camped here on the banks of the Little Bighorn River, with more than twice that number of horses steadily denuding the surrounding countryside of grass. Everything was so normal that She Wolf could never have guessed that today, the twenty-fifth of June 1876, would be the day that she and Wild Wind would fulfil Red Bird's vision and contribute to history.

Just over two miles to the east of where She Wolf was walking, Lt. Col. George Armstrong Custer had already made the fatal error of splitting his forces, sending Major Marcus Reno with three companies down the left bank where Reno would lead the first attack into an enormous village that they hadn't even seen.

Reno called his troops to a halt. The air was as thick as syrup. Private Zach Riley felt he could hardly breathe and the density of the air was only increased by the swirl of dust that the horses had kicked up. He wiped away sweat from his forehead that had been leaking out from under his hat, but all he did was create a gritty, greasy slime that was just as irritating. He checked his horse's girth was tight and double checked that his carbine and Colt .45 were loaded. He felt comfortable with the guns, it was his horse that worried him. Despite being in the cavalry, he was an almost novice rider and every time they went into a gallop he feared for his life. He looked down at the baked earth, which looked just as hard as rock and felt a sense of dread almost overwhelm him. Without warning Major Reno yelled, "Chaaaaarge!" and one hundred and fifty horses shot forward as one, propelling Zach Riley into a cataclysm of fire.

She Wolf couldn't tell who liked the cold river more, her, or Wild Wind. They had both revelled in the water and the glorious chill of their exit from it. As they climbed out of the river Wild Wind sank to his knees and then rolled sideways onto his back and wriggled, making She Wolf skip away from him in case she got caught by a flailing leg. It was so good to see the horse enjoy himself. As he got back to his feet and then shook, She Wolf slipped his bridle on and she jumped up onto his back to walk him back to the herd.

Suddenly, the air was rent with the screams of women and children. Panic was spreading in a wave heading downstream, so the soldiers, for what else could cause this much panic, must be coming downriver. She Wolf put her heels into Wild Wind and raced to her tipi where she leapt off, dashed in and picked up Half Bear's lance. With a heavy weight of foreboding crushing in on her she pushed Wild Wind into a gallop towards the source of the panic. She was rueing taking Wild Wind into the river, because now the red birds had been washed from off his hips and there wasn't time to repaint them.

As She Wolf galloped to the outskirts of the village she could see already that the battle was lost. Most of the men in the village, having been caught off guard, were amongst the horse herd trying to mount up and weren't in a position to stop the cavalry charge. To make matters even worse, a lot of men were out on a buffalo hunt and it would take time for them to come back in. The women and children were scattering towards the hills, but were going to be cut up piecemeal.

Despite the impending implosion of her life, She Wolf charged onwards with nothing left to lose.

At first Reno had been swept up in the dash and excitement of the charge, but as he approached the village and he could see the growing number of tipi tops appearing over the rise, he feared a trap. Thoughts of the Fetterman Massacre entered his head and he suddenly decided that he could be heading into an enfilade. He called a halt to the charge and ordered a dismount. The cavalry were grouped in fours and smoothly and crisply, as if on a drill, ones, twos and threes dismounted, clipping their mounts' halter rings together with a leather strap so that they could be led to safety by the number fours. The un-mounted troops now formed a skirmish line and began firing at the village. Reno's idea was for a rolling skirmish to advance carefully into the village.

She Wolf couldn't believe it. The cavalry had stopped the charge just when it looked as if all was lost. Now the warriors behind her would have time to mount their horses and join the fray. The soldiers were firing wildly. They were still well out of range of the village, but they weren't deterred from shooting. Incredibly, She Wolf saw some of them firing at the sky. They paid little attention to her as she galloped onwards.

Wild Wind drifted right, towards the slope of the valley side and She Wolf was content to let him go, thinking it would be better to swing in at the end of the skirmish line, rather than charge at it face-on.

Zach Riley fired steadily in the direction of the tipis. He was full of himself now that he was on his own two feet and firing at enemies so far away that they couldn't hit him with their arrows. To his left, where the ground rose up on the hill, he saw a girl galloping a horse, an eagle soaring lazily high above her head. He watched her for a moment and then turned his attention forward, where a large cloud of dust was forming behind a shimmering heat haze.

The roiling dust-cloud was being kicked up by hundreds of warriors charging towards Reno's command. She Wolf turned her head back to watch them. She could just make out the shapes of men and horses at the head of the charge and she grinned maniacally knowing a storm was about to break over the soldiers. She turned Wild Wind in towards the end of the skirmish line and hefted the lance in her right hand, tilting the tip down like a medieval jouster. The steel tip glinted wickedly in the hot sun and it wavered like a living thing, seeking blood to cool it.

The dust cloud in front was huge. An enormous, malevolent entity travelling at great speed towards them. Zach Riley was now wishing that he hadn't fired almost a third of his ammunition without even aiming at a target. He felt a sudden rush of fear and his sweat ran cold.

By swinging to the right and travelling a greater distance, She Wolf had timed her attack to arrive as the warriors would clash with the skirmish line. The soldiers were creating a bedlam of fire as the warriors closed in and She Wolf saw several shot from their horses, but hundreds more rode on, yelling and screeching with war whistles. The noise of the battle was stupendous, but Wild Wind bore down on the skirmish line unfazed, as if reaching for the finish line in a race. He was just the most beautiful horse, She Wolf thought as she aimed him at the soldier on the end of the line, Private Zack Riley.

Riley turned as the horse bore down on him. It was the girl! The lance wavered, now only fifteen yards out, seeking his chest as it bore on, propelled by a half-ton harbinger of doom. In a fumbling panic, Riley raised his carbine and sighted on the girl's chest. The .45 calibre shells the carbine used had copper casings. Unlike modern brass ammunition, the copper went soft when hot. After several shots in quick succession, the carbine's extractor mechanism had a tendency to rip into the bottom of the shell case and get jammed. Riley's gun was jammed. A split second after finding his target, She Wolf's lance smashed into his chest.

At the last second the soldier's gun lifted to greet her and she knew she was dead, but she didn't waver. The lance hit the soldier before a bullet came and the impact ripped the lance from her hand, breaking her thumb, but she didn't feel any pain. The soldier landed on his buttocks, poleaxed and blinking, mouth agape, with the lance thrusting out a full two feet beyond his spine. She Wolf turned Wild Wind hard left, to head back towards the village. She was now unarmed and could do little else, and besides, the fury of the warriors was now being unleashed on Reno's men.

As she galloped through it, the village was eerily still. The men were fighting Reno's companies and the women and children had fled downriver, away from the battle. At the far, downstream end of the village, where the Cheyenne were camped, She Wolf dismounted and ran in and out of the tipis of people she knew. She was looking for a weapon to borrow. On the fourth attempt, in Calling Crow's tipi, she found a war hammer. The stone it was made of was beautifully smooth, polished by millennia in running water, but one side had been chiselled into an edge, though even the gouges where the flakes of stone had come out were smooth to the touch. The stone was lashed to a wooden handle that was carved and painted with horses and buffalo. She hoped that both she and Calling Crow would live to see it returned to its proper place.

Custer had paused with his command on a ridge above Medicine Tail Coulee. From here the situation didn't look good. He could see that Reno was in a large engagement to the south, though the dust cloud covering it meant that he couldn't see how that was going. Captain Benteen and his three companies were still way behind Custer after being with the pack train and their much-needed ammunition. Custer had already sent Captain Keogh and two further companies away to the right and now, realising for the first time how massive the village was, he didn't have enough men to charge into it. There was a way out though, he thought. The Indians might be savages, but if you had hold of their women and children, they could be used as hostages and a large mass of the enemy could be brought to heel as they would try to protect their loved ones. Below him, to the right, on the far, village side of the river and downstream of where the coulee met it, was a slow moving group of between fifty and a hundred women and children.

Custer, sat on his horse, snapped his head back around and called out, "Lieutenant Reily!"

"Yessir," Reily called back, dancing his mount up towards Custer at the head of the group.

"Get the scouts and five men and bring them with me. We're going down this coulee and straight over the river at full speed and we're going to capture that group of women down there. D'you see them?"

Reily looked down and did see the women right at the far end of the village. Other than those women, there seemed to be no life in the village at all. He couldn't believe that eleven of them were going to charge into a village of a thousand tipis on their own, but that was Custer all over. Still, he thought, if it really is that quiet down there, they might survive it and come back with hostages to bargain with. Two minutes later the horses were skittering down the coulee, their dusty wake hidden from the women below by the coulee wall. As they hit the flat valley floor they charged for the river and were blasting sun glittered rooster-tails of water up into the air seconds later.

As She Wolf came out of Calling Crow's tipi she saw Custer's party explode across the river heading for a group of women and children. She leapt onto Wild Wind and kicked him on, turning him to head for the centre of the group of squaws. As she left the village and came out into the open, the group was already surrounded and one woman was tied up and being dragged to Custer by an Arikara scout. Custer had dismounted to take possession of the woman. A soldier stood between She Wolf and Custer and he looked her way as Wild Wind pounded the last twenty metres towards him. He turned, raising a pistol, as She Wolf swung her arm up and back, bringing the war hammer up level with her shoulder. She let out an almighty scream as the hammer began an arc downwards and backwards. The soldier fired his pistol, but the bullet went high and wide and unmolested, the hammer reached the bottom of its swing and began to rise again in an uppercut, its speed creating a low moan in the air. It smashed into the man's chin like a locomotive, obliterating both his lower and upper jaw and sending out a spray of blood and teeth that landed long after Wild Wind had rushed past him.

She Wolf, still in mid-scream, was only vaguely aware of the bullets flying in her direction as she steered Wild Wind directly at Custer. The scout holding the squaw pushed her away in order to pull a pistol from his belt, but it was too late. He dived to the side to avoid being trampled by the horse that suddenly spun around and kicked out. Wild Wind's right rear hoof caught Custer a glancing blow just below his ribs and dumped him flat on his back. The war hammer flew downwards again, smacking onto the top of the Arikara's head just as he was stumbling back upright, recovering from dodging the horse. With another scream She Wolf charged at the far side of the circle of men, who were already mounting and trying to get to the aid of Custer.

The women and children had become a maelstrom of panic and were running in all directions away from the soldiers, who now no longer had any interest in them. Custer was helped back across the river by his men as She Wolf brought Wild Wind to a stop and turned back to watch. Custer looked at least partially incapacitated as the soldiers fled back up to the main group on the hill, but ultimately, they would find no safety there. She Wolf watched as Cheyenne and Sioux warriors gathered around the soldiers like a plague of grasshoppers. Custer had finally run out of luck and he was going to pay with his life and those of his men.

She Wolf didn't stay to see the demise of Custer and the humbling of the Seventh Cavalry. She felt she had played her part and retired to her tipi to prepare for a journey. In fact, as the sun set over the prairie, she knew, with a sense of grim satisfaction that Wild Wind had finally fulfilled Red Bird's prophesy. On the banks of the Little Bighorn River the two of them had certainly changed the course of the battle, for by preventing the capture of the women and children they had prevented Custer from defeating Sitting Bull's village. She Wolf was also pretty sure that the injury Custer had sustained from the horse's kick would have at least reduced his ability to lead his men. Despite all of that she also knew that this battle marked the beginning of the end for Sitting Bull and Crazy Horse. After the defeat of Custer, the whites would be like an agitated wasps' nest and reprisals would be ferocious. It was time to take Half Bear's advice and find a new life beyond the Shining Mountains because the Indian way of life on the plains might soon be lost and a life on a reservation wasn't an option, as she knew many people in Sitting Bull's village who had already fled reservations in the face of starvation.

She Wolf crossed the Shining Mountains in glorious sunshine. She had been apprehensive about the journey all the way up to the continental divide, but once she had crossed that and was heading downhill, even thoughts of sudden bad weather didn't worry her. The horses coped well and avoided accident or injury and she kept them fresh by alternating riding Rain, Dragonfly and Wild Wind. Wild Wind was once again sporting red birds on his hips and that fact alone, kept She Wolf's spirits up.

She Wolf had no idea where she wanted to be, but she felt she was going to keep moving until she found somewhere that felt welcoming. She was confident she would know the right place when it came. The right place appeared with the coming of autumn. The fireweed had flowered at the top and its fluffy seed was blowing in the breeze like snow when she set out on the morning she came across the fence. It was solidly built of three layers of pine poles, presumably to keep cattle in a pasture, though She Wolf couldn't see any cattle. What she did see, was a woman on a horse riding towards her on the other side of the fence.

As the woman got closer she could see that she looked as though she had Indian parentage, though she was dressed like a white woman, with chaps over trousers, a blouse, a jacket and a Stetson. She was also wearing a smile and that encouraged She Wolf to use the only English word she knew.

"Hello."

"Hello," the stranger replied with a wave of her hand. With no more English left, She Wolf launched into Cheyenne, hoping upon hope, that it would be understood.

"*Do you speak Cheyenne?*"

"*I do. My mother was Cheyenne and my father a white man. My name is Susan, welcome to our ranch.*"

"*Thank you. My name is She Wolf.*"

"*Hello She Wolf. Have you travelled far?*"

"*I've come from the other side of the Shining Mountains. I was camped with Sitting Bull on the Little Bighorn, but we were attacked by soldiers and I am looking for somewhere safe to build a new life away from war.*"

"*Well in that case, I think you should come with me and join us at our house,*" Susan said, intrigued by this stranger. She turned in her saddle to point. "*There is a gate in the fence just back that way. Follow me and I'll take you to my home.*"

As the two women rode side by side separated by the fence, Susan admired the red birds on the Cheyenne woman's horse. "*I like the red birds on your horse's hips. My half-brother was called Red Bird.*"

She Wolf pulled Wild Wind to a stop and looked at Susan, stunned. "*Susan Sumner?*" she asked. Susan halted her horse, similarly stunned.

*"Yes, I was Susan Sumner. How..."*

*"Red Bird was my husband and this is his horse, Wild Wind. I can't believe it, meeting you."*

*"Is Red Bird dead?"* Susan asked, noting She Wolf's use of the past tense.

*"Yes. I'm sorry. He was killed at Sand Creek."* The two women were silent for a few minutes as they rode towards the gate, sending a party of pronghorn racing away like comets under the vault of the sky.

It was after midday by the time Susan and She Wolf reached the ranch house. They put the horses in a paddock at the front of the house and then climbed the steps up onto the porch. Susan motioned for She Wolf to take a seat and she was about to step inside to bring out some food, when Dale Jackson walked out.

"Hi Dale," Susan said and opened her hand towards the visitor, "This is *She Wolf*. She is Cheyenne and has travelled over the Rockies to escape the army. Incredibly, she is the sister-in-law I never knew I had. She was married to my half-brother, *Red Bird*. Isn't that amazing?"

"That is amazing. Hello *She Wolf*. My name is Dale Jackson. It's a pleasure to meet you."

She Wolf stood and beamed a smile, not understanding the words, but accepting the hand that was offered for her to shake.

*"She Wolf, this is Dale, my husband,"* Susan said. *"I'm just going to go inside to fetch some food. Please take a seat and relax. When we've eaten, you must tell us about your journey here.* Dale what do..." Susan's question died on her lips as she looked at Dale, who was now standing and staring out into the paddock.

"I don't believe it," he said, "That's my horse, U.S. Son-of-a bitch it's incredible!" Dale jumped off the porch, bypassing the steps and jogged over to the paddock fence, leaving Susan bemused and She Wolf confused and a little anxious.

*"Don't worry, he says that your horse was once his. He's just surprised."*

They watched as Jackson vaulted the fence and threw his arms around Wild Wind's neck and then together, they followed him over to the horses. As Jackson put his face against Wild Wind's nose the horse gave a loud stamp with his rear hoof and nodded his head up and down and then pushed it into Jackson's chest, blinking against his shirt. As Susan and She Wolf reached the fence Jackson turned to them with tears in his eyes. He spoke to Susan, "Can you tell *She Wolf* that this horse was the best horse I ever had. I'm afraid I took him from an Indian I found unconscious in the middle of nowhere. I called him U.S because of the brand on his chest."

Susan translated for *She Wolf*, who replied, *"His name is Wild Wind. He belonged to my husband, Red Bird,"* She Wolf began to cry as she told Wild Wind's story and of her husband and friend, who were no longer with her. She paused after every phrase to allow Susan to translate back to Jackson. *"Red Bird had a vision that Wild Wind would do something of huge significance by a river. Red Bird was killed at Sand Creek and his friend, Half Bear, took him to look after. I decided to paint red birds on his hips in memory of Red Bird and to give him strong medicine. It was Half Bear you took the horse from. He fell over and banged his head when he nearly stepped on a rattlesnake."*

As Susan caught up with the translation Jackson interjected into the narrative. "I'm sorry to tell you that I was once in the militia, though I promise you that I am a friend to any Indian I meet now. Wild Wind was with me at the Battle of Beecher Island and he was taken from me by the bravest man I ever saw."

*"That was Half Bear. We wanted Wild Wind back to fulfil his destiny. And we loved him. Half Bear was killed in an accident only a few weeks ago."*

"I'm sorry about Half Bear. He was a great warrior. Has Wild Wind done anything to fulfil his destiny?" Jackson asked before Susan asked it again in Cheyenne.

*"I think he has. I was camped on the Little Bighorn with Sitting Bull and we were attacked by the cavalry. Their leader was Custer and as he was about to make prisoners of about a hundred women and children, we rescued them and injured Custer."*

Jackson stood with his mouth agape. "Yes, I'd say that was significant. Much of the Seventh Cavalry was wiped out and Custer killed on the Little Bighorn. You and my horse have certainly made history."

*"Wild Wind is beautiful to me. He saved my life when I fell into a frozen river."*

Jackson let go of Wild Wind and strode back to the fence. He took hold of She Wolf's hand and beckoned for her to follow, which she did. "Susan, come on," he said, "Can you tell She Wolf I have something to show her," and he strode off towards another paddock to the side of the house, still holding She Wolf's hand. They climbed over the fence and Jackson put She Wolf's hand on the neck of a young stallion. "This horse is called Mountain. I called him Mountain because he was born in the lee of one. His mother is Bess," he pointed at Bess nearby, "and his father is Wild Wind."

She Wolf looked at the beautiful stallion and back over in the direction of Wild Wind, who let out an enormous whinney as he saw Bess and Mountain and cantered over to the fence as close as he could get to where they were. Tears began to stream down She Wolf's face. Jackson continued, "Mountain is now your horse. I want you to have him. You must stay with us here for as long as you wish. I'm sorry I stole your horse, but I can tell you I was honoured to have him the little time I did. I have to tell you I would be overjoyed to ride him again, if you would let me."

She Wolf Nodded, *"Of course."* A moment later she asked, *"Shall we put them all together?"*

*"Good idea,"* Susan said, turning on her heels and heading back for Wild Wind. When they put Wild Wind into the paddock with Bess and Mountain all three were clearly delighted to see each other. For a few seconds they touched noses and sniffed and snorted and then they took off for a canter around the paddock in a tight

bunch, shoulders rubbing and bumping together. Their excitement was clear and Wild Wind bucked his rear up several times. As they settled to a stop all three knelt down and rolled around on their backs and the humans had to laugh.

Wild wind had never felt such excitement and contentment at the same time. He was breathless with emotion. As the three of them settled and Mountain began to graze, he laid his head across Bess's withers and they stood together for a long time.

# EPILOGUE

## Hell and Back ranch, Oregon
## June 1886

The little boy burst from the front door of the 'Hell and Back Ranch' and out into brilliant sunshine. He skipped down the porch steps and ran full pelt to the corral fence, where he climbed up and over with the ease of the well-practised. Despite the cool morning air, the rails under his hands were becoming warm in the sun. She Wolf followed her son out into the day at a more leisurely pace. She kept her eye on the boy as he scooted in amongst the horses. "Samuel, don't run behind them!" she called, wincing as he brushed against Bess's back legs and through her tail, though the horse wasn't perturbed at all.

"Okay mommy," he called out into the wind ahead of him, unconcerned if his mother could hear him or not. He bore down on his target who turned to watch him with forbearance through a steady brown eye. "Wild Wind!" called the boy, as he laid his hands on the horse's shoulder and pushed his face into muscle. They had been learning to ride together and truth be told, Wild Wind was enjoying it, but this morning he felt very tired.

Wild Wind turned gently, sidestepping his back legs to get the full force of the sun on his flanks, without greatly disturbing the boy, who was trying to stroke him. The boy was babbling softly and it reminded Wild Wind of the man in the mountain meadow who used to talk to him gently. He thought back to the cabin where he had lived inside with the man through the winter and it was a pleasant memory. Locked away in his brain were memories of many things, good and bad, from his twenty-five years of life.

The sun was beautifully warm and the boy's presence was comforting, but he did feel very tired and he settled down to his knees, bringing his rump down after them, to lie on his belly in the grass. The boy laughed at the horse, whom he'd never seen lie down before, and he ran back to the house, suddenly keen for breakfast before his riding lesson.

"Mommy, Wild Wind laid down!" Samuel called as he ran back with the wobbly sprint of a young child. She Wolf turned back towards the house and called, "Tom!"

"Yep," came the reply.

"Come out here. Wild Wind laid down and it don't look right." Tom Eagle Feather stepped out onto the porch.

"Daddy, Wild Wind laid down to sleep. Just like a person!" Samuel squealed as he ran up the steps.

"So he did, son. He must be tired. Shall we go eat breakfast while he has a rest?" Tom said, taking the boy by the hand and nodding at She Wolf to go check on the horse. As she took the step off the porch, a small hand squeezed on her heart and she began to jog. Behind her, signalled by Tom, Dale came striding out, wiping shaving soap from his face.

It was difficult for She Wolf to climb the fence with her heart squeezing and the breath taken from her lungs and now her legs were beginning to tremble. Wild Wind had laid his chin on the grass and his body slipped over sideways, flipping his head so that his cheek lay on the pasture and one beautiful brown eye looked up into the sky. He watched an eagle pass overhead and a white cloud moving slowly in the wind and then he shut his eye. He felt She Wolf land on his neck. She was even warmer than the sun and he relished her touch, not noticing the tears that fell on his coat. He knickered his thanks and his heart stopped.

She Wolf was weeping inconsolably into Wild Wind's neck by the time Jackson reached her. His own vision blurred and tears slipped out unchecked. He knelt down and put one hand on She Wolf's and with the other stroked the velvet of the horse's nose. It was amazing how soft his lips felt, despite spending a lifetime ripping up brittle grass from hard soil.

"He had a good life, I think," Jackson said. "He was loved by all those who owned him. He was a wonderful horse. He's died at peace."

Tom joined them kneeling in the grass and put his arm around She Wolf's shoulder. "Don't be worried for him, She Wolf, he's on the way to the afterlife now."

"I know," she nodded, "He won't be frightened, because Red Bird will meet him and ride him across the Milky Way. If there are no clouds tonight, we might even see them."

They were quiet for a few moments until a strong gust of wind blew against them and was gone, cantering off across the prairie.

# AUTHOR'S NOTE

In the autumn of 2012 we bought an ex-racehorse called Shayla. Though my wife, Melanie, could already ride, I was a complete novice and Shayla has, to some extent, taught me. As I stumbled beyond walking and into trotting, cantering and galloping, riding became thrilling and being with such a wonderful creature is a constant source of joy. That Christmas I looked to buy Melanie a 'horsey' novel, but couldn't find one (we'd already read Nicolas Evans' excellent novel, 'The Horse Whisperer') and so I thought that perhaps I'd try and write my own novel about a horse.

At the same time I was searching for a horsey book, I was finishing reading 'Bury My Heart At Wounded Knee', by Dee Brown. Dee Brown describes the American expansion westward from the viewpoint of the Native Americans and it is a real eye-opener, which I highly recommend. The main 'Indian Wars' took place between 1860 and 1890. As a horse typically lives for 20+ years I thought that perhaps a horse could be involved in many of the engagements of the wars, going to and fro between sides.

Whilst the main characters in my book are fictional, their lives are interwoven in real historical events and with real people. All of the battles between the U.S army and the Cheyenne that I described were real events. Readers may have been surprised that the appalling mutilation of bodies was committed first by the U.S troops at Sand Creek, but this is true. It also surprised one of my proof readers that Custer organised his companies by the colour of their horses, which was also true, as is the fact that he rather recklessly attacked villages of unknown size.

Could She Wolf and Wild Wind have influenced the outcome of the Battle of the Little Bighorn? I think it's possible. I cannot recommend highly enough Nathaniel Philbrick's, 'The Last Stand', which details that battle. Custer was seen on the bank of the river with a bound native woman and a Native American male whilst Major Reno was fighting on the opposite bank. Perhaps out of view of the eyewitness was She Wolf, Wild Wind, and a larger body of non-combatants. Of course, if they'd been seen by the eyewitness, Private Peter Thompson, then they would have made it into the current history books and their story would have been written long ago.

Throughout my novel I have referred to horses, but many of the Native Americans' 'horses' would have actually been ponies, being below 14.2 hands in height, with relatively shorter legs and thicker bodies. I make no apologies for this lack of exactitude on my part, as it would have been confusing to try refer to horses and ponies in the story. One of my own 'horses' is a Dales pony, but to me she'll always be our horse. My other 'simplification' regards the names of US states. At the time, Montana, Colorado, Dakota and Wyoming were territories rather than states. Oklahoma was known as Indian Territory, which might leave some readers puzzled as to locations, so I have used the modern state names.

In order to gain an insight into the lives of the Cheyenne I have read two books by George Bird Grinnell, 'The Cheyenne Indians – Their History and Lifeways' and 'The Fighting Cheyennes'. I would thoroughly recommend them and the books I have already mentioned to anyone interested in this period of US history.

I hope you enjoyed reading my story as much as I enjoyed writing it.

25857914R00092

Printed in Poland
by Amazon Fulfillment
Poland Sp. z o.o., Wrocław